Behind the Gem

SECOND EDITION

KEN HART

World Castle Publishing, LLC
Pensacola, Florida
Copyright © Ken Hart 2016
Paperback ISBN: 9781629894201
eBook ISBN: 9781629894218
First Edition World Castle Publishing, LLC, January 18, 2016
http://www.worldcastlepublishing.com

Licensing Notes

Editor: Maxine Bringenberg

Prologue

In deep space, an exploration probe materialized out of the blackness. A star plot of all visible pulsars showed many of them closely matched the distances to the nearby star, based on the radiating image shown on an alien gold plaque stored in memory. When it scanned the region, the only planetary system within range had nine planets, matching the image of the gold plaque. Scans of the third planet revealed it had an atmospheric composition closely matching what was stored in memory. Comparisons of the planet being viewed to images stored in memory indicated a ninety-seven percent probability of being correct. The probe accelerated toward the third planet at near light speed.

As the probe slowed to penetrate the dense atmosphere, it scanned the surface of the planet. When sensors indicated millions of life forms, a small pod bubbled out and dropped to the ground. Floating in a stand of trees, the pod singled out a life form and compared it to the images on the gold plaque. Calculations indicated it had the correct configuration, and the pod moved slowly toward it.

***

Tanner Watson was awakened by a very early telephone call. He was told to report to the White House immediately to meet with the president some time that morning. Although this annoyed him, when the chief advisor from the Office of Science and Technology was summoned by the president, he had to show up.

Just before dawn, Tanner arrived at the White House. Other than the secret service agents and the kitchen staff, there was no one around. After reporting in, he left his briefcase in his office and took a walk outside. The cool, early morning air was refreshing in the solitude of the floodlit garden, but as he paused near a fountain he felt his hair stand on end. As he absently tried to smooth it, his hair sparked and crackled in his hand with static electricity. Suddenly alert, he turned and saw a silver, egg-shaped object floating near him. Startled, he backed away, but it slowly followed him, stopping at the edge of the fountain. He watched in amazement as fragile looking manipulator arms extended from the shell, holding a sizeable object out to him.

Tanner slowly reached out and gently pulled the object from the manipulator arms, and quickly backed up. The arms silently retracted into the silver shell, and it shot into the air.

"Nobody's going to believe this," he mumbled, looking up, but the silver thing had disappeared from sight. In a daze, Tanner returned to his office and saw he had been given an oversize book written in English.

"This has to be a joke," he said, looking around. "Okay, you got me. Ha, ha, very funny."

Fully expecting someone to try and surprise him, he checked his closet and under his desk. Secret service agents were the only ones in the hallway, and he knew they were too serious to be involved in any kind of joke.

Still holding the book, he sat in his chair, wondering what to do until curiosity got the better of him. He opened the book and began to read.

Chapter 1
TAKEN

My name is Raymond Meinhardt, and this is my record of events since I arrived here, wherever here is.

This morning, as I sat down to drink a cup of coffee at my home computer, a news headline caught my eye. *A Seventh Building is Missing.* I scanned the article and read that another building had disappeared, scooped out of the ground near Atlanta, Georgia. The first six buildings had disappeared from other countries, and I wanted to know more about it; but there was very little to be found online. Joining me and reading over my shoulder, Kim wondered if the bank could disappear like that, and despite the cold chill crawling down my spine, I told her it wouldn't.

I felt something was wrong, but I couldn't put my finger on it. So, instead of voicing my fears, I reminded her that the first building to disappear was a pub in England crammed with people, as were all the others, and I assured her the bank never got crowded.

My job at the bank suited me because I enjoyed computer operations and I was able to work alone in a secured room, with few people able to bother me. When it was time to go to my fortress of solitude, Kim packed my lunch, reminded me to get my notepad that I was always forgetting, and we loaded the saddlebags. I've had a Harley since my stint as an army ranger in Vietnam. I kept it over the years, but Kim has had been trying to get me to sell the old classic. I'd give it up if someone could pry my cold, dead hands from the handlebars, but even then, I wasn't sure I would. They would probably have to bury me with it.

Before I put on my helmet, we enjoyed a long kiss. I'm sure we annoyed the neighbors with our open affection for each other, and it may not have been the way a pair of fifty-eight year olds should act, but we didn't care. In fact, we got even longer and sloppier with our kisses when we saw the neighborhood busybodies peeking through their curtains.

Just before I pulled out of the driveway, she was standing in the grass in her favorite tight T-shirt and really short cutoff jeans. No shoes. It was an alluring change from the politically correct dresses she wore when she didn't have the day off. Another chill spilled down my back, but her smile reassured me as she waved, and I rode off to work.

I had just settled down at my desk when everything started moving in slow motion, with a hum I felt more than heard.

***

The next thing I remember was darkness, except for the emergency lights. I tried to call the branch managers to warn them about our power failure, but the phone was dead.

"Ray! You gotta see this!" Ann's voice sounded anxious from the hallway.

"The only thing I gotta do is pay taxes and die," I said, walking to the hallway. "What am I supposed to see?"

When I looked out, most of the parking lot was gone, replaced by a smooth sandy beach with waves gently lapping along it. The sun was floating like a red rubber ball on a watery horizon under a sky streaked with vapor trails. After several minutes of confused silence, I noticed something strange.

"That's not right. The sun's rising, and that way's west. Or, at least it was."

We watched for several more minutes until another sun slowly rose beside the first.

"You know what? That looks like a binary star."

"A what?" Ann said.

"A binary star. You know, two suns circling each other."

"You're crazy, you know that?"

"Maybe, but there are two suns out there."

"Ray, what's going on?" Cherie said when she joined us from the lending office. I'd known her since I started working at the bank. Her infectious smile, curvaceous figure, and laid-back attitude always made her comfortable to have around, even when she got a little flirty. The ring on my finger didn't have to remind me to keep my pants zipped up.

"I'm not sure. Let's go downstairs and check it out."

When Cherie and I reached the lobby, the entry doors were mangled and glass was scattered across the floor.

"Let's look around, but be careful. Whatever broke through those doors might still be here."

Heavy office doors had been ripped from their hinges, and torn clothing was scattered around the usually spotless carpet. I was confused by empty shoes still tied and leather belts broken apart.

"Cherie, do you see any blood?"

"No, and I don't want to," she said, clutching my arm. "Where is everybody?"

"Judging from the clothes, I think they're still here, what's left of them. Let's get back upstairs."

We carefully made our way upstairs, guided by a commotion in the spacious break room. Everyone had gathered there, huddling together like frightened sheep. Everyone was talking but nobody listening. The two bank annoyances, Tonya and Rico, were there as well. Tonya was a demanding, know-it-all bitch who used to be my supervisor.

9

Pulling a few strings and using office politics, I helped her leave the computer room. I was a very happy man the day she took a position elsewhere, away from me. Rico was an ass-kissing little weasel, following anyone in charge. The grapevine said an office romance raged between them, not that I cared.

Nothing was getting done with thirty-seven people talking at the same time, so I decided to give them something to focus on.

"You're all gonna die!" You could've heard a pin drop when the conversations ground to a halt. "That's right. You're all gonna die. You'll be dead in a week if you don't get your act together. We've got to figure out what happened, and we need someone to take charge."

"And you think you're the one?" Tonya said.

"No, thanks. I enjoy being a peon in the computer room, but I think I know what happened."

"You don't know anything."

"What do you think happened?" Ann said me.

"You're not going to listen to him!" Tonya said with a distinct whine to her raised voice.

"Tonya, you know better than to interrupt me. Ray, what do you think?" Ann had been hired to manage the department after Tonya left. She was knowledgeable, calm, and unlike Tonya, she let me do the job without getting in my face. She surprised me when she confronted Tonya, because I thought she was too mild mannered for that.

I spoke up, pointedly ignoring Tonya. "I'm sure you've heard the news about the buildings that have been disappearing. This morning another one disappeared from Georgia, and I think we've been taken, like they were."

"I think you're crazy," Tonya said.

"Do you have a better explanation?"

"I don't need one. You say someone needs to be in charge. I'll do it." Several of her friends quickly agreed with her.

"That's fine with me. Lead on," I said, and left the break room.

My priority became finding my way back home. I figured we'd gotten there, so there had to be a way back, and I was going to find it.

While I was packing some supplies, I felt a gentle pushing inside my head, like a tentative finger testing a fragile object.

You are the one I have chosen.

I was glancing around for the owner of that whispered voice when Cherie walked in.

"What're you doing?"

"I'm getting out of here. I'm not staying to die with this bunch. With my army training, I can survive very easily out there, and I'll be a lot better off than they will."

"You can't leave. I need you to stay here, with me."

"I'm not staying with Tonya in charge. Did you see how quickly her friends sided with her when she opened her mouth? She knows I was behind her getting booted out of the computer room, and I'm not hanging around to be a target for her."

I grabbed a fire extinguisher, went to the break room, and broke the glass on the candy machine. Astonished looks greeted me as I took a handfuls of candy and bags of chips.

"What are you doing?" Tonya said.

"I'm leaving."

"No, you're not. I'm in charge now, and you'll obey my orders to the letter," Tonya said.

"I don't think so," I said, and left the room.

Tonya followed me, grabbed my arm, and said, "You're not going anywhere. Rico! Keep an eye on him. Nobody's to leave, especially him."

11

"Tonya, you don't have the first clue how to survive, and you're going to get a lot of people killed trying to figure it out. By that time, they'll kill you, and as tempting as that sounds, I'm not going to be a part of it."

The distinct click of an opening switchblade got my attention, and when Rico pressed it against my throat, he said "You'll do what she says."

"For now." I must be getting old. Once, I would've easily taken the knife and shoved it up his ass with his hand still holding it. Instead, I surprised myself and backed down.

Tonya said, "I know you, and I need your Ranger training and experience in survival. I want you to stay and help me. If you do, I'll go easy on you."

"Do I have a choice?"

"No, but most of these people trust you, and you'll do what's right for them."

"I'll stay for them, not you."

Leave them and come to me. You will be safe with me.

"Fair enough. Give me some suggestions, and I'll tell them what to do," Tonya said with a pained expression, pressing her hand on her forehead.

"We need the basics; shelter, fire, water, and food. Shelter's taken care of, and we have lighters for fire. Being near the shore, and with the jungle around us, it will rain. We can use the plastic trash cans to store fresh water from the downspouts. Food's a problem. All we have is what we brought with us today, and what's in the break room. We need to gather what food we can and ration it until we can figure out what's in the jungle to eat. We'll test the plants to see what's safe and edible."

"We don't have anything to test with," Tonya said.

"Sure, we do. Rub a sample under your forearm hard enough to get a stain. After about an hour, if you don't have a reaction, then it's probably safe. It's a primitive method, but it works."

"What kinds of reactions?"

"Reddening on your arm, or feelings of nausea or dizziness. Keep a sample of what was tested so you can start a list of what's good and bad."

"I'll get a group started on that. What else?"

"We need to know if we're alone, so you could send a four-wheeler along the beach to see what's out there. You could use one of the repos the bank has," I said.

"Rico, see if you can find the keys to the king cab pickup we just got."

"What about him?"

"Don't worry about him. What else do I need to do?"

"We need to know what's outside, so everyone should go to the windows and watch for anything that moves."

"Follow me. David, find a hacksaw and cut the hinges off the soda machine. Everyone else, stay upstairs and go to the windows and watch for anything that moves. Yell if you see anything."

***

When the soda machine was opened, we took the bottles to a corner office that became the supply room, and we gathered all the food we could find. It was disappointing how little there was.

"Tonya, make sure everyone gets two of these plastic bottles. With their caps, they'll act like canteens, so make sure they keep them. The front doors are smashed in, so you'll have to block the stairwell to keep anything from getting up here."

"I'll take care of that later."

"Ray! Ray! Something's outside!" Cherie shouted.

"What is it?" I said, running to her.

"I don't know." Cherie moved close to me as I went to stand beside her at the window. "Something flew by. It was shiny and kind of egg-shaped."

13

Tonya raised her voice above the increased ruckus. "Cherie, you call me if there's a problem, not him. Don't think for one second either of you will take charge over me."

"I think it's time for a break." I wanted to add "from you," but gazed out at the beach and jungle around us instead. My thoughts flashed, *You're not in Kansas anymore. I wonder what would happen....*

"Did you just click your heels together?" Cherie whispered from close beside me.

"It worked for Dorothy."

"Uh huh. What's the word with you and Tonya?"

"She and her attack dog convinced me to stay and work for her."

"But you don't want to, do you?"

"When you have a knife at your throat, your options are somewhat limited."

"Oh." She frowned. "Well, I'm glad you're staying."

Finally, I saw a large silver egg hovering deep in the jungle canopy. The moment I saw it, it backed into the jungle and disappeared. When I started toward the back door for a closer look, Tonya appeared and said, "Where do you think you're going?"

"I have to take a leak, if it's all right with you."

"Use the toilet."

"There's no water to flush with," I said.

"All right, make it quick, and stay in sight."

When I walked toward the jungle, the voice returned and said, *Come to me.*

"What do you want?"

Someone is coming.

"Tonya sent me to keep an eye on you." Cherie answered the question as she walked up behind me.

"Don't take this the wrong way, but I think I'm hearing voices."

"Really?"

"Yeah, and I think the flying egg you saw has something to do with it."

Come to me.

Cherie groaned and pressed her hand to her forehead.

"What's wrong?"

"I'm getting a headache."

"Come on. Let's get back inside before Tonya gets upset."

A pickup drove around the building and stopped by the back door. Tonya came out and gave everyone their orders.

"I need to know if anyone else is around here. You four drive along the beach for a couple of hours, then come back and tell me what you found. Rico, get ten people from the windows and send them down here. They're going to do some plant testing. Ray, go upstairs and watch the truck from the drive-through lanes."

When I walked upstairs, the voice returned.

Please talk to me.

"Who are you?"

You are the only one I would choose. Come to me.

I had the feeling I wanted to leave. The feeling quickly became a craving, demanding my attention.

"I can't leave. I have to stay and help my people survive."

You have given them what they need. Come to me.

"Who're you talking to?" Cherie said when she caught up to me.

"Nobody. I was just thinking out loud."

"Are you sure it's not the voices you told me about?"

"Actually, it's only one voice."

"Does it answer you?"

"Yeah, and that's a bit scary."

"Do you know where it comes from?"

That female does not need your help.

"Oh, damn." Cherie groaned and pressed her hands against her forehead.

"Headache again?"

"I don't know where it's coming from. I don't get headaches like this."

"Come on, let's go watch the truck."

We opened a large window and crawled out on the teller lanes roof. While we watched the truck's slow progress along the beach, a ground-shaking boom jolted us. We looked up and saw a flaming meteor streaking across the sky. When it disappeared over the horizon, we looked for the truck, but it was gone.

"Where'd it go? It couldn't have gone out of sight that fast," Cherie said.

"Yeah. Tonya, the truck's gone! It just...disappeared!"

"Go find out what happened to it! Cherie, go with him!"

We followed the tracks until they suddenly ended, as if the truck had been lifted into the air. When I saw the head of a large creature resembling a plesiosaur rising out of the water, I grabbed Cherie by the arm and ran toward the jungle. It watched us run with the crushed roof of the truck in its teeth. Then, it tossed the metal aside, dipped its head, and disappeared. We waited, desperately hoping someone would surface.

"They're dead. They're all dead." I sagged to my knees and knelt in silence, until Cherie insisted we leave.

When we approached the building everyone was standing outside. No one spoke, but their silence was as devastating to my thoughts as trumpets blaring into my ears. That is, until Tonya's annoying voice shouted "This is your fault!"

"What? How's it my fault?"

"You told me to send them!"

"No, I didn't. You sent them! You took over, not me!"

She wants to send you on the Long Walk. That is unacceptable.

The silver egg flew over the building and dropped to a hover in front of us.

"Is that what you've been talking to? Is it alive?" Cherie said.

"I don't know," I said.

Tonya said, "You've been talking to that thing? Since you're friends with it, go talk to it." She shoved me hard in the back.

Trying to keep my balance when I stumbled off a concrete step, I thought I was going to run into the silver thing, but it rose before I tumbled to the ground. Then it took up a position between me and the others.

You must leave.

I scrambled to my feet when it moved toward me, and when I put my hand on it to push it back, I recoiled from an electric shock that knocked me down. Everyone suddenly scattered and disappeared.

You must leave, now!

With the egg bumping me, shocking my ass as I was moved north, I hoped someone would follow me and give me a hand with the silver thing. When I turned out of sight of the building, the egg stopped.

The pod will stay there to keep anyone from following you. You must walk in this direction. I turned my head in response to a pull from inside my head.

The heat and humidity were oppressive and I was going to take a break at a stream until I glimpsed movement out of the corner of my eye. There was a head, like a giant alligator, just skimming the surface of the water as it came toward me. I ran upstream, and then circled back through the jungle, looking for whatever it was. I didn't see anything until a creature suddenly lunged from the water. I scrambled into the jungle, tripping and stumbling through the thick brush until I couldn't see it anymore. Then, I circled toward the beach again and peeked around a tree. The creature had half its body on the beach, peering intently into the undergrowth until the silver pod swept in and shot it with some kind of energy weapon, driving it off the beach. I slipped back into the jungle and moved quietly northward.

After slogging through the thick growth for a while, I headed toward the beach again. I didn't see anything around, so I kept a wary eye and walked on.

Are you safe?

"What? Yeah, I'm safe enough."

Continue in this direction. You will come to a place where the water is far from the vegetation. When you arrive, my people will come for you. Then, she was gone again.

I should've been freaked out. I'd been speaking to a voice that came and went inside my head. I'd been knocked down and pushed around by some silver thing that could've easily killed me. Certainly, I had fears and doubts, but somehow they seemed minor. Maybe suppressed is a better word, but I wasn't doing it, that's for sure.

I began to wonder if this was how it started when people lost their minds. Despite popular opinion, I was not crazy…I was sure of that. To leave everyone behind was not the most sane thing to do, so I decided to head back, but felt resistance from inside my head. I wanted to turn around, but I kept walking until I saw the silver pod flying toward me along the beach. I stepped aside, hoping it would fly by, but it bumped against my leg, giving me another nasty shock. It kept blocking my way so I turned around, and the pulling inside my head disappeared. When I looked back, the silver pod was gone. It had to be somewhere nearby, and I wasn't about to go another round with that thing so I kept walking.

It was early evening when the jungle curved away and a large beach spread out before me.

My transport is approaching. Go with my people.

The transport crossing the shoreline was large, oval-shaped, and flat-bottomed as it silently floated above the water. When it approached, my hair crackled and sparked with static electricity that stopped when it settled to the sand.

A curved seam pulled back, and something stepped out that was about twelve feet tall with dark gray skin, wearing a snug fitting top blending into shorts that revealed tattoos etched on the upper thighs. The head and face resembled a horse with large eyes; the hands had three fingers and a thumb, and it had a tail carried upward in an arc behind it. The legs were double jointed like a kangaroos, but were more muscular. There was a gentle rise under the shirt, making me suspect this was a female, and was not a reptile, but a mammal, or maybe both. Her long hair was easily ruffled by the breeze.

Another one stepped out behind her and was apparently male, judging by the absence of a shirt and the tight fitting shorts covering the waist to the upper thighs. He was shorter than the other one, with brush-like hair going down the back of his long neck.

The female walked toward me with a smooth, easy grace that belied her gangly appearance. She squatted in front of me, and even in her seated position she towered over me. Part of me wanted to run, but I could only stand in fascination. She gently smiled and slowly extended an open hand to me. Curiosity extended my hand to touch hers, bending at the waist because my feet seemed rooted to the sand. Her hand was warm, and as she closed it around mine, I felt a powerful, controlled strength. I knew I couldn't resist these things, even if I tried, so I surrendered myself to whatever fate had in store for me, and took a step toward her. With a toothy smile that scared me at first, she stood and gently led me to the transport. The male had squatted and extended his hands to me, palms up, his chin on his chest.

It is a greeting. Touch your hands on his.

When I touched my palms on his, he lifted his head and stood up. As I turned back, I noticed the female had assumed a similar stance, but her palms were down.

Turn your hands up to her. She gently pressed her palms on mine. *Get into the transport. I want you here.*

When we entered, the male moved to a control panel, squatted, and wrapped his tail around a thick post set in the floor. The female wrapped her tail around another post, and when I sat on the floor, she easily picked me up and set me in her lap. It was very uncomfortable for me, on many different levels.

When the transport lifted and pivoted toward the water, the walls became transparent. Quickly gaining speed, we left the sand and sped low over the water. Suddenly, a plesiosaur-like creature reared up in front of us and opened its jaws. A surprised squawk came from the pilot as the female wrapped her arms around me. The loud thudding impact caused the transport to lurch and shudder. I squirmed around to see the thing thrashing in the water as we sped away.

Are you damaged?

"Damaged? No, I'm not hurt." I looked up, and the female smiled at me again.

You will be here soon. You will be safe with me.

After a short flight we approached a volcanic island. The craft we were in climbed steeply and slowed, drifting over a large plateau until we settled to the ground amid many domes and a large pond. When the door opened the female took my hand, and we walked to an elegantly-dressed female wearing robes. The first thing I noticed was a large blue gem suspended between her eyes by a circlet on her head; the second, a scepter wrapped in her tail held above her right shoulder.

I stood very still, placed my chin on my chest, and extended my hands, palms up, like I'd been told. She closed the distance between us, squatted, and covered my palms with hers.

Welcome to my colony, Raymond.

"You know me, but I don't know who you are. Do you have a name?"

I am Ambrisseethsss, the High One of my colony.

"Can I call you Amber?" I couldn't believe I'd blurted that out.

Amber is acceptable for conversations between....

Suddenly, a raging headache grayed everything out.

Chapter 2

DOWNLOADED

I was struggling with consciousness until I heard rustling sounds, like someone walking through grass. A gentle pushing began inside my head again, so I kept my eyes closed in case someone was watching.

I have reestablished the link, but I cannot hear him. Why is he still damaged?

This is a new species, and I can only estimate his condition until I can examine him in detail. I must remind you about the Kalmarins. He is similar to them in many ways.

I have not forgotten the Kalmarins. It is very sad they could not endure our contact. Can you do anything for him?

It will take time to complete my examinations. Oracle! You have not been summoned.

I will examine this new species. I felt something touch my forehead, hard and warm with an electric tingle. *The male will recover on his own. Leave him to rest.*

The light faded and I was left in silence, so I took a chance and opened one eye, just a crack. I was naked and alone on a table in what resembled a hospital operating room, which didn't give me a good feeling. Looking over the side of the table, I saw the floor a long way down, so I sat up and quietly dropped to it. What felt like grass caressed my bare feet, but it felt strange because it seemed to move. When my eyes adjusted to the darkness, I located my clothes and got dressed, then I crept to the door and peeked out, but there was no one around. I walked out and saw the first light of morning beginning to show on the horizon. These people would be waking soon, and I thought I'd better go back to the hospital before I was missed.

When I turned I bumped into someone, even though I hadn't heard anyone approach. I could see it was a female as she squatted, looking at me, and as strange as it may sound, I still felt no fear. I extended my hands in greeting as I had been told, and she pressed her palms down on mine.

How do you feel?

It was Amber. I recognized the soft feeling in my head as the voice who had been speaking to me at the bank.

"I'm getting better."

I was very concerned when you fell.

"I was fine until we left the transport, then it hit me all at once. It may be dehydration."

The High Draasen? Do you have Draasen on your home world?

"Uh, no. Is that what you're called, Draasen?"

Yes. Our healer wants to examine you, but not until we bathe and have a feeding. I will stay with you to be sure she does not damage you. She spoke inside my mind as she smiled at me.

"I'm not sure if I should bathe with you. I'm a stranger here."

You are not a stranger to me.

She extended her hand, and with only a little hesitation, I took it. When I did, my mind was filled with incredible notions, not the least of which was that I was comfortable, like I'd always been there.

The bathing pool was at least three hundred feet across and about forty feet deep at the base of a volcanic mountain, getting shallow toward the steep cliffs where water ran over to the sea far below. Amber removed her clothes and sprang into the air, twisting to land on her back with a splash that drenched me.

Coming in?

"Why not? I'm already wet."

After undressing, I eased into the water and found a rocky ledge where I could sit and watch what was going on.

One female jumped in, and it was easy to follow her movements in the clear water. She stayed under a very long time, and didn't seem to be in any distress when she surfaced to take a breath. Amber surfaced beside me and cleared her nose with a blast of air.

Why were you watching that female?

"I was curious to see how long she could stay under water."

Amber turned to look at the female, and then said, *She is not for you to look at. Come with me to the scrubbing ledge.*

I pushed off the side and started swimming until Amber surfaced under me, supporting me. We arrived at the shallow end of the pool and I slipped off Amber's back. Touching bottom, I found the shallow end was still just over my head. She picked me up, placed me on the hip-deep scrubbing ledge, and handed me a firm, sponge-like object she called a scrubber. The bathers washed their own backs with their tails wrapped around the scrubber, although mutual back scrubbing appeared to be very satisfying.

Amber was scrubbing her back with her tail and her stomach with one hand when she offered to scrub my back. I became self-conscious because I was butt-naked in front of everyone.

Is something wrong?

"No, not really."

She turned me around and washed my back with the scrubber, vigorously at first and then more gently. I arched my back because it did feel good, but no matter how good it felt, I had questions needing answers.

"Why have I been brought here?"

Other things need to be done. We will have first feeding, and you will be seen by our healer again. Before any of that will happen, you need to rub off the scrub. She slipped her tail between my legs, flipped me into the air, and I landed with an awkward splash.

As I tread water, I watched Amber swim deep into the pool. She was very graceful, arching her back to change direction, rolling repeatedly while she swam with others near the hot springs at the bottom.

When I sat on my ledge again, Amber surfaced and placed her chin on the rocks beside me.

Are you ready to begin?

"I guess, but I don't want to take you from your bathing," I said, extending my hand to rub the side of her wet cheek.

She closed her eyes, apparently enjoying my attention. I couldn't understand why I was so much at ease with these people, with her in particular.

Do you like me?

"Yes." I was surprised by my answer because it didn't seem to come from me.

Good. We will begin. We rose from the water and walked to a nearby dome.

Inside, Amber took a piece of light gray fabric from one of the shelves. The fabric was smooth like satin, and elastic like spandex. She put the fabric over her head through a hole in the middle, and settled it over her shoulders. Then, she took a thick rod from a shelf, pinched the fabric together under her right arm, and touched the rod on the fabric beside her fingers. Right before my eyes, the fabric sealed the side from under her arm to the bottom. Changing sides, she created the left seam. She then pinched the fabric together between her legs, touched the rod there, and the fabric sealed all the way up her legs. When she spread her legs and it split up the middle to become shorts, and when she pressed the rod on her stomach it formed around her, close to the skin. The fabric became the clothes these people wore.

Amber took another fabric and wrapped it around my waist. There was a large overlap where the fabric ended, and it hung below my knees like a long skirt. She pinched the fabric at the overlap, touched the rod to it, and it formed around my waist. She then pinched the fabric between my legs, touched the rod there, and it formed around my legs. When I spread my legs, it ripped easily up the middle, and I was wearing pedal pushers.

"That's amazing. How does it work?"

It is time for first feeding.

We made our way to a covered area where everyone was gathering. Several males arrived with heaping trays of food from one of the caves.

Everything is safe for you to eat. Please try everything.

When I settled on a tall stool set out for me, I looked for the basic eating utensils, but there were none. Everyone waited until Amber squatted beside me and her tongue speared out, wrapping around what appeared to be a large round steak on one of the trays. When she drew it back to her mouth, it sparked a flurry of tongues from all around the table. Those closer to the trays were using retractable claws, which looked more like daggers when they appeared from their fingertips. Feeding could be mistaken for a food fight, because those who couldn't reach a tray had items tossed to them, using either tongue or claw. I watched in amused fascination at the food being thrown around, but no one missed a catch.

Not hungry? Amber said.

"My tongue is not like yours, and I don't have claws. Should I just grab something with my fingers?"

Suddenly, a steak-like item was hovering in front of my face on the end of Amber's tongue. I took it in my hands and closely looked at it.

"What are these?"

They come from a nearby colony. We harvest them from fast growing-trees and process them in the preparation area.

That was the last time I asked about anything on the table, because I really didn't need to know. After years as a Ranger, I was accustomed to eating strange stuff. I was hungry and there were trays of food heaped in front of me, so I bit into the steak-like offering, and smiled at the thought, *It tastes like chicken*. I sampled everything, and although nothing was inedible, there were some things I wished I hadn't tasted.

Are you still hungry?

"No, High One, thank you." I noticed when I spoke aloud, their ears turned toward me. "High One, whenever I speak to you, others appear to be listening. Do they understand what I am saying?"

Everyone is listening and learning. Almost everyone is happy with my choice, and they want to know you.

"You don't seem to have any problem understanding me."

I have watched you since your arrival, and I have listened to you very carefully. You were the only one who would speak with me.

A floating ball, the size of a softball with shifting, multicolor hues, sped to the table and landed on Amber's forehead.

"Hey, get off her!" I sprang up to yank the ball from her head.

In mid-jump, I was lassoed by tongues and fell on the table. While I struggled with the bindings, the ball left Amber's forehead and landed on mine. The connection was powerful and direct, with none of the gentleness I felt with Amber.

You would defend the High One at the risk of your own existence. The thing seemed to contemplate what had happened. No, not contemplate, calculate. *You are acceptable.*

The ball left me and moved back to Amber, touching her forehead again. I wanted that thing off her. I didn't know why, I just did. When Amber was released, she opened her eyes, and they had changed to a bright green. Amber picked me up and held me tightly to her, excitedly stroking her long chin across the top of my head.

I knew my choice was correct! I knew you would be acceptable!

"What happened?"

I was going to tell you why you have been chosen, but Oracle disagreed. I was disobedient to protocols and Oracle came to remind me, but when you came to defend me, Oracle made its decision about you, and we agree you are acceptable.

"Would it hurt you?"

No, but Oracle can be insistent with reminders.

"What happens now?"

I want you to become a member of Draasen society. For non-Draasen hatched individuals, there are three steps to be taken for acceptance; Escort, Consort, and Surrogate. Will you take the First Step of Acceptance with me?

What's the First Step of Acceptance?

The First Step of Acceptance is called escort. You would become escort to the High One, and I would become your escort as well. Our pledge is to accept each other, nothing more. You will be linked to me, and the connection must be renewed every suns rise, or it will dissolve on its own like it did when you arrived. Raymond, will you accept me as your escort?

With the feeling I was being led somewhere, I placed my chin on my chest, extended my hands, palms up, and said "High One, I accept your offer as escort."

Amber squatted and pressed her palms down on mine, and then gently squeezed my hands. Somehow, I felt she was very happy.

I cleared my throat, unsure what to say. "What do we do now?"

We go to see our healer. She took my hand and a path cleared for us as others moved aside.

When we arrived at the hospital, Amber approached the healer and they pressed their foreheads together. When they separated, Amber picked me up and put me on the table.

"What was that head bump about?"

The one who hatched me is happy for me, Amber said.

"What's your name?" I asked the healer.

I have selected Ssurlanaseethesess.

"Can I call you Lana?"

You may call me Lana.

For the remainder of the morning I was subjected to the typical poking and prodding all doctors do. Lana must have used a dozen devices on me, but I didn't feel anything, but one device she used I found especially interesting. She wore it like a gauntlet extending halfway up her arm, and when she pressed and rubbed it all over my body, a hologram-like image formed in front of me. She removed the gauntlet and picked up a device similar to a large TV remote she used to manipulate the image.

You are very similar to a Kalmarin.

"What's a Kalmarin?"

She tapped the device and a new image appeared. It looked like an aquatic human; about eight feet tall, long fingers and toes, with webbing between them extending outward like flippers. The head was bald with slits for a nose and a circular mouth. Openings in the side of the head showed where ears would've been, and the eyes were large and round.

"Can I see what's inside this thing?"

The skin disappeared, leaving a transparent skeleton with the internal organs behind it. There were some differences, especially the lungs, and it had an extra organ of some kind near the heart. I wondered why it looked so human.

"Are we finished?" I said, suddenly feeling heartbroken.

I have what I need for now, Lana said, looking at Amber.

Amber squatted in front of me, held my chin in her fingers, and gently lifted my head.

Why are you unhappy?

"Why am I here? I've been taken from my home and family, and I don't know why."

Oracle may be able to help.

"Will Oracle help after I tried to knock it off you?"

Amber and Lana exchanged a knowing smile.

Oracle may have the answers you need.

As if on cue, Oracle floated into the hospital, stopped just off the end of my nose, and said *Come to my structure,* and floated out again.

"I guess we go see Oracle."

You will see Oracle. I must wait outside.

When we approached Oracle's dome, the door slid open. Amber let go of my hand and gestured for me to go inside. Oracle was in the center of the dome on top of what looked like a shaft of light. Light glowed from the walls when the door closed.

Welcome to my center.

"What do you want?"

I want to take your memories to study.

"No, whoa, wait a minute. I need my memories. You can't have them."

I will rephrase. I want to assimilate your memories into my reasoning centers. Your intellect will remain undisturbed. It appears to be similar to the Kalmarins. I already know how to assimilate memories from them.

Oracle left his post and floated over me, stopping just in front of my forehead.

Close your eye coverings.

"Eye coverings? Eyelids, they're eyelids."

You are safe. Think of nothing.

I waited for something to happen. When I opened my eyes again, Oracle was back on its post.

The scan is complete. I will summon you when I have completed my analysis. The High One requires your attention.

Amber was where I'd left her, and the suns were already high in the sky.

How do you feel?

"Tired, confused, thirsty, and hungry."

We will get a feeding.

When we walked toward a cave entrance, I suddenly got a headache that almost split my head open. As everything grayed out, my last memory was of Amber carrying me.

***

When I came to, I recognized the ceiling of the hospital with Oracle at the center. I saw Amber and Lana examining an enlarged image of my brain.

Feeling better, I sat up and swung my legs over the edge of the table. Oracle dropped from the ceiling, attached itself to my forehead, and I passed out again.

When I came to, Amber was holding me upright, and she looked like she might burst into tears at any moment. Oracle floated to Amber's forehead, and she leaned toward me, took my head in her hands, and touched my forehead to Oracle. I felt unusual sensations inside my head; pressure and buzzing.

Can you hear me? Amber said, with much more clarity than I had heard before.

"Yes, what happened?"

Oracle said, *Your brain structure can now maintain telepathic contact on its own, but only with modifications I have made.*

"What modifications? You could've fried my brain!"

The reason you lose consciousness is the link the High One established deteriorated each time contact was made and disconnected. My scan of your memories accelerated the speed of the link deterioration. Return to my structure. There are many items in need of explanation.

He will not return until we have had a feeding and rest. We will come to your dome next suns, Amber said in a manner that would not tolerate argument.

We went toward the feeding table where everyone was gathering for second feeding.

When you fell, the link stopped again. I was very worried I'd lost you.

"It feels different this time," I said, pointing to my head. She seemed very happy as she picked me up and carried me to the table, where she sat me in her lap and got various items for me to sample.

All day long, I had been poked and prodded, quizzed and modified, and Amber had been at my side every moment.

"High One, am I keeping you from whatever you do?"

I have shared duties with junior females who can use the experience. Everything is as it should be. It is time to rest.

"That's a good idea. Which dome is mine?"

We share the same structure and rest together. There is no safer place anywhere.

I caught my tongue and my thoughts. I hadn't anticipated we'd be sleeping together as we walked toward her dome, hoping an out would present itself.

When we arrived at Amber's dome, the walls glowed with light. Shelves on the wall displayed her scepter, robes, and the blue gem circlet prominently. The center of the floor was dominated by a depression with a blue covering, and when Amber walked on it, it distorted with her steps. She settled on her side and looked at me.

It is very comfortable. Please join me, she said, patting the space in front of her.

The out I hoped for didn't appear. I walked onto the depression, which was covered by a material similar to what we wore. When I tried to settle myself in a space of my own, Amber bounced her hips against the cover, and I rolled against her.

This is much more comfortable. She pulled me against her chest and stomach. *But, you are not comfortable with me.*

"I am comfortable with you," I said, struggling to a seated position. "But I'm not so sure about sleeping together."

I think I understand. You do not have all the information you want to make satisfactory decisions. Perhaps we should have seen Oracle this suns. Should I make other arrangements?

She sounded disappointed. She had been the gentlest and kindest of people toward me, more so than most others in my life, and I really didn't want to hurt her feelings.

"I just need time to think about what I've seen and heard. I've been writing some notes, and if I could go back to the hospital, it would give me time to update them and consider everything."

Where will you write your notes?

"I need light to write, and I don't want to disturb you by leaving a light on in here."

You will not disturb me. Recover your items and return here.

"Thank you."

Excited by the reprieve, I hurriedly left the dome. Suddenly, someone grabbed my hand and pulled me to the hospital, where the light came on. Lana squatted in front of me.

Keep contact with my hand and speak softly so no one else will hear. I felt my hatchling is unhappy but she will not say why. Can you explain?

"This is a new situation for me, and I need time to think."

Do you think sharing a rest together will damage this situation?

"Maybe. She claims to have chosen me, but what if she wants someone else? What happens then?"

That will not happen. She has already had all the males she needs. She has chosen you.

"Why has she chosen me?" I said as Oracle entered.

Do not say. It violates the first protocol.

Lana stood to her full height, looking down at Oracle, still holding my hand.

When I was the High One, I maintained the protocols. He is a new species, and this is a new situation for him and us. He has the right to know, because he is not bound by our protocols.

He agreed to the First Step of Acceptance.

He agreed out of ignorance. Medically, he is acceptable. Your own acceptance of him shows he is intellectually acceptable, but he is not Draasen. Different protocols apply to him.

Oracle rose, touched her forehead, and I was left in silence. Not knowing what else to do, I was going to get Amber, but she already was at the door.

Do you have your notes?

"There's an argument going on, and I'm the center of it."

Do not be concerned. Do you have your notes?

When we returned to the dome, Amber settled herself in the blue bed again. I sat near the wall where the light was better and wrote several pages. Eventually, I was going to run out of paper, and I wondered if I could get more from the bank without getting caught.

When I finished, I looked at Amber. What would it hurt to sleep with her? Nothing bad would happen to me; of that, I was certain. When I crawled into the bed, she helped me settle, and I fell into a deep, comfortable sleep.

***

Unknown to me until much later, there was a discussion of me while I slept.

I feel the influences you are sending, Lana said.

I need him.

Are you sure you want to guide him without his knowledge?

I am following our first protocol.

Give a male only what he needs, not what he wants; I know this. He appears to be a good male, but he needs a tail around him.

34

I selected him. It is my responsibility to keep my tail around him. I will listen to him and watch him very carefully.

We must consider how he will fit into our plans for the most High One.

It is too early for that. My eggs have priority, and I am late extracting.

Everything has been delayed until your eggs have been hatched. Oracle said the next suns rise will determine how far he will go with us. Stay close to him, especially after the next meeting with Oracle. He does not know it yet, but he will need you. Constantly remind him you will always want him, even beyond the long walk. He will need that reassurance. Rest well.

Thank you, Mother.

Chapter 3

MEMORIES

I was rousted out of comfortable sleep by a hand shaking my shoulder.

You can wake now. We can bathe and feed, Amber said happily to me.

"Go away. Let me sleep." I hated cheery people in the morning.

Come, sleepy. She jumped on the bed, bouncing me into the air where she caught me. *I need to bathe, and so do you.*

When she carried me toward the bathing pool, I was comfortable with it. I had no idea where the feeling came from, but I was happy with it as I snuggled in her arms.

Take a breath. She jumped into the air and we landed in the bathing pool together. *Are you still sleepy?* she asked with a smile when we surfaced.

"This is not how I want to wake up in the morning," I grumbled at her, trying to be serious, but my smile gave me away.

After a leisurely scrubbing and a stop at the clothing dome, Amber squatted in front of me.

Will you renew the First Step of Acceptance with me?

"Yes, High One, gladly." I placed my chin on my chest and extended my hands, palms up. She pressed her palms down on mine in acceptance of our agreement, but this time, I felt a gentle pressure inside my head again.

Thank you. She took my hand, and we walked to the first feeding. On the table was a plate, a fork, and a large spoon for me. Along with the other trays being brought to the table, a large steaming yellow mound was placed in front of us.

Oracle floated to me and said, *Verify the molecular structure of the new item.*

"Verify the what?"

Taste it.

I took a fork full from the tray and tasted the concoction. "You've got to be kidding me. Scrambled eggs. How did you get so many?"

They are not eggs. They are —

"No, no, no, don't tell me! Yesterday, I was eating trees. Today, I'm eating eggs, and they're delicious. Thank you, Oracle. What other surprises do you have for me?" For some reason, Amber and Lana were closely watching Oracle.

You can have anything you have eaten in your past. They are prepared based on your olfactory memories, using a combination of items that produce similar molecular structures.

I shoveled a mound of eggs onto my plate and sat back to enjoy it. Using her tongue, Amber sampled the eggs.

It has an unusual taste. It is good.

With that proclamation, tongues and food began flying in all directions. When I reached for more eggs, my fork fell off the table. I was going to get it when I saw what looked like white worms were rising from under the ground and sliding all over my fork. I picked up my feet and put them under me.

What are you doing? Amber said.

"Something came out of the ground and is all over my fork."

The ground cover is brought from our home world to keep the colony clean. It also keeps the natural vegetation from reclaiming the colony area. It has finished cleaning your fork. You can use it again.

"I don't think so," I said, suddenly losing my appetite.

After breakfast and a stop at the water tank, Amber said, *Are you ready to see Oracle?*

"Sure, let's go."

High One, you may leave, Oracle stated after we entered the dome.

Amber picked me up and placed me in her lap with my legs straddling hers.

I will stay.

There was a pause while Amber eyed Oracle intently. Then, she gently placed her muzzle on top of my head.

I understand. I will begin with images from your memory I cannot identify. An image of me as a child appeared out of the air. *What is this?*

"This is a picture of me when I was about four years old."

Another image appeared. This time, it was a picture of my parents with me as a baby seated between them.

Is this similar?

"Yeah, it's similar."

Oracle displayed my memories for most of the morning, many of which I had long forgotten, and some of which should've had stayed that way. When no more appeared, Oracle said, *I am cataloging your memories for storage. What are your questions?*

"Why can I hear the High One, you, and the healer, but no one else?"

An image of a Draasen head appeared that opened like a clamshell. There was a large, teardrop-shaped area glowing in the front part of the brain.

This is the organ that gives the Draasen their ability to communicate by what your species calls telepathy. You hear the High One because she has established a link across which you speak to each other. You hear me electronically. You hear the colony healer through the High One. You are at the First Step of Acceptance, and you have not been given the ability to communicate with others. That will be established later.

"Lana insisted I hold her hand while we spoke last night."

Direct contact allows for private communication.

"On my planet, it has been suggested telepathic communication implies control. Can they control actions by using their minds?"

Draasen telepathy cannot control your actions any more than your telephone can control you.

"What was the pulling in my head that brought me here?"

You are susceptible to what your species identifies as subliminal suggestion. It attempts to influence you to a certain course of action.

"That's nice to know. Do they have space travel?"

The Draasen transit the void by manipulating magnetic fields.

An image appeared that I recognized as the gold plaque on the Pioneer Ten spacecraft; the nude man and woman standing beside lines and circles representing something an intelligent species could understand. I had seen it on TV once, but didn't remember what it meant.

I understand the significance of this image. The two circles represent what your species calls the hyperfine transition of hydrogen. Your Periodic Table of Elements identifies hydrogen as the simplest, lightest element your species understands. The male and female of your species standing beside a spacecraft shows relative size and appearance. The male has his hand up showing an opposable thumb, suggesting dexterity and motor skills. From this representation, your species is on the third planet of your planetary system. The intersecting lines represent relative distances to what your species identifies as pulsars. With this information, I have located your home world. An image appeared that I recognized as our galaxy. Yellow and green spots flashed in one of the spiral arms. *This image is of the galaxy we are in. The yellow pulse represents the location of your home world. The green pulse represents the location of this planet. I calculate you are approximately seven hundred light years from your home world.*

The importance of this fact did not strike me immediately. Amber held me closer to her.

"Can you explain why I'm here?" I said, hoping Oracle would explain what the Draasen wanted with me.

There is duality in your question. I will answer in this manner.

An image of another species appeared. It stood about six feet tall and was very dark red. The neck was long and thick, topped by a relatively thin, flat head with jaws and teeth vaguely resembling those of a shark. It had four muscular arms with two arms ending in claws, and two ending with circular hands with eight fingers each. The arms extended from a fat, pear-shaped torso with six legs and a long thin tail.

You and your companions were brought to this planet by this species, called the Baleorans. Five thousand years ago, an exploration probe attempted contact with them. That contact indicated they did not want peaceful interaction because they see other species only as a source of food. Probes have been studying them as they move between star systems. Before they descend on a planet to capture and store the population for feeding, they take samples of the species and transport them to compatible planets, possibly to repopulate a planet to feed on in the future.

I guessed the Baleorans might be galactic farmers. They placed people on other planets, like seeds in a field, and they took people from their planets with no more regard than humans had when taking livestock to a slaughterhouse.

"How long would it take for the Baleorans to travel from Earth to here?" I said with a very bad feeling.

Amber said, *I will always be here for you. I will never leave you.*

If the transport carrying you traveled at what your species identifies as light speed, it would have taken seven hundred years.

Fighting back a surge of despair, I got off Amber's lap.

"Send your fastest probe to Earth. Record all radio transmissions on all frequencies and return it here so I can hear them," I said as my voice cracked.

That is my command, Amber stated, rising to her full stature.

Command accepted. Is there anything else the probe should be programmed to look for?

"Life."

A probe has received navigation instructions and has been launched from the northern defense platform.

The revelation that Kim was dead suddenly burst forth as abject despair took control of me. With a twist of my body, I shunned Amber's hand on my shoulder and I bolted toward the opening door. Running only a short distance, I stumbled and fell to my knees, doubling over, holding my head and crying uncontrollably. Everyone, everything I had known, had been dead and gone at least seven hundred years. My wife, my only friend of twenty-five years, was dead. I'd promised I'd take care of her, and I'd failed her.

Go to him. He needs you, Lana said urgently.

Amber picked me up, and I struggled against her.

"No! No! Leave me alone!"

Amber said nothing while I struggled against her powerful embrace. I fought her touch, beating my fists on her chest, trying to push her away. When my struggles sapped the last of my strength, I collapsed against her, wailing like a baby. I couldn't guess how long I was like that, but it seemed like a very long time, as exhaustion gradually replaced despair. I felt ancient and unwanted.

"Can I have some space, please?" Amber relaxed her hold, but did not let me go. "I'm sorry you saw that. I always thought I'd be the first to die, and I'd have been spared what you saw."

I knew you had a mated pairing. We bond until the long walk, and we act similarly when one of us goes on the long walk, but we allow others to comfort us during such times.

"I'm sorry. When I arrived here, on this planet I mean, I hoped I could find a way back home and everything would be okay. Now, I have nothing; nothing to hold on to."

If you would accept me, I will become the one you could hold on to, and I would never leave you. Please, take the Second Step of Acceptance with me.

"What's the Second Step of Acceptance?"

Oracle floated in and said *The Second Step of Acceptance is consort. It is a commitment that is permanent and irrevocable. Only the long walk will break the bond. There will be a new link, unlike any other, that connects you to each other, and you become as one. Before this bonding can occur, there can be no reservations by either participant, or by any of those who are gathered. If there are reservations, they must be expressed for discussion and resolution. Do either of you have any reservations to this commitment?*

I do not have any reservations, Amber said clearly and firmly for all to hear.

"I...have reservations." All eyes were on me. "Oracle, I need to see you and the High One in your dome. There is much to be discussed," I stated, squirming out of Amber's grasp.

I entered the dome without slowing a step. Oracle floated through the door and landed on his post, and Amber came in and squatted, curling her tail behind her.

Am I not acceptable? Amber said.

"Being acceptable is not the issue, truth is. Do you value truth?"

Truth is very important.

"Oracle, do you value truth?"

Accurate presentation of facts, as they are known, is my primary function.

"Then, let's have some truth. What have I been chosen for?" I said.

As High One of my colony, I must uphold the protocols that have been in place for millions of years.

"That's not an answer. Oracle, you were constructed by the Draasen. You are a machine. Thus, you are not, and cannot be, Draasen. I call on your function. Give me the truth about being chosen by the High One."

When Core was first brought —

"What's Core?"

Core is the center of my functions, and is operational on the Draasen home world. When Core was first brought online, the Draasen were very much like your people; warlike, violent, sending others on the long walk for greed, power, and control of females. During the final Draasen war, an engineered virus was released. When it spread throughout the home world, it had an unforeseen consequence. The females were altered at a level your species identifies as DNA. The females lost the ability to carry their eggs to birthing, and the Draasen nearly became extinct. The one who is called the First Most High One organized the females and took control of Draasen from the males. It was discovered that a fertilized egg could be transplanted into a birthing animal, where it could be birthed at its normal time. Animals were selected and bred for the sole purpose of birthing, and have successfully repopulated the Draasen people. At extremely rare times in Draasen history, a High One with fertilized eggs cannot use a birthing animal. At those times others are asked to help. There have been eight occurrences when a High One was unable to transfer her eggs into a birthing animal, and it was offered to other species that were available at the time. Two accepted, the others refused, and some of them went on the long walk rather than accept becoming a birthing animal. The birthing animal for this colony was very old and did not survive the final birthing of the previous High One's eggs. Another birthing animal will not be provided from the home world due to the restriction of travel commanded by the current Most High One. Ambrisseethsss has ten fertilized eggs that are ready to be implanted. The High One has chosen you to be her birthing animal.

I felt a gentle suggestion inside my head that said to accept this fact. I ignored it.

"Oracle, can these people return me to my home world?"

Yes.

"How long would it take to get there?"

Approximately one suns rise per one hundred light years traveled through the magnetic tunnel with life forms stored as passengers. Probes are smaller and travel much faster without life forms to be damaged by the intense magnetic fields required at their highest speeds.

"What is the status of the probe sent to my home world?"

The probe has reached your home world.

"What do you have so far?"

The third planet has one natural moon and thousands of non-functional manufactured objects in high orbits. There are no artificial emissions detectable. The magnetic field is disturbed. There is a layer of dust in the high atmosphere.

"Can you show me the planet?" An image appeared that looked like a splotchy, tan ball. "Are you sure this is the right place?"

The location is confirmed.

"Can your probes go into the atmosphere?"

The probe is on the surface.

"When will the pictures be ready?" A moving image appeared out of the air as a dark blur. "I can't see anything."

The probe is in a dark environment.

"Can you speed it up and get to some daylight?"

The images moved quickly forward until they became lighter blurs, and then slowed. There was nothing but a flat, featureless surface.

"Can you show me where the probe is located on the planet?"

The image changed to an orbital view and a red dot blinked on the dusty atmosphere.

"That's not very useful. Can you show me the surface without the dust?"

The dust disappeared and the probe was east of the South Carolina coast. Racing ahead of the sunset, the probe moved inland and slowed as it passed over a town. I could see intersections between the buildings, but there were no lights or any activity. What looked like deep, dirty snow covered everything.

When the probe headed west, it passed over a major city that looked like it had been bombed. Then, the images stopped.

"What happened?"

What you observed is what has been received and processed.

Amber was closely watching me, and I felt a gentle pressure in my head again.

"I have several decisions to make. Come on, let's get in the tub," I said to Amber, and we left Oracle's dome.

My mind was racing as I tried to relax on my ledge. What had happened on Earth? Should I tell the others about these people? No, not after what Tonya and Rico did to me. They might try to kill these people. They'd have to know about them sooner or later, but for now, they had all the essentials for survival and were in little danger if they stayed away from the shore. What did the Draasen want with me? What did it mean to be a surrogate? Using the human definition, I already had an idea of what it meant, but before I could get that far, I had to become consort, which was the equivalent of being married. I knew so very little about them, and they knew everything about me from my downloaded memories. Maybe it hadn't been such a good idea to let Oracle download my memories, but it was far too late for recriminations now.

Your mind is overly active with thoughts, Amber said when she surfaced beside me.

"We need to discuss what's involved with my being a surrogate."

It is the highest position we will offer a non-Draasen hatched species.

"I want to know what will happen. I'm guessing it involves putting your eggs in me, right?"

Yes.

"I need to know the process from beginning to end. How many eggs did your mother have?"

Eleven.

"How many did you watch being hatched?"

None.

"Why are you being evasive?"

I do not want to frighten you.

"This is ridiculous. Where's Lana?"

I am here, she said, surfacing beside us.

"Please tell me what is involved being a surrogate."

It is the highest position we will offer a non-Draasen hatched species.

It was obvious they weren't going to tell me anything.

As I swam, Amber surfaced under me. When she placed me on the scrubbing ledge, she gently took my head in her hands and pressed our foreheads together. When she did, I felt something race down my spine that made me gasp and curl my toes. I clutched Amber around her long snout as the sensation playfully tickled in all the right places. Lust ignited in my loins and burned upward, and as it rose, Amber pulled my head so hard she almost crushed my skull against hers. When it exploded into my head, Amber snorted with a quick headshake, and her tail shot straight out behind her. The brief experience was erotic, sensual, intoxicating, affecting every single part of me, and it left no part untouched. It left me breathless, weak in the knees, and my insides quivering. It left me wanting more, much more.

I am happy to feel your urge to mate is easily influenced, Amber said.

I see you have a return from him, Lana said, looking at Amber's rigidly quivering tail. *That could influence his decisions, and you know you cannot be a mated pairing.*

There is very little a High One cannot do. Amber smiled and turned me around to scrub my back. Still savoring the experience, I could barely move as I slowly went through the motions of my bath, carefully avoiding certain sensitive areas—areas that seemed to be everywhere.

After bathing, we arrived at the feeding table. Beside the scrambled eggs were large green bars.

Sample the new item, Oracle said as it floated to the table.

"I don't remember eating anything that looks like this."

The combinations of ingredients are correct for your olfactory structure.

"It's bacon," I said, nibbling on a green bar.

Amber flicked out her tongue and got one of the bars.

You are going to change me from my usual feeding with these interesting foods, she said, crunching on the new taste sensation.

"When we're done, can we go back to Oracle's dome? I'm anxious to get information on becoming a surrogate."

***

After feeding, Amber took my hand and we walked to Oracle's dome.

"How far have you progressed on your report of my planet?"

The final report will take at least ten more suns before it is ready.

"Did your probe detect any life on the moon orbiting my planet?"

There were no artificial habitations detectable anywhere except on your home world.

"Do you know why the magnetic field is disturbed?"

The most probable answer is an intense magnetic burst from the nearby star.

"How many electromagnetic pulses would be able to disrupt the magnetic field like that?"

Explain.

"Examine my memories for thermonuclear explosions and their effects."

It is probable many electromagnetic pulses from uncontrolled releases of fission energy would have a disruptive effect on the

47

magnetic field. There would have to be several hundred simultaneous pulses to create such a disturbance.

I had once read the United States had over nine-thousand nuclear weapons. Those in other countries would easily double that. "What's the radiation level on the planet's surface?"

Your memories do not contain sufficient information to answer your question. The Draasen would not be permitted to go there. They would be overwhelmed by the radiation and go on the long walk within one suns.

"I need a date from somewhere. Can your probe explore inside buildings?"

The probe is carrying two exploration pods that can enter confined environments.

"How big is a pod?"

An image of an oval-shaped device appeared in front of us, it was about two feet in diameter and three feet long.

"Hey, that looks like the thing that was stalking me."

I commanded Oracle to send a pod so I could easily talk with you.

"This is what I want to do. We need to search a building with the windows intact. Select a building far from any destroyed areas. Since the probe has two pods, search two buildings in different areas. When they're inside, I'd like an examination of the walls and desktops on all floors of the building."

Are you searching for calendars and documents containing a date?

"Exactly. How soon can the probe be ready?"

Programming has begun. The search has an undetermined time resolution.

"Inform me when the search is done. Now, I want details about a surrogate."

The High One has ten eggs ready to be implanted. You have been selected for this.

"Details, Oracle. I need details."

A Draasen's eggs are independently mobile and are approximately the size of your thumb. All fertilized eggs are expelled by the female into a single incision made in the birthing animal's abdomen. After they are inserted, they seek places of nourishment and attach to the birthing animal. They will go into a biological stasis until telepathically activated by the birthing female. The average gestation is twenty-nine suns. When the hatchling signals the need to be birthed, it is surgically removed.

While Oracle was explaining the process, I was looking at my thumbs. There would be ten of those things running around in me.

"How large do the eggs grow?"

An image appeared, showing a segmented, oval egg about twelve inches long and ten inches in diameter.

Each egg weighs nine pounds at hatching. There are variations in size and weight between each hatching, with a female egg being larger.

"For me to give birth to ten eggs in the sizes you describe, they would kill me. My body would not be able to support them."

A birthing animal supports three eggs in various stages of growth. The healer has examined you for compatibility, and you can birth a single egg with a recovery period between each birthing.

"It's impossible for a male to give birth. We are not equipped to do it," I said, frightened and fascinated by the explanation.

In your home world oceans, the female seahorse and the female pipefish give their fertilized eggs to their males, who birth their offspring.

"It's not the same thing. When an egg hatches, it'll have to be cut out of me. It'll take weeks for me to recover."

The length of the healing process is greatly reduced by medical techniques using medicinal and magnetic means.

While Oracle was explaining this, I was watching Amber. Except for an occasional eye blink, she showed no reaction.

"If I survive the birthing, what happens to me?"

My mother will closely watch you during each birthing. You will be safe with her.

"Okay. When all the eggs are hatched, what happens to me? What happens to us? On my planet, breakups of...pairings are frequent and not always friendly or pleasant."

Amber got on all fours to look directly into my eyes. *When a bonded pairing is formed, it is permanent and irrevocable until one goes on the long walk. The survivor will not bond with another. Pairings last a lifetime. We will last a lifetime together. You can help me, but only if we take the Second Step of Acceptance. Afterward, we will take the Third Step of Acceptance, where you become Surrogate to the High One; my surrogate. Then we can begin the birthing process.*

I had become lost in her eyes and I felt her great affection for me. The thought of being with a human female suddenly seemed foreign to me. That was not right.

"High One, can I have some time to consider what you've offered?"

Yes, it is an oversized decision.

While I walked alone with my thoughts, I struggled to make sense of the confusion. So much had happened since I came here. I had to consider the memory of my wife. She was dead; killed over seven hundred years ago by the Baleorans. That chapter of my life had been forcibly closed. Now, I had the opportunity to help Amber and the others who had come with me. The decision was mine alone; there was no one to ask for advice.

Then, there was Amber. Alien, but pleasant enough to look at considering some of the movies I'd seen. All said and done, I may as well stay there. When I turned to find Amber, I walked into her as she squatted behind me. These people snuck around so easily despite their size.

I felt a change in you when you turned into me.

"I made a decision I feel good about."

I have seen when you make a decision; you have visited a dark, confusing place in your mind I cannot look into. I cannot understand how you can make decisions from what I see there.

"I guess it's part of the human experience."

Have you decided to take the Second Step of Acceptance with me?

"Yes, High One. I'll take the Second Step of Acceptance with you, without reservations of any kind."

Oracle floated to the top of my head.

It has been recorded that those who have taken the Second Step of Acceptance lived a long life. I do not understand happiness, but my research indicates those who have taken the Second Step of Acceptance recorded they were happy with their decision. You are going to face a situation different from those who preceded you. You must encourage this High One in all of her efforts, and obey her decisions without question. This High One must succeed.

While Oracle was explaining, we were being surrounded by every Draasen in the colony. They changed positions to all fours with their tails in the air, quivering rapidly, creating a deep, intense buzzing that bounded around in my lungs and head.

"Why are they doing this?" I said, clamping my hands over my ears.

We are happy! We have been accepted by almost everyone in my colony.

"What happens now?"

Oracle will assist me in establishing a permanent link with you to complete our bonding. She took my head in her hands and looked into my eyes. *Are you ready?*

"For you, I'll try to be ready."

Her smile lit up her whole face, and her eyes turned a brilliant blue.

This is new to you, and you will resist without meaning to. Let me guide you. Follow me wherever I go.

When I looked into her eyes, I felt I was being drawn into her. She gently pulled our heads together and when they touched, my vision blurred, and I felt my knees weaken. When they buckled under me, I was supported under my arms by someone from behind.

Be calm.

Silence. Darkness.

Relax.

I tried hard to relax but all my senses had fled.

Follow me.

How was I supposed to follow if I couldn't see?

Suddenly, an explosion of images and sounds overwhelmed me. My head felt like it had been hit with an iron bar, and I passed out.

Chapter 4

BONDING

I think. Therefore, I exist.

He has returned to us, Lana said.

Amber, what is going on? I heard myself say, but I did not move my lips.

Amber pulled back from me, gently holding my head in her hands.

How do you feel?

I clamped my jaws shut and tried it again.

I feel fine. Can you hear me?

I hear you clearly.

Amber looked intently into my eyes, searching for something. Suddenly, we connected, merged, and swirled into each other. An intense desire was surrounding us, binding us together. We shared everything willingly and openly, yet greedily…we had everything all to ourselves. It was love, strong and pure, and I knew it would last forever because it could not do otherwise. I knew it for the indisputable, unalterable fact it was. This was our flawless space. No one could enter here but us.

I had to find Amber to tell her about it, but where was she? I felt her everywhere, inside me, inside us. She appeared in front of me, her eyes a dazzling blue. She was not the statuesque queen I had learned to love, but smaller, equal to me. Or maybe I was equal to her. I could see with my eyes, but there was more, infinitely more to see with my eyes closed. We snuggled close to each other, her tail and arms wrapping around me as I embraced her, and we floated without direction or care. Nothing mattered except our love for each other. Nothing mattered—we had each other, and it was all we needed. We were filled with an incredible longing and desire that overflowed. We could not contain it all, and parts of it slipped away to become a gift for others. Then we were slowly descending, descending into the reality awaiting us. We did not want it, we did not need it. Too soon; it was too soon. Sights and sounds assailed our senses when we returned from the bonding.

When Amber released me, I staggered back and dropped to my knees. I was gasping for air, completely breathless. Amber fell on her side, nostrils flaring in response to her labored breathing. It had been hours since we bonded and the suns had nearly set, but it seemed like only minutes, very short minutes; an eternity of minutes.

"Can we get that back?" I begged hopefully.

"We can, any time we want," she said aloud in a breathless English voice.

Surprised by her voice, I reached for her, but the best I could manage was to flop on my face.

Lana said, *That was one of the most intense bondings I have experienced. It affected everyone. We have four new-mated pairings.*

I would have liked to look around, but I had no strength to move.

A young male said, *There are twenty-eight others on the ground. It is amusing, and it felt very good. I cannot wait until I can become a pairing.*

"I think we could be more comfortable in our dome, but I cannot move," I said.

With a rapid series of commands, Lana took charge. Since most of the paired Draasen were unable to help, unpaired females picked up Amber and took her to our dome. Lana carried me as my arms and legs dangled uselessly.

"Does this always happen?"

Yes, and we take care of our own when it does. At next suns rise, everyone will be back to normal and better for the experience.

When Lana and I arrived, Amber was being situated on the bed while Lana waited with me in her arms. Then she stepped onto the bed and arranged me with my back to Amber and her arm over me.

Rest well, my hatchlings. Lana smiled and left, the light going dim when the door slid shut behind her.

Neither of us wanted to break the feelings that had settled over us by talking about what happened. While we relaxed, I had a mental image of a puppet. I watched strings drop to the puppet and when they attached, I fell deeply asleep.

Chapter 5

IMPLANTS

I woke early, energized and ready to go. Amber was still sleeping, yet I felt her affection ripple between us as I smiled in remembrance of our bonding. I marveled at being married to an alien species, but discovered that I had one regret: I did not know these people a long time ago. Peace and love in abundance flourished here. There was no pursuit of the almighty dollar, or the accumulation of wealth and possessions, and there was no fighting or war.

That thought brought me to something Oracle had said. It launched a probe from what it called a defense platform. By my way of thinking, defense suggested there must be weapons, and to defend a planet, there must be some tremendous firepower on that platform. I would have to ask Oracle about it. Then I wondered how the humans were doing, and if Cherie was okay.

With that thought, I found myself disembodied, soaring over the cliffs, whisking across the water at high speed until I stopped outside the door of the bank building. I wanted to go inside, but suddenly felt shaky and uncoordinated, and instantly I was snapped back into my body with a raging headache.

What is wrong? Amber said.

Nothing, I said, not wanting to upset her.

You are in pain. What did you do?

Nothing. Technically true, considering I had no idea what I did.

Mother, I need you!

I am coming. He extended himself too far, just as you did when you were learning.

Lana opened the door and the light came up, stinging my eyes and making my headache worse. She held one of her medical devices on my head, and the pain melted away.

"Ah, that is better. Thank you."

Lana took my chin in her hand.

I am pleased you are trying to learn to do things that are new to you, but do not hurry. As you discovered, it can be painful. The High One is your guide. Listen to what she has to say.

"I am sorry for anything I have done wrong."

Very good. Rest now, Lana said, then left the dome.

I did not go that far my first time. Amber was impressed with what I'd done, however painful it was to me.

I will be more careful. When can I begin learning about my new gifts? I said, snuggling closer to her.

I can see you are not ready for training. We will rest until first bathing, and then we will have first feeding. Then I will have a conversation with Oracle.

I understand Oracle has been operational for many thousands of years and has achieved sentience. What if it has developed beyond its programming and has its own agenda? Can anyone turn it off?

Mother, please speak with me.

It seems your new consort does an excellent task of keeping you, and me, awake, I heard Lana say.

He has many excellent thoughts. He suspects Oracle may have its own plans. If we need to, can we turn Oracle off?

I felt Lana's surprise. *Oracle must remain operational. I have had many discussions with it, and it has always obeyed without question. I will consider this and let you know what I discover.*

I seem to have started something, I said, with an uneasy feeling.

Do not be concerned. If something is happening, my mother will discover it. She has an insight others lack.

How long do your people live? I said.

If we do not have an injury that sends us on the long walk, three-hundred years is average.

What reference are you using for this?

Oracle has given us your time and space references. When we speak with you, we will be using your references. It will be easier for you, and is an excellent exercise for all of us. We are learning, so please be patient with us.

If your skill is an example of your people's abilities, I will not need much patience.

Since we are not going to get any more rest, we will go to the bathing pool, Amber said and sat up.

While I relaxed in the warm water, a male was picking up discarded clothing.

"Good morning," I said to him.

"Good...morning, Consort to the High One."

"How is your morning?"

"It can be...tedious...boring...I am sorry. I am not sure which word is correct."

"Either word is correct. Practice will make you a better speaker of English."

"Thank you, Consort to the High One. I must continue my duties," He left with the bundle of clothing in his arms.

You want to ask me about something? Amber surfaced beside me.

Are you hearing my thoughts before I have a chance to tell you about them?

I can feel when you have a question, and I am always ready to help you.

Why are the males so formal when they speak to me?

You are Consort to the High One and my bonded choice. You are the leader of the males.

Uh, oh. Something else I did not know. How do I provide for them?

When something is needed, one will approach you and say what is needed. You will bring it to me, and I will decide the merits of the need. Then, you gather resources and fill the need. Since this is an established colony, needs presented by males are few.

I will try not to bother you too much.

I already know you will act correctly for everyone.

***

After feeding, Amber said, "I must see Oracle before we can continue your training. You can write your notes while I am gone. Why do you write those?"

"They may be important someday. If nothing else, it will be a record of what I have done since I was taken from Earth," I said sadly, because they might be the only thing I could leave behind when I died. No other record of the human race would exist.

"I will return to you quickly."

"I would like to go in with you."

"I know you would. I will find you when I am finished." I watched until she entered Oracle's dome and the door slid closed behind her.

I felt very alone when the link between us closed with the door. After pacing for a few minutes, I decided I might as well do something, so I went to our dome, got my notes, and started writing. The pen ran out of ink and I had to suppress a few choice words. An empty pen may not seem like much to anyone else, but to me, it was a disaster because I had not brought a spare. It meant I had to return to the bank building, and I was not ready to face them. Not yet.

Consort to the High One, there may be another solution, a male said from the doorway.

"Do you have a pen?"

We have our recording tablets.

"Can I have one?"

Please follow me.

I noticed he did not walk with the graceful ease the others did. He limped, and his skin was a lighter gray than the others, as was his hair.

"How old are you?" I said.

I have 307 years. I am not as functional as I used to be, and I hope to be allowed to go on the long walk soon.

I decided to call him Elder. I had a feeling something was bothering him, and he was hanging on for some reason.

"I have a lot to learn, and you can be a great resource for me."

The High One will be training you.

"You can teach me about Draasen society from a male perspective. I am sure the High One would not have any objections."

She might.

"Really? Well, I have the impression you are not one for following all the rules," I said, smiling up at him.

When we entered one of the caves, I felt a hot breeze flowing out. Inside was an enormous cavern that looked like a warehouse.

I like the heat in here. I like the deep, hot water of the bathing pool, but I cannot hold my breath as long as I used to.

"I know the heat feels good on the old bones. Have you considered using a tube to breathe through when you bathe?"

When he squatted in front of me, a knee popped so loud I was almost certain it broke.

Can you show me your idea?

"Do you have something to draw on?"

Elder looked puzzled for a moment, and then said *I forget you have not been instructed. May I show you how it is done?*

"Sure." When he reached for my head, I stepped back. "Are you going to put our heads together? I thought that was for pairings."

Pairing is one thing. There are others. May I show you this one?

Elder took my head in his hands, and we pressed our foreheads together. I found myself in a place similar to the Flawless Space, but it was more like a painter's canvas, or a workspace of some kind.

With Elder's patient instruction, I created a crude version of the bathing pool. I managed to cut it in half, creating a profile of the pool. I put a passable image of him in the pool near the hot springs on the bottom, then drew a tube to a breathing mask on him, and attached the other end above the waterline. I was no artist, but it was enough for him to get my idea.

We use something like this to move around under the water. You might want to breathe in through your nose and out of your mouth to circulate fresh air.

With this, I will be able to stay under the water as long as I want. Thank you, he said.

The workspace dissolved around us, and we were back in the cavern. I was not weak, but I was disoriented and dripping with sweat.

"It is a little too hot in here for me. Can we get the tablet and go outside?"

I had not noticed he had already left and I was talking to myself. When he returned, he handed me a very large book, light for its size. When I opened it, the pages were blank and the paper, if you could call it that, was very thin and looked like parchment, but very smooth to the touch. In the binding was a long, pointed rod.

The rod is similar to your pen, but does not stop working. Try to use it.

I took the foot-long stylus from the binding and wrote my name on the first page. The letters were similar to what a fine marker would make.

"How does it work?"

The rod absorbs magnetic fields and concentrates them at the point. When you write on the tablet, it reveals what you write, but it is not permanent. You can remove the writing by pressing the stylus firmly on what you want to remove, and pulling it across the writing. The page cannot be damaged by doing this. Try removing your writing.

When I followed his instructions, the writing quickly disappeared.

"Can it be made permanent?"

Only when you are sure you have completed writing, a device can be used to make it permanent. After that treatment, no stylus or magnetic field will be able to remove the writing.

"After the writing has been made permanent, can I write on a blank page?"

Yes, and the new writing can be removed. Only the parts that are made permanent cannot be changed.

When I looked down at the open tablet, a drop of sweat fell from my chin onto the page. I made matters worse by wiping the page with a sweaty hand.

I made the page wet. Do you have a paper towel? I said.

Close the tablet, and open it again, Elder said.

When I did, the page was completely dry.

The tablets are durable, and they are not affected by water.

"This will be very useful. Thank you. Can we leave now?"

I will stay here and make the breathing tube. The High One is waiting for you at the water tank.

I left the cavern at a run, anxious to be with her. When I rushed toward her, she caught me up and held me off my feet at arm's length.

"You are wet with inside water."

"It was hot in the cave."

Drink water. Keep your blood thin, Lana said.

"You were kind to the old male," Amber said.

"He needed someone to help him feel useful."

"He is very happy with your idea of a breathing tube. I will remember it, because I will need one when I get old."

"I cannot imagine you getting old. Speaking of age, how old are you?"

"I am three years old," she stated proudly.

I was robbing the cradle. Amber must be big for her age...she certainly looked older. She had never told me how old she was.

Why are you concerned about my hatchling's age? Lana said.

"In my society, we do not marry...bond with anyone until they are at least eighteen. There are special circumstances that might, but...certainly not...."

You move too quickly between human and Draasen thinking. You have been accepted by our society, and you are subject to our protocols. Human protocols have no value here.

"When is a female able to bond with a male?"

Hatchlings are considered able to make their own decisions within six months. Some finish their education earlier, like my first hatchling. She finished her education at the end of two months. She is a very fast learner.

Amber was smiling at me.

"You are enjoying this," I said.

"It is amusing."

"Your mother seems to hear me whenever I think about something, just like you do."

"She is linked to you through me."

I felt something else needed saying, but the moment slipped away.

Eventually, Amber said, "Will you take the Third Step of Acceptance with me?"

"What is the Third Step of Acceptance?"

Oracle appeared and hovered in front of me.

It is the highest position Draasen society will offer a non-Draasen hatched individual. As part of the Third Step of Acceptance, you are assigned the duties of protecting and birthing the High One's eggs. This is offered to you as the bonded pairing of the High One. It must be accepted without reservations of any kind.

Will you accept the position of Surrogate to the High One and complete the Third Step of Acceptance? Oracle said.

A ring of Draasen had gathered around us. They were on all fours standing on their fingertips and toes, with their tails high in the air, anticipating my answer.

"My queen, I accept your offer," I said, placing my chin on my chest, extending my hands, palms up.

Amber pressed her palms down on my upturned palms and then squeezed my hands.

"Thank you, Raymond."

With that, she picked me up and gave me a breathtaking hug. An intense buzzing bounded around in my lungs as they rapidly shook their tails again. The buzzing became deafening as Amber carried me toward the bathing pool.

Suddenly, I saw everything clearly for the first time, like a veil had been lifted from my mind. I was being held by an alien, surrounded by them, and I was terrified by everything I saw. As I struggled in Amber's arms, trying to get away, the males stood up and looked directly at me. Strangely enough, with that, my doubts and fears disappeared. Why would I question any of this?

"Is everything acceptable?" Amber said.

"Yes. Why, did something change?"

Silence! Both of you! Lana said.

The males were rushing toward domes and caves while Lana and several females ran toward Oracle's dome. Amber set me on my feet and ran after Lana.

"What is happening?" I said when Elder ran to my side.

"Oracle tried to influence you through the females. When we felt its influence, we stopped it. What did you feel before the High One put you on your feet?"

"I felt as if I did not belong here, and I wanted to run away."

"It is curious. Oracle was violating you without any effort to hide it."

I noticed all the males, except Elder, had disappeared.

"Where did everyone go?"

"Hiding. We may be held responsible for what happened."

"You are not hiding."

"You would have been unprotected. There is no danger to you in this colony, but it is not correct to leave you alone."

"I think they need reassurance. Will they come out if I call them?"

"We will respond to you."

I would like all males to come to me. Please, everyone, gather around me.

While they slowly gathered around me, they took uneasy looks at all the females who had gathered around Oracle's dome. Amber said I represented the males, and it made me uncomfortable because I thought it was a ceremonial position. I would put it to the test.

Everyone put out a hand. I pressed my palm on each hand to reassure them. *None of you are at fault. You were able to stop Oracle, and I thank all of you for it. When they have finished with Oracle, we will be on our guard for future influences. In the meantime, we will wait together until we find out what happened.* I stood in front as we faced the direction of Oracle's dome and waited.

***

Nearly an hour later, the females left Oracle's dome and came toward us with Amber in the lead, and Lana beside her. Elder stepped up beside me. I greeted Amber with my palms up and my chin on my chest. When she returned the greeting, I said, "High One, are any of the males at fault for what happened?"

"This was Oracle's doing. None of the males are at fault."

"Elder was the first to feel the influence by Oracle. Can he be complimented for alerting us?"

"He is commended for his detection and alert."

"Can the males be complimented for assisting in stopping the influence?"

"All the males are commended for their actions."

"High One, may we return to our duties?" I said.

Smiling, Amber picked me up and carried me toward the bathing pool while the two sides dispersed.

When we arrived at the bathing pool, Amber set me on my feet, took my head in her hands, and pressed our foreheads together in a private, and intimate, conversation.

I am very proud of you. You represented them surprisingly well. Some of the females wanted to punish them.

Why should they be punished? They did nothing wrong.

Because they are males. Your request made directly to me stopped protests from the females. The respect you demonstrated to me won over several females. There is only one who does not approve of you as my choice.

I thought your decision was final in everything.

It is, but I would like everyone's approval. It will become important.

She smiled, and I could not help returning the smile as my apprehension melted away. After we removed our clothes and dove in, I wondered what had happened with Oracle. Amber surfaced beside me.

Oracle's intellect was not in its sphere. We do not know where it went, and we could not get it back. We will be feeling for its presence, and when it returns, we will ask it then.

Why was Oracle trying to influence me?

I do not know. It has not been the same since it took your memories.

Elder was walking toward the bathing pool with his arms loaded with equipment.

"He is ready to try his snorkel. I want to watch this," I said, diving toward the back of the pool.

He asked another male to attach one end of the tube on the rock above the water. Then, he placed the mask over his muzzle, covering his nose and mouth. I noticed he had installed valves on the mask to let air out.

He gently entered the water and slowly sank toward the hot springs at the bottom.

Does it work?

Yes. Thank you for your suggestion, he said as he squatted on the bottom.

"You have made him very happy," Amber said.

"He deserves it."

At the scrubbing ledge, Amber was very meticulously cleaning herself. She insisted she scrub me as well, even after I had already done so. I figured this was in preparation for the egg implanting. This sounds strange, but I was about to become a mother, and I wondered why I was doing it.

You have accepted me and my people, and we have accepted you. You have bonded with me, and I know you have no reservations. Why do you have doubts about my eggs?

"Normally, it would take weeks, even months, to adjust to something like this. Why have I been moving so fast? It is not natural, and I am not comfortable with it."

Amber looked at me for a long time before she spoke. *What I am about to tell you is the truth. Please do not reject me for not revealing this before now. Until this suns rise, I had been influencing you and your actions. The way you feel now is how you would have felt much later in our relationship, if there was time to do so. You could have refused anything at any time, if you wanted to. I am happy you have accepted what has been offered. Those who support you and me together had been sending influences to you as well.*

More than anything else she said, her request not to reject her surprised me, but what she said made sense. It was the will of the people, and everyone wanted me to succeed with her. There was a lot to consider while I was on the fast track to success.

"When can I begin learning about your people and your history?"

It is correct to say our people. You have taken the Third Step of Acceptance, which has not been offered in many thousands of years. I will delay your education until our first hatchling achieves sentience. Then the two of you can learn together.

After a stop at the clothing dome, I noticed the humidity seemed more oppressive than usual.

There is going to be a storm. The air has the feel of it. Oracle would warn us if a storm is coming, but without it, we will have to be watchful, Amber said.

The food trays were brought out with what appeared to be large dinner rolls.

"High One, have you ever seen anything like that before?" I said.

"This must be a new item."

Each item on the tray was brown all over, and as big as a softball cut in half. I got one from the tray, and took a bite.

"Cheeseburger," I mumbled as I chewed through a mouth full, pointing at it. There was no meat inside, but no matter where you bit into it, it tasted like a really good juicy cheeseburger.

Amber smiled as she speared two with her tongue.

"It is very good."

That set off a frenzy of competing tongues and clawed hands as the pile on the tray quickly disappeared. The males tossed me items from other trays that were out of my reach. As I ate, I wondered what nutritional value these foods had.

Be sure to take something from every tray to get the nutrients you need, Lana said.

I do not like some of this stuff.

When hatchlings do not eat the correct foods, we hand feed them, Lana said, drilling me with her eyes.

Is that a challenge? I said, looking directly back at her. I did not get a response, but I did get the feeling she would turn words into action.

While I wondered if I could finish the last bit of the burger in front of me, I leaned back in my seat and closed my eyes. I fondly remembered the first bonding with Amber. It was an experience I wanted to relive. Suddenly, I found myself back in our Flawless Space, floating effortlessly with Amber holding me.

How did we get here? She said.

I thought about you, and here we are.

To be pulled into a Flawless Space is unheard of.

I am sorry.

Do not be, but we must control it.

When we returned to ourselves, I was slumped against the table. The feeding was long over and the trays had been cleared. I felt sluggish and disoriented, but managed to sit upright.

What happened? Lana said.

Amber looked as if a roof had caved in on her, and she was not very steady as she squatted at the table.

He called me into the Flawless Space.

It is the strength of your bonding. Your bondings make me wish my pairing was here.

"There is a storm coming," Amber said aloud, changing the subject.

In the distance, I could see a dark line of clouds backlit by lightning, and it was moving very fast. "It looks like a bad one. I do not think we can trust the domes."

"Tell the males to get to the caves," Amber said.

There is a storm coming. Do not go to your domes. It is safer to go into the caves.

When I delivered the message, all eyes turned to the ocean. Then everyone started moving toward the caves. I did not hear Amber give an announcement to the females, but they were moving as well. I looked at Amber, who was looking back at me.

"What did I do?" I said, knowing I must have done something wrong.

"The females are obeying you."

"They may be moving because they know this is a dangerous storm," I said defensively.

"Yes, that must be the reason," Amber said in a way that did not convince me it was true. "We must get to the caves as well."

When we walked to the caves, I remembered my notes and made a detour to pick them up. I saw Amber's robes, scepter, and circlet still on the shelves, so I wrapped everything up in the robes. A crack of thunder sounded very close and I made a hurried exit.

The speed of the storm was incredible, because I had been in the dome only a few seconds and it was already on us. When I was running toward the nearest cave, a powerful bolt of lightning struck the mountainside, making me run even faster as lightning crashed all around, and a blinding rain pelted me. While I was running blindly, hoping I could see a cave entrance, I was picked up and carried into the preparation cave. When we skidded to a stop, I thanked the male who had rescued me, and I saw everyone was far back from the entrance.

I looked for Amber, but she was nowhere to be seen. I knew she would be worried so I tried reaching out to reassure her, but I could not hear her. The thunder was deafening, even inside the cave, and I noticed everyone had their ears folded against their heads. When I tried reaching out to anyone in the cave, I realized I was telepathically deaf. I saw Elder and I tried to contact him without success, so I touched his arm to get his attention and pointed to my forehead. He pointed to the cave entrance and then covered his forehead with his hand. Apparently, storms like this blocked telepathic contact, probably because of the lightning, which was severe to say the least. The constant thunder made it impossible to be heard, so I settled on the floor to wait out the storm.

Eventually the thunder faded, and there were cautious movements toward the cave entrance.

Where are you? Amber's telepathic voice was suddenly very loud in my mind.

I am in the preparation cave.

Stay where you are!

I saw two males outside, low to the ground on all fours with their tails flat out behind them, carefully looking over the area. After a few minutes they stood, and Amber said it was safe to come out.

The devastation was surprising. All of the domes were either damaged or completely gone, replaced by blue, water filled depressions where they'd once stood. The feeding table was gone, as was the water tank, ripped from its mounts.

When I approached Amber, who was standing near the location of our dome, she shot a look over her shoulder that stopped me in my tracks. She spun around and roughly picked me up off the ground, pinning my arms at my sides.

You should have stayed with me. If you went on the long walk, what would happen to my eggs?

"High One, there is nothing more important than the safety of your eggs, but your eggs are in you, not me. Please put me down, you are hurting my arms. I felt these were important."

"My robes! My scepter and circlet! They were not lost. Thank you, thank you, thank you!" She picked me up again and gave me a breathtaking hug.

"Amber, I need to breathe." She set me back on my feet and gently nuzzled my face before she took my head in her hands. "High One, I am sorry. I should have stayed with you."

"You saw to our people before yourself, and you were concerned for things that are important to me. I should have gone for these."

"Was anyone hurt?"

"Because of your warning, everyone was in the caves when the storm arrived. One cave was blocked by the falling rocks, but no one was damaged inside. It is being cleared first."

"We should take a look around and see what needs to be done to get our colony back together."

"What do you think should be done?"

"Well, since Oracle is unavailable, we should set a guard facing the sea to watch for more storms."

"I will tell one of the males to be our watcher until Oracle returns."

"The area needs to be cleared and new domes set up."

Amber pointed to several individuals taking armloads of items into one of the caves, and others bringing out what resembled closed umbrellas.

"Do I need to ask about clearing the bathing pool?"

Several males surfaced from the bathing pool and handed off damaged items.

A sudden earth shaking explosion knocked me off my feet, and Amber was quick to cover me with her body. Several females made a tight ring around us while others rushed to investigate the explosion.

"Are you damaged?"

"I just got the wind knocked out of me," I strained to say. *Oracle's dome exploded! Five are damaged!*

I saw Lana and two others run to an injured pair who had been blown against the rock wall. Three others were hurt by flying debris. Lana reported that the damage to everyone was minor and was easily repaired; if you could say broken bones and deep cuts were minor.

The place where Oracle's dome once stood was scoured in a dark circle. As we watched, a shaft of light rose from under the ground and stopped about five feet in the air. Everyone was wary of it as they walked around it.

High One, the personal transport of High One Sialisannsee is approaching. Her consort asks for your permission to arrive.

Welcome to my colony, Sialisannsee. The way is clear for you to arrive.

When the transport swung up the cliff, I noticed the bottom of the transport was smooth except for a four-pronged object pulled tight in the center. As the transport drifted sideways over the ground, the air energized with static. Amber looked at me as arcs of static electricity jumped around me. She picked me up and it stopped.

"Is this better?" she said.

"Always, when you hold me."

When the transport settled, Amber set me on my feet and walked toward it. A seam opened and High One Sialisannsee stepped out. When they met, they placed their palms together, like high fives, or in their case high fours, and pressed their foreheads together. Then Sialisannsee greeted Lana and three other females.

Elder stepped up beside me, put his hand on my shoulder, and started a private conversation.

The pilot of the transport is the mated pairing and Consort to High One Sialisannsee. You saw the High Ones greet each other as equals, palms facing each other. You are the birthing animal to the High One, and you must greet him as his superior, not as an equal.

The pilot came out and walked directly to me. When he stopped, he was so close he almost bumped me. While we stared at each other, I had the feeling I was being challenged as he gave me a sneer. Out of the corner of my eye, I saw the two High Ones watching us. I stepped back and offered my greeting with my palms down. He shouted several bagpipes-like tones at me that I did not understand. High One

Sialisannsee spoke in sharp tones to her consort that made him turn and run to their transport. She came to me, and I gave her the greeting with my palms up.

Do not be offended by my consort's behavior. He will stay in the transport for the remainder of my visit, and I will instruct him to greet you properly in the future.

Thank you, High One. Being polite is always appropriate.

High One Sialisannsee smiled and turned to Amber. *Despite your surrogate's lack of education, he has demonstrated he can act correctly; but my visit is not to compare consorts. I have this for you.* She gave Amber a purse she carried with her tail. *Do you need assistance in re-establishing your colony?*

Thank you for your offer, but we are almost finished.

Very well, I will take my leave of you. They touched palms and when they separated, she returned to me and lifted my chin in her hand.

Ambrisseethsss is fortunate to have you. When she told me what she was going to do, I disagreed with her. Now that I have met you, I know it was the best decision she could have made under the circumstances. She is your guide. Listen to what she has to say.

I have heard that before.

From your healer? she said.

Yes, how did you know?

Ssurlanaseethesess is my mother. She smiled at me before returning to her transport.

Amber picked me up to insulate me from the static electricity as the transport lifted and pivoted toward the cliffs. It soared in a graceful arc toward the sea, where it leveled off above the whitecaps, and disappeared in the mist.

I did not know High One Sialisannsee was your sister.

Did you know the other females she greeted are my sisters as well?

No, I did not. When I looked at her sisters, one of them gave me what I felt was a flirty little smile as she cocked her head at me. When Amber looked at her, she quickly looked elsewhere. Another female approached and said *High One, we are ready to establish an Oracle.*

Two males were waiting at Oracle's light post with one of the large umbrellas. Amber opened the purse and brought out a shiny black sphere.

"Take this and set it on the top of the light post," she said as she handed it to me.

"You are supposed to do that."

"I want you to do it."

I held out my hands and the weight of the softball-sized sphere surprised me. It weighed about thirty pounds. When I placed it on top of the light post, it landed with a solid thump and changed into the familiar, multicolor sphere when it rose from the post and resettled.

Enclose the Oracle, Amber said.

Two males took the umbrella and set it up as a soft dome. Another solidly hit each of the support members with a heavy silver rod, and with a sound similar to rubbing your fingers over a balloon, the dome filled out and became hard. A door was attached and left open.

High One Ambrisseethsss, your presence is requested. Bring your consort.

When we entered Oracle's dome, Amber placed me in her lap.

Welcome to my center. High One, please update the relevant events since the shutdown of the previous Oracle.

"Shutdown? Is that what you call it? People were hurt."

Ignoring my outburst, Amber related the activities including my defense of the males during the attempted control by the previous Oracle. Lana and each junior queen were called to relate their version of events, and then Elder was called. When he entered, I got off Amber's lap and stood in front of him.

Consort to the High One, there has been no violation of protocols by this male. I am gathering information to update colony records from different perspectives.

"Oracle, I stand with the males in all things."

Amber smiled at me, and then looked at Oracle with narrowed eyes.

Male, relate the relevant events, Oracle said.

After Elder spoke and left, Amber placed me in her lap again.

"What happened to the other Oracle?" I said.

During attempts to repair the previous unit, it refused commands to shut down. Central determined it had become an entity, and when Central attempted to shut down the malfunctioning unit, it destroyed itself.

"What is Central?" I said.

Central is a unit installed on each colony planet, deeply buried to protect it. Its primary function is to gather and transmit data to Core on the home world. High One, I have updated the necessary information. The colony members are waiting for your arrival at the feeding table.

"When we have finished feeding, we will bathe. The next suns is special for us."

I had not given much thought to carrying Amber's eggs and I felt nervous about it.

"The implanting procedure is simple and painless. You can sleep if you want."

"I have to admit, I am curious about it. I will decide when the time comes."

When we arrived at the feeding table, trays of steaming foodstuffs were brought out. Amber told everyone to eat.

"Why are you not eating?" I said, spearing an item with my fork.

"I do not want a feeding inside me at the time for implanting."

When we finished eating and went to the water tank, Amber stumbled against it and drank so much I thought she might explode.

"Thirsty?"

"Not any more," she said distractedly.

When we reached the bathing pool, I settled on my ledge. When Amber eased into the pool beside me, I realized our link was quiet.

"Is something wrong?" I said. Her face was blank, and I held her head as she began to sink. "Lana, I need help!" I shouted when her weight started pulling me off the ledge.

My shout brought females from every direction. Those in the pool helped me support Amber until others pulled her from the water. Lana arrived with her equipment and performed a scan.

Quickly, bring the High One to my dome. Bring the consort.

I was swept up by one of Amber's sisters, and we ran behind the group carrying Amber.

Did the High One say or do anything unusual before you called me? Lana said to me.

She was being careful with herself when she entered the bathing pool. Before that, she did not eat, and she drank so much water I thought she would burst.

When we entered the hospital, Amber was placed on the table as the light became very bright from all sides.

Set up the second table and put him on it.

"What is going on?" I said.

Implanting will take place now, and you are going to sleep.

As I was eased onto my back, Lana placed one of her devices on my forehead and tapped it.

"Hey, wait, I...."

***

"...want to watch." I finished mumbling my sentence long after the surgery was completed. There was a dull ache above my belly button and a general discomfort all around my middle.

The eggs are attached to you, and they are all healthy.

"Can we wake her yet?" I said, greatly missing Amber's presence inside me.

Not yet.

"How is she?"

She had to wait a very long time to implant her eggs. Usually, we remove the eggs from a female and implant them into a birthing animal within two suns of fertilization. For her, it had been twelve suns.

"If she wanted to implant her eggs earlier, she should have told me."

She wanted you to be comfortable with your decision. There is nothing more for you to do. You can leave.

Elder was walking by the door, and I noticed he was limping a lot more than usual.

"Lana, can you do something for his leg?"

It is of no concern, he said.

I will decide that. Come in and stand still, Lana ordered.

Lana tapped the diagnostic device on her arm and passed her hand over Elder's hip. She went to her shelves and retrieved a long rod that she attached to the device on her arm. The rod glowed with a blue light that made my hair stand on end. She swung her arm and hit Elder's hip with a heavy thump.

"Hey, I wanted you to fix it, not break it!"

It feels much better. Thank you.

As he walked out of the dome he still limped, but not nearly as much as before.

A time is coming when I will not be able to heal his pain and damage. He will soon go on the long walk, Lana said as we watched him walk toward his dome.

"Whenever I see him, he is always alone. Does he have anyone to be with him?"

His bonded pairing has gone on the long walk. He is available, so he is not lonely. We all must walk within the Great Ring until our end.

"It sounds like the circle of life. Maybe some music would cheer him up. Do you have any music we can listen to?"

The Most High One has forbidden song to be sung.

"Do you know why?"

She has forbidden it! Go to your dome and rest.

That was unusually snappish, and I felt a flash of fear from her.

As I walked, there were bumps in different places I felt inside, but only if I moved in certain ways. I felt I had to walk differently to keep them comfortable.

They cannot feel anything yet, Lana said.

The dome we shared was very empty without Amber. I pulled out my paper notes and continued transcribing them to the Draasen book.

After writing for a while, I decided to turn in. Without Amber, I was an uncomfortable empty shell, and I could not sleep until I found myself in the workspace with the puppet in front of me again. A string dropped toward the puppet, and I fell into a deep sleep.

Chapter 6

SHIELD

Wake up. Wake up! I am ready to wake the High One.

Suddenly wide awake, I was up and running to the hospital.

"Lana, how is she?"

She has nearly healed.

I climbed to the top of the table and sat beside her head. When Lana tapped the device on Amber's forehead, our link reconnected and I was happy to feel her presence inside me again.

Good morning, beautiful.

She smiled at me, and then her eyes popped open. *My eggs!*

Your surrogate has them. They are all healthy and firmly attached.

Do they cause you any pain? Amber said.

No, but I can feel them when I move, I said, placing her hand on my stomach.

Lana said, *You will go slowly today. The healing accelerator has healed most of the incision, but the bindings could release if you put too much stress on them.*

"You did not tell me to go slowly last night," I said.

Your surgery was small compared to hers, and your body adapted surprisingly well to the accelerator. She pointed to a long, light green line across Amber's mid-section. *The eggs had started migrating, and I needed a longer incision to reach them.*

"Why did you hide your pain from me?" I asked Amber.

I did not want you to know.

"Are you sure it was me you wanted to hide your pain from, or your mother?" They exchanged glances, but said nothing. "Whenever you are in pain, you will tell me. How can I care for you if you hide it from me?"

I will keep you informed, she said.

"Excellent. How do you feel?"

I am not in any pain, and I will move slowly this suns.

"Can she bathe?"

Yes, she can do most activities, but she must do them slower.

"Good, we will go to the bathing pool and relax."

As we walked, I caught myself admiring her. Then I thought of a human female, but I did not feel the same. Somehow that was right and wrong at the same time. She was walking faster than I thought she should, so I gently restrained her.

"Slow down. The bathing pool will still be there."

I am not a hatchling.

"No, you are not," I said, grabbing her hand with both of mine, pulling her to a stop. "You are the High One, but I will not allow you to hurt yourself. You can run, tomorrow. You can carry me, tomorrow. Today, you will move slower. Since you have to slow down, it would be a good day to continue my training. I do not have thousands of years of conditioning to show me how to use telepathy. You have to show me."

It appears he has a tail wrapped around you. I wish he was here when my eggs were ready for implanting, Lana said as she passed us.

There was humor in her thoughts, and I was grateful for that because I belatedly realized I had been speaking out of place.

"Very well. I will walk slowly."

When we arrived, she set her feet to jump in, but I took her hand and shook my head.

"No diving today. Ease yourself in."

While I enjoyed the water, a female surfaced beside me and placed her hand on my thigh.

I heard your conversation. You are speaking out of place and embarrassing the High One. As she spoke, I felt a tingling pressure in my head.

Maybe, but if a little embarrassment is what it takes for her get healthy again, so be it. She is my bonded pairing, and I will personally see to her health and safety.

She released my thigh and swam toward the hot springs. Then Amber surfaced beside me.

What did she want?

She said I am embarrassing you.

Did you feel anything unusual when she spoke to you?

I did feel a tingling inside my head. Does that count?

She was testing you, she said, and submerged again.

There was something going on, and I wished she would give me a clue about what I was supposed to do. Unlike my life on earth, things here were so peaceful and simple. Maybe something was going to change. I hoped not.

Please concentrate on our eggs. I will see to your needs and the needs of our people.

That left me confused. The more I thought about it, the more I was convinced something was going to happen. Amber surfaced again and looked at me.

You are too inquisitive, she said, and took me to the scrubbing ledge.

I wondered if there was a way I could shield my thoughts. As an experiment, I envisioned a shield on my left arm, like an ancient warrior might have. Amber stopped swimming and looked over her shoulder at me. I did not feel or hear anything from her. The longer I held the shield in place, the more uncomfortable I became. I mentally dropped the shield from my arm and was very relieved when our link re-established.

I heard nothing from you. How did you shut me out? Amber said.

I was testing a new idea. If it is any consolation, I could not hear you either.

What happened? There was emptiness where I usually feel him, Lana said when she surfaced beside us.

How can I do something you do not know how to do? You have more experience with the telepathy thing than I do.

I would like to learn about this, Lana said.

Amber started a private conversation with me.

This is something I have been fearful of. You have different ways of thinking, and I suspected you might go in new directions. Please do not pursue the idea of change. Do not think about it. The less you know, the more orderly things will be at the appropriate time.

If I could have a simple reason why I should not consider what I have heard, I would be able to put it out of my mind.

It is too dangerous for you. Your thoughts are too easily heard by others. Please, do not ask for more information. For your safety and the safety of everyone involved, do not think about anything you heard. I can help you put it out of your thoughts, if you want me to.

My interest was piqued and I wanted to ask detailed questions, but I knew they would not be answered.

You are thinking again, Amber said.

"Sorry. I will stop thinking," I said without much confidence. How can you stop thinking?

We will work on controlling your thinking.

***

When we left the clothing dome, the female who had spoken to me in the bathing pool approached Amber. They were both standing at their full statures as she spoke.

High One, I apologize for my lack of acceptance of your surrogate. I had doubts that have been answered satisfactorily. I accept your position and I will follow your decisions in all matters. She squatted and offered the Gesture of Respect.

Amber lifted her to a standing position, pressed her palms down on hers, and had a private conversation with her. When they were finished, the female turned and squatted in front of me. I offered the greeting, palms up as was the position of a male before a female. She gently turned my palms down, pressed her palms up under mine, and started a private conversation.

Ask your pairing why the Most High One abandoned our colony planets. You will find the answer interesting. She walked away and left me confused. Amber was smiling at me.

It is a Gesture of Respect to you as my surrogate. As my surrogate, you have been placed above all females except High Ones. After my last egg is birthed, you will become my consort again, and you will be placed only above the males, where you will continue to represent them.

I decided not to ask about the colony planets. I felt it was a bad idea because it sounded a lot like something was changing, and I was not allowed to think about that.

When Amber started a fast walk toward the feeding table, I took her hand with both of mine and dug in my heels to get her to stop. She gave me an annoyed look, but I was adamant. We looked at each other for a few moments before I started walking at a slower pace, still holding her hand.

You are doing well to keep her moving slowly, Lana said.

Amber's tongue shot out for the eggs and with that, everyone was tonguing or clawing at the food. For some reason, I passed my plate and was given a little of everything. I did not like the flavor of what looked like boiled spinach, but I was given some anyway. I continued to look at the leaves and wondered why something was on my plate I did not like. Amber and Lana were looking at me, and I felt I was being influenced again.

"Come on, you know I do not like this stuff." I felt amusement from around the table.

"You need the greening for my eggs."

I held my breath as I gobbled them down, and quickly followed up with a bacon bar I hoped would cover the taste. It did not.

"Blah. That stuff is nasty." My male tablemates broke into laughter.

"I am sorry, but the greening is full of nutrients that are important to my eggs, so you will have to eat them at every feeding."

"Is there a way I can get the nutrients without the flavor?"

Oracle floated to the table and said, *If you request, I will create a food item with better flavor that has the botai leaves as the main ingredient.*

"Oracle, I request...." I stopped because every request to Oracle had to be presented to the High One for approval first.

I faced Amber and offered the Gesture of Respect. "High One, can I make a request?"

"Present your request."

"I request a better-tasting food item be made using the greening leaves as the main ingredient."

That is my command, added Amber.

Command accepted. Oracle flew off.

"Thank you. I never liked botai, but I ate them anyway," Elder said, with quiet agreement from around the table.

"If you would bring such things to my attention, I can make a request to do them. That is what I am supposed to do, right?"

The males cast nervous glances toward the females.

85

"Surrogate to the High One is a position that has not been used for many thousands of years. Guidance is needed," Elder boldly said.

"What applies to the consort should apply to the surrogate," I said.

Oracle sped back to the table and said, *When an alien surrogate was first needed, it was decided Surrogate to the High One would become the highest position a non-Draasen hatched individual can hold. It is higher than Consort to the High One, and holds all the duties and responsibilities of that position.*

Amber held my thigh under the table and started a private conversation. *Your thoughts tell me you are troubled again.*

I have to be responsible for your males, but I am not a leader.

Just be yourself.

I wondered how many times I would hear that before it would make sense in the overall scheme of things.

Careful.

Apparently, that thought strayed into the forbidden area of change again.

"Is there anything anyone needs?" I said aloud.

I did not expect an answer. While females were nearby, the males might not express any of their needs openly.

"If anyone has a need, come to me, and I will act on it."

Very good, your education is proceeding, Amber said.

After feeding, I was watching her closely as we walked to the water tank for a drink.

I am much improved since last suns, Amber said when she saw me watching her.

"I want you healthy. Besides, I enjoy looking at you."

When we arrived at our dome, Lana walked to us and said, *It is time to continue training your telepathic abilities, with an emphasis on control. Before we do that, I am curious about the shield you used.*

"How would you like me to show it to you?"

We will go to what you call the workspace, Lana said, and the three of us telepathically entered the workspace together.

This is what I did. I concentrated on creating a shield I mounted on my arm to protect me, and this appeared.

Again, I had the large shield on my left arm, and I lost all contact with them. I waved to them as they looked around. It was a very lonely feeling being disconnected from Amber, so I dropped the shield.

Did you see me waving at you?

No, you disappeared completely, Lana said.

Could you see the shield I set up in front of me?

I could not see or hear you at all. It is curious you completely disappear to us in here, but not outside.

Why are you worried about this? I said, feeling Amber's concerns.

I do not like it. When we were separated during the storm, I thought you went on the long walk.

Just because I have found something new does not mean I have to use it.

Lana was looking at us, but not really seeing us.

Lana, you have something on your mind, I said.

I need a private conversation with my hatchling, she replied, and went into head to head private conversation with Amber.

While I waited, I wondered if a smaller shield would be as effective...a buckler perhaps? Then I thought I should let go of the idea of a shield on my arm. Dropping my arms to my sides, I concentrated without the image of the shield, and I felt it worked because my link to Amber was gone again. Amber and Lana separated and looked around in confusion. I walked behind Amber and dropped the shield. When the link established again, she spun around and looked at me.

I tried using the shield without having one on my arm, and it worked!

Your shield may be useful, but I cannot work with it when you are invisible. We will leave here and see what we can do with it, Lana said, and the workspace dissolved around us.

***

Because I could not telepathically hear anything with my shield in place, we set up hand signals for me to raise and lower it. We worked with my shield for what seemed like hours so Lana could learn from me. I was becoming bored with my new toy, and when my concentration strayed, Lana sharply told me to focus.

I have learned all I can. This is adequate, for now, Lana finally said, and went into another head to head private conversation with Amber.

"Amber, what is happening?" I said when they separated.

Please do not ask. I would tell you if I could.

Would the others of your colony accept us? Lana said to me, distracting my attention.

"They would probably try to kill you."

Why?

"Humans believe they are the masters of everything they see. When they discover they are not, they think they must conquer and control. Failing that, they will destroy it so no one can have it."

The humans that came with you are too few to cause damage to anyone except themselves, Lana said.

"It already started before I was brought here. I hoped we would be able to go home and everything would be okay. Now, the human race is on the brink of extinction, and there is nothing I can do about it."

Oracle! I want you here, Amber commanded.

Oracle swept in and hovered in front of us.

Is there any evidence of my surrogate's species on any Draasen-settled planets?

I will request Central ask Core for information.

"Oracle, is there any progress on my request for information from my home world?"

One pod has completed its programmed tasks and has returned to the probe for data retrieval. The second pod is searching the interior of a selected structure.

"Do you have any details about how I was brought here?"

A Baleoran transport vessel approached this planet....

You did not inform us the Baleorans were here. How did this happen? You are supposed to protect us! Lana was afraid, as was everyone else, judging by the bagpipes-like tones that resounded across the colony.

Mother, I am the only one who needed to know. Oracle will explain, Amber said.

A Baleoran transport vessel approached this planet close to one of the suns. Due to solar interference, it was not detected until it was in orbit. The Baleorans detached a drop vessel and placed the structure the surrogate arrived in on the surface. Before the transport left orbit, it was destroyed.

"How many buildings could be stored inside one of those transport ships?" I said.

Drop vessels were not stored inside the Baleoran transport. There was space for eight-drop vessels attached to the sides of that type of vessel.

"The defense platform probably killed hundreds of my people."

There were six empty spaces when it was destroyed. It is likely the others were dropped elsewhere.

"Did the Baleorans find out we were here?"

That information is not known. The Baleoran vessel may have scanned limited areas of the planet surface to determine a suitable area to place your structure.

"Did the defense platform detect any communications from the Baleoran ship?"

There were no detectable emissions during the destruction of the Baleoran vessel.

"Good. Whoa, wait a minute. On my home world, certain ships have a distress beacon that is launched when it is in trouble. The beacon allows a searching vessel to locate the last known position of the ship to begin a search. Did the Baleoran ship drop something like that?"

That information is not known.

"The meteor showers must have been the remains of the Baleoran ship burning up. I wonder if they had a beacon that burned up as well."

There was a large quantity of debris after the Baleoran vessel was destroyed, most of which vaporized when it entered the atmosphere.

"Send probes to search the debris and monitor for communications."

A probe has been launched and is programmed to monitor for Baleoran communications within the remaining debris.

Oracle obeyed my command, but it should not have. Everything must be approved by Amber as the High One of the colony. Despite that, I pressed on.

"Can your probes be programmed to push the debris into the atmosphere?"

The remaining debris does not need to be removed from orbit. It will eventually enter the atmosphere without assistance.

"If the Baleorans come looking for their ship and find the debris in orbit, they might find us."

Remove the remains of the Baleoran vessel from orbit. That is my command, Amber said.

Command accepted. Probes have been programmed and launched. It will take many suns to clear all debris.

"If the Baleorans come here, do we have weapons to defend ourselves?"

Central has been monitoring our interface and has requested an explanation why you have requested access to restricted information concerning warrior's weapons.

"I thought the Draasen were peaceful. What do you need warriors for?"

Central requires an answer. Why do you request restricted information?

"My species is nearly extinct because of the Baleorans. If I am to remain with the Draasen and have any chance of saving my own species, I have to defend those I care for. If we are to defend ourselves, we need warriors, and warriors need weapons."

Amber and Lana went into a head-to-head private conversation.

As a result of the duality in you, Central provides the following information. Until 195 years ago, the Draasen were explorers, seeking new worlds they could inhabit and draw resources from. Before the arrival of the Baleorans, there were thirty-eight billion Draasen on the home world and twenty-two colony planets. Now, there are nine billion Draasen on six colony planets and the home world. Because of this, the Most High One has restricted travel in the void.

"Can the Draasen be removed from a planet before the Baleorans arrive?"

There is not enough time to relocate if the defense platforms fail, or are destroyed.

"I wonder where the warriors were when the Baleorans arrived. Oracle, I want to know about the warriors and the weapons available to them."

Access to restricted information is denied.

"Who has access to the restricted information?"

The Most High One has restricted access.

"When was the restriction put in place?"

The restriction was placed 195 years ago.

"That was before I arrived, so the restriction applies to all Draasen except her, but I am not Draasen. Since I am human, the restriction does not apply to me. As a human, I request access to warrior information."

I was overconfident with my status, and did not think it through. I was struck by a flash of light that knocked me off my feet and left me with the strange sensation of vibrating from the inside out. Amber immediately covered me with her body and several females rushed to us, gathering in a tight ring around us.

Are you damaged? Amber said.

"I do not know. I am numb. What hit me?" I said, straining to speak.

An energy pulse of some kind, Lana said.

Amber rushed to Lana, who quickly squatted with her chin on her chest and hands behind her back. Amber stood at her full stature as she shouted down at her.

Did you know Oracle would damage any of us? This is completely unacceptable! My surrogate is carrying my eggs!

I was helped to my feet, and I wobbled to Amber on rubbery legs. When I stumbled against her, she picked me up, and I felt she was angry, but, thankfully, not at me this time.

"Are the eggs okay?" I said.

They are safe. Your body insulated them, Amber said.

The Most High One has ordered that anyone attempting to gain access to warrior information is to be sent on the long walk. Central modified the order and used an enveloping energy field to stun your surrogate as a warning, instead of sending him on the long walk, Oracle reported.

Amber glared at her mother and then took a clawed swipe at Oracle, which quickly retreated out of range.

"Did you know Oracle would attack me?" I asked.

I am greatly annoyed with Oracle, and my mother, for keeping information from me.

"Central could have simply denied access instead of attacking me."

It warned you, but you attempted access again with authority you do not have, Lana said.

"To kill anyone who attempts access is stupid. The Most High One must be crazy to order such a thing. And how can a computer disobey its programming?" Curiosity may yet kill me.

Oracle said, *I will keep this session of instruction simple so your limited intelligence will understand. Core, Centrals, and*

Oracles are sentient, interactive units with telepathic and vocal inputs. Programming differs from orders. Telepathic inputs are programming. Programming cannot be disobeyed or modified in any way except by the Most High One, who inputs the commands. Vocal inputs are orders and can be modified. The Most High One's command regarding access to warrior information was a vocal input. Your position within this colony indicated a change of instruction was necessary. You are advised not to attempt access to any restricted information. You will find programming that will be obeyed without regard to position.

A computer modifying its instructions. My mistrust of this computer system grew by leaps and bounds.

Do you think it may try to take control? Lana said.

"Any computer that can change its instructions is a threat, and I do not trust it."

It is what we have, and we must depend on it.

I was confident I would not get blasted again if I asked another question while I was in Amber's lap.

"Oracle, how long has the Most High One been in charge of the Draasen society?"

Two hundred one years, since the Most High One forced the former queen from the position.

Leave us, Amber commanded.

"Please, do not be angry. I brought the attack on myself with my curiosity."

It was not your curiosity that prompted the attack, but your love for me and our people. I am certain you would defend our people even if you were to go on the long walk doing it.

"If I am going to live the life I have been invited to live, I must be willing to defend it."

When the time is correct, I will assign my first hatchling to you. I will do this because new directions are needed in our society, and your experience and influence will help them grow into our society in new and different ways. Our society is stagnating, and you will give our society new directions through my hatchlings, Amber said with an encouraging smile.

"I do not want to change what I have found here," I said, as fear rose in the pit of my stomach.

You do not have to make changes, just be yourself. You are peaceful, despite the aggressive and fearful influences of human society. My hatchlings can learn from that.

"They will have to accept the things that are good and bad."

I will be responsible for accepting what is needed.

I had been forbidden from thinking about change, and now I was being encouraged. Amber looked at me for a very long time before she said, *Mother, I want your presence.*

I could tell by her tone she was still unhappy with her mother. Lana arrived and squatted before her.

"We are going to speak to Oracle. I want you to update your diary while we are gone," Amber said.

"It is a journal, not a diary."

I reread some of what I had written because I noticed I had stopped using contractions when I spoke and wrote. It was a curiosity that may have had something to do with my bonding with Amber, since the Draasen did not use them. I looked outside and saw many walking toward the bathing pool for second bathing. I looked for Amber, but she was still with Oracle.

When I arrived at the bathing pool our link reconnected, and I saw a streak fall from above and land in the water, creating a wave that drenched me as it pushed me backward. As I gathered my dripping senses, Amber surfaced and leaned against the side of the pool with a mischievous smile.

"Come in, get wet," she said happily, and dove for the hot spring.

"Too late for getting wet," I mumbled as I eased into the water.

I sat on my ledge wondering about Draasen possessions, or the lack of them. None of them had any things except for Amber and Lana, and I could not include Lana because she was using the equipment for the health of everyone in the colony. I wondered if Lana had robes of her own when she was the High One.

Robes, scepter, and circlet are passed to a new High One, just as I passed them to my hatchling. We are happy you saved them because they are not replaceable. My hatchling would have been required to surrender her position as High One, and we would have had to submit to another colony, and its High One, if they were lost.

A sudden blast of air splattered water on my face and sent me scrambling out of the pool. Lana had surfaced and cleared her nostrils at me while I was listening to her.

Your reactions are quick enough, but your body is slow. We will have to work around that.

"Stop sneaking around! What if I had a heart attack and died while I was carrying Amber's eggs?"

She squawked and disappeared when Amber pulled her under. They briefly struggled before Lana swam toward the hot springs.

She will not frighten you like that again.

"Thank you. I never liked anyone sneaking up and scaring me."

You should feel safe here, because you are.

"With all the activity, I am concerned for the eggs. When are you going to activate one?"

I can release an egg after second feeding, if you are ready.

"There is no being ready about this. Information would be good...if it does not violate protocols."

When I release an egg from its sleep, it will move to a place where I will direct it. As it moves, it will extend a filament from where it is attached to you. That filament will grow as the egg grows and will draw nourishment from your body. After the egg reaches its final position, two more filaments will extend. I will guide these filaments to attach to your ribs. They will thicken to support the egg as it grows. We expect you will be able to move around normally for the first twenty-one suns. My mother is concerned the weight of the egg will be uncomfortable for you, so I will carry you after that.

"I do not want to be a burden."

You will never be a burden to me. She helped me onto her back and swam to the scrubbing ledge.

"Am I a birthing animal?"

You are intelligent, so my answer is no.

"Can I be called a birthing surrogate? It sounds better to me."

It will be done.

***

While Amber and I were relaxing at our dome after bathing, I wondered why I had not received the tattoos, like very one else.

"When will I get the marks of ownership on my legs?" I said, seizing an opportunity to tease Amber.

"They are not marks of ownership. They are symbols of position, and are worn by order of the Most High One. You do not need them."

"Why not? I want everyone to see that you own me."

"I do not own you." She turned to stare at me. The look on her face was precious when she belatedly realized I was teasing. Before I could scramble to my feet, she swept me up in her arms and ran to the hospital, where she squatted and held me close to her until Lana came out.

I am not going to stand here just to watch you slobber all over each other.

He wants the symbols of position, Amber said seriously.

He needs the symbols of position. Bring him inside.

When I was placed on the table, Lana said, *We had better use this.* She placed one of her devices on my forehead and tapped the controls with a delicate claw point.

"Hey, wait. I want...."

***

"...to watch. I wish you would stop that! How can I learn anything if I am asleep?"

You did not need to experience the placement of the symbols of position.

My thighs were burning and itching at the same time, but it was tolerable. The symbols were like bright, colorful tattoos extending from mid-thigh to ankle on both my legs, and anyone who read them would know my position within Draasen society. I could not read them yet, but that was fine with me.

When Amber and I walked to the feeding table for second feeding, there was a new item that looked like a jumbled pile of large hockey pucks.

Sample the new item, Oracle said as it floated to the table.

"I do not remember any food that looks like this."

Amber got one of the hockey pucks for me to try. "Pizza. Cheese and pepperoni pizza. It is good, too!" I said when the taste hit me.

The botai leaves are the main ingredient, Oracle said.

Amber got one of the hockey puck pizzas and sampled the flavor.

"It is much better than the botai leaves. I never liked them. Thank you," she said as she got five from the tray for herself and passed another one to me.

After feeding, we walked to the hospital and I was placed on the table. I looked up and saw Oracle at the top of the dome.

Amber said, "Oracle will record the release of our first egg. Are you ready?"

"Uh, okay. What do I need to do?"

"The egg I have selected is located here," she said, gently pushing just below my waist with her finger. "Lie on your back while I guide the egg. It will not take long."

Amber placed her forehead on my stomach, and the eye closest to me changed shades to bright green. I felt movement deep inside near my waist, and I became nauseous as it continued to move. Determined to stay awake and keep my food down at the same time, I moved my arms up, grasped my wrists, and placed them on my forehead, just in time to block Lana, who was moving toward me with one of her devices. When I gave her the meanest look I could muster, she stepped back.

The egg settling into the final position was the worst. It felt like it suddenly enlarged, and I went into a cold sweat as my stomach went sour. My arms slipped off my forehead and Lana was quick to place and activate the device that put me to sleep.

***

I was still nauseous when I was allowed to wake, and I wondered if it could be considered morning sickness.

The move is complete. The egg is positioned and the filaments have attached, Amber said.

Open your mouth and swallow this, Lana said.

I got a squirt of an overly-sweet liquid that immediately calmed my stomach.

"It may be a bit late for this, but I should have told you when something is placed in our body, the body tries to reject it, even if it kills it. It is called tissue rejection. My upset stomach may be the beginning."

My examinations showed your body would see the eggs as something neutral, like metal or plastic your species uses in your primitive medical practices. I will keep a tail around you as a precaution.

I would like to know what it is like to birth my own eggs, Amber said wistfully.

"You might be able to experience the birthing though me. Maybe Oracle can do something."

Oracle could set up a link and let the females experience the birthing process through your surrogate. I would like to experience it as well. Oracle, what would be needed to set up such a link? Lana asked.

The bonded link between the High One and her surrogate will be adequate. I will record the birthing through the surrogate, and you will be able to experience the birthing at any time.

Amber was happy with my idea, and her happiness had become the most important thing in my life.

Lana passed her diagnostic equipment over Amber's midsection. *You are healing, but do not stress the bindings or I will keep you here, in restraints, if necessary.*

***

Amber and I spent much of the suns relaxing outside our dome while I wrote in the journal, but it was getting boring.

"I have not explored the caves yet. Can I see what is in there?"

"We can go together, but I want you to be careful. Some things in there might damage you."

When we entered one of the caves, I was only briefly aware of the heat as an immense panorama opened before me. Inside was a cavernous dome carved out of the mountainside with all the trappings of a maintenance hangar. Shelves cut into the wall were filled with all kinds of neatly-arranged equipment. There were two transports on one side, and another, larger one was in the middle of the floor with several males working on it. Clinging to the ceiling was a large inverted silver dome, from which a faint, shimmering light spread around the transport. On the transport were open areas where several males worked. It was stable while they walked on it, even though it floated several inches above the floor.

An order was given for everyone to get away from the transport. The shimmering light intensified as the transport rose on one edge to a forty-five degree angle, and stayed there as several males went to work under it. When one of the males was putting away his tools, I went to him to ask how the transport worked. When he noticed me approaching, he backed up, shooting a nervous look at Amber, who had stood up. When he was comfortable with the distance between us, he launched into a highly technical explanation of transport operation that I did not fully understand. I understood there were magcoils, which were hot and cold coils of some kind that stored and balanced magnetic fields to power the transport. Suffice it to say the planet's magnetic field and the transport's manipulation of it played a great part in its operation.

At another signal for everyone to get clear, the transport returned to its original position and then rose several feet above the floor. With a loud click, a cross on the bottom detached and gently lowered to the floor on a thin wire. A female went to the place where the cross was housed and began looking inside. When I started to go under the transport, I stopped to look around, but no one seemed to object.

"What is this?" I said, pointing at the cross and wire.

It is what you call a grappling hook. It is used to carry large items that will not fit inside.

"How much weight will this transport carry?"

She picked me up, hefted me a couple of times, and placed me back on my feet. *This transport will carry seventy of you.*

Twelve thousand pounds. Remarkable technology these people have, I thought.

Our people, Amber gently corrected me.

Our people, I agreed.

Leave the cave and cool him, Lana commanded.

I was sweating and leaving wet footprints where I walked. When I walked out of the cave, I was drenched with cold water from a pot held by one of Amber's sisters, who seemed to enjoy the task. I was about to protest the drenching until I saw Amber walk back into the cave.

"Did you see my symbols of position?" I asked Elder as he stood nearby.

Yes. We are required to read them.

"What do they say?"

They are read from the lowest position to the highest position starting here. He pointed to my ankle and touched each symbol appropriate to each word or phrase. *This is a new symbol that is exclusive to you, and has been recorded by Oracle. It means Raymond. This one says, Escort to the High One, with her symbol and the symbol for this colony. This one says, Consort to the High One, with her symbol and the symbol for this colony. This one says bonded pairing to the High One, with her symbol and the symbol for this colony. This says, Surrogate to the...* Elder stopped his translation and looked carefully at the symbols. Then he switched sides to look at the symbols on my other leg.

"Is something wrong?"

There is a space here, as if a symbol is missing. It reads, Surrogate to the — there is the space — High One, and her symbol. The symbol for this colony is also missing. He stopped and stared at the symbols on my leg. *Do not think about the spaces in your symbols of position, because your safety depends on it. Keep the eggs safe because they are the key to the future of the High One.* He quickly backed away just before Amber left the cave.

Come, it is time to bathe, Amber said.

When I had settled on my ledge, Lana surfaced and said, *You are good for my hatchling. She draws new ideas from you, and I can feel the changes in her. You will be a great benefit to our society.*

I am just a human. What can I do that she could not do better?

Be yourself.

There was definitely something going on. I wished I could think about it, but I did not have any privacy with everyone going through my head like a rummage sale.

You are very important to my future, Amber said when she surfaced next to us.

Careful, hatchling.

I do not like being called that. I am High One of this colony! Amber snapped at her.

"Excuse me," I said.

Take care, hatchling. I am still your mother.

"Excuse me!" I raised my voice.

Every female Draasen in the bathing pool had surfaced, their heads resembling alligators as they peeked above the water.

You will address me as High One! Amber said heatedly.

"Can I say something?"

I will address you as I please. I was the High One before you were accepted for the position!

I grabbed Lana and Amber under their chins and pulled them to me, their eyes swirling with yellows and reds. "What is the problem? Stop it, both of you, and switch off those nasty eye colors!"

The argument stopped, and the color in the eyes that faced away from each other slowly shifted back to light gray. The eyes facing each other were still swirling, and I covered them with my hands.

"Stop it! What is wrong with you two?"

The males had disappeared and the females drifted to the far side of the pool as I stood alone between the two most powerful females in the colony. Then I remembered what happened when the previous Oracle had tried to influence Amber and me.

Hey, old man! Do you feel anything? I said.

No, not this time, Elder said.

"I need you to work together. The eggs will not birth themselves. Can we do that, please?"

Excellent. This was better than I expected, Lana said.

It was a test? Amber said.

"I am confused."

It was necessary to know if your surrogate would be able to suppress his human instinct to fight, and accept a peaceful resolution. It is a skill he will need, Lana said, watching me as she slowly sank under water.

"I thought it was a good idea to get between you two, because I thought you might attack your mother."

I would never do that!

"Really? Your claws are dug in. I am glad my foot was not under them."

She looked down to see that her six-inch claws had sunk to her fingertips into my ledge. She gave me a guilty little smile when she pulled the claws out and retracted them.

"Are you hungry? We will finish bathing and eat. I am hungry," I said.

Chapter 7
FATE OF EARTH

Oracle finally reported the probe sent to earth had completed its mission, and the information was ready for viewing. When Amber and I arrived in Oracle's dome, it produced images midair in front of us. The search of the first building had revealed nothing useful, but the second was far more interesting.

The pod rammed through a window and glowed for visibility as it entered. It used its manipulator arms to move items as it went through cubicles and offices. On the fifth floor, an open newspaper revealed the headline BALEORANS TAKE 93d BUILDING. As the pod went about its examinations, it picked up a desktop calendar showing a date nearly a month after we had been taken.

I became profoundly sad as I sat in Amber's lap. What happened to my wife? Did she suffer? What kind of husband was I? I had not thought of her as much as I should have. I did not even have a picture of her. I looked at my wedding band and spun it on my finger.

These images are making you unhappy. You must stop seeing them, Amber said.

"No. I have to know what happened. Only by knowing what happened can I help myself, and anyone else who needs to know. Oracle, I remember seeing snow. What was the air temperature at the last building?" I said with a terrible sinking feeling.

Ninety-seven degrees below zero.

"Show me where that temperature was taken."

A pulsing spot appeared in south Texas. I had to ask the obvious question.

"Oracle, is the planet dead?"

The planet is unable to support your species.

As near as I could tell, there was a nuclear winter. The destroyed cities, high radiation count, and the dust blocking the sun pointed to it. I surmised that armies were sent to stop the Baleorans, and they had been beaten. Those with nuclear weapons had launched them, creating the nuclear winter. No one could have survived the Baleorans, radiation, and extreme freezing cold. Now, there were only a few thousand humans left, scattered across the galaxy. I sat back against Amber's chest, and she wrapped her arms around me.

"Well, I suppose that is it. There is nothing left to be done."

Amber stood and carried me outside.

May I make a suggestion?

"You do not need my permission to make suggestions."

There are some things I desire permission to speak about. You have possessions; your journal and the metal on your hand. It is the metal I want to discuss with you.

"What do you suggest I do with it?" I began spinning the ring on my finger again.

Only that you remove it. It is a source of memories that makes you unhappy.

"It holds happy memories as well. It has been on my finger for over twenty-five years. I just cannot take it off and throw it away."

If you would give the ring to me, I have a plan for it that I know you would agree with.

She knew I could not refuse her anything, but the memories the ring held were special to me.

I promise you will agree with my plan for the ring. She held her open hand in front of me.

I felt a very subtle influence cross our bonded link. I was being guided again.

"Why is the ring so important to you?"

I want you to be happy with me.

"I am happy with you, but you are evading the point. Are you jealous of my past relationship with my wife?"

I am not jealous. How can I be jealous of a female who no longer exists?

"You tell me. You are the one asking for the ring."

I felt my answer hurt her, and I did not want that. With some difficulty, I removed my ring and held it over her outstretched hand.

"Kim gave me this ring a very long time ago. It symbolizes our love for each other. If I give it to you, what happens then?"

We do not show love by giving material items, but you hesitate over a ring of metal, a possession you do not need here. Do you trust me?

"Trust is not the issue. What, exactly, will you do with it?"

I would never do anything to damage you.

Somehow, Elder was involved because he arrived and waited a short distance from us. Despite my misgivings, I gently placed the ring in her hand. It looked very small as she closed her hand around it.

Thank you, she said, and affectionately stroked her chin along the top of my head.

Amber handed Elder the ring, and as he walked away he smiled at me. I was more reassured by his smile than by anything else.

I felt naked without the ring, and I became sad to the point of tears as I watched him walk into one of the caves. Amber dropped to all fours and looked into my eyes.

Do not be unhappy. Your ring will be a gift from me you will like very much. You display the ring as an outward sign of bonding to others. Our outward signs of bonding are much larger than your ring.

She stood and extended her leg, showing me her symbols of position. Using her tail, she pointed to the symbol near her upper knee and touched each symbol appropriate to each word or phrase as they went up her leg.

This is the symbol that is my name. This symbol says I am first hatched of my mother. This symbol says I am favored by my mother, which is important. These say I am the High One of a colony, and this is the symbol for this colony. This is important because this is a birthing colony. This symbol is very important to me. It says bonded pairing to Raymond, and this is your symbol. Your symbol is new and has been added to our written language.

My name was permanently imprinted on the most important female in the colony, and it appeared on the top of her thighs. It did not matter to me the symbols were read from the bottom up. My name was high above all the rest.

I knew this would make you happy.

Just as I thought about the ring again, Elder returned and Amber retrieved something from him. She opened her hand and held what resembled a large snow globe with my ring inside, floating as it slowly turned on an invisible axis.

Touch the base with your finger.

An image of Kim appeared in my mind as I last saw her, standing in the grass, wearing her favorite T-shirt and cutoff jeans, no shoes. I took the snow globe from Amber and held it close to me. Words could not express how it made me feel. My tears flowed for a long time while I clutched it to my chest, and allowed the image to remain in my mind.

I placed it on the shelf beside my journal, where it would remain as a remembrance of my beloved wife.

Chapter 8

BIRTHING

I now had a unique perspective into childbearing.

After the egg was released, the growth rate was phenomenal. I could actually feel the swelling of my midsection increase daily. It was also a tremendous physical drain. By the second suns, I was weak and light-headed. It got to the point where I struggled to walk, and I could barely stay conscious. Lana provided a medical remedy, and she had Oracle prepare certain high energy, high nutrition foods that were good for the egg, and me. I had become especially fond of raw botai leaves, and no one liked the dill pickle pretzel rods I requested, which was good, because it meant more for me.

While the egg was growing, Amber was very protective of me around everyone, and when we relaxed in our dome, she would gently lay her chin on my chest and keep her eyes on the door. The eyes revealed the emotional state of a Draasen, and it was a beautiful sight to watch her eye color swirl in the contented happiness of blue patterns.

There were no mirrors there, but from what I could see, I was losing weight, although I was getting as big as a house. Lana assured me the growth would slow by the end of the third week as the egg approached its full size. As my stomach swelled, it itched all the time. Amber frequently restrained me from scratching because my fingernails left red streaks, and she thought I was damaging myself. I carried my swelled stomach around by interlacing my fingers under it, and I waddled like a fat, barn sized duck.

During the third week, an uncomfortable tugging on my ribs became increasingly painful when I walked. Lana called me to her dome and performed another scan on me. When she finished, my image was embarrassing when I was displayed in all my pregnant glory. I could not believe the size of my belly when I saw my profile. Amber said I looked cute, but her assessment did little to help. Lana used her equipment to reveal the two support filaments hanging from my ribs. After a close examination, she said the filaments were normal but my body was not adapted to their function. When the support filaments first attached to me, they were as thin as sewing needles but had grown to belt-sized straps supporting the egg.

Lana explained a birthing animal had a specific bone the egg hung from on the filaments. Using her equipment, she displayed an image of a birthing animal. It was the size of a hippopotamus with very short legs and a face only a mother could love, and the bone she mentioned was the swayed and fused backbone of the animal itself. She said a birthing animal was a very gentle creature who enjoyed the attention it got, but I was warned to stay away from it if I happened to encounter one because it ate constantly, and because of my smaller size, it might mistake me for something to eat. It was kept under a large dome, protected from sun and rain. During storms or other emergencies, it would be carried away for protection. Lana explained a birthing animal was very well cared for only by the birth mother and females she trusted, similar to how I was treated.

I had become Amber's birthing animal.

***

On the twenty-first suns after the egg was released, the day started with our routine of waking and walking to the bathing pool. Without warning, a piercing, painful sound filled my head. It was not a sound as you might understand it, but a telepathic screech. It dropped me to the ground and I pressed my hands over my ears, trying to shut out the sound inside my head. Amber quickly rolled me onto my back and placed her forehead over the egg. After a painful eternity, the screech faded into many softer sounds. When I looked around, we were surrounded by females, all facing outward in a defensive circle.

"What happened?"

The hatchling has achieved sentience, Lana said.

The swirling mix of Amber's eye colors defied description. Our link was quiet as she pressed her forehead on my stomach.

"What is she doing?"

Silence, she is very busy.

While I lay on the ground, I thought about things I needed to do. How was I going to write about this in my journal? I needed to bathe. I needed a drink, and not just water. Lana leaned over and gave me a look that said I was doing something wrong again.

"What?"

You think loud. She placed her hand on my forehead, and I felt one of her medical devices hidden under her hand. Before I could protest, I was asleep.

***

When I was allowed to wake, I heard distant murmurings. Nothing intelligible, just soft sounds. Several hours had passed and most of the females had left us. I wanted a word with Lana. I wanted to experience everything I could, but she kept putting me to sleep at critical times.

You were thinking loud, and I did not want you to disturb the bonding the High One was having with her hatchling. There was

110

nothing for you to experience unless you consider lying on the ground and doing nothing a critical experience.

Amber rose and our link reconnected with all the love and reassurances I would ever need.

"When a hatchling achieves sentience, immediate bonding is most important. The birth mother opens her intellect to the hatchling so it can receive information to develop pathways for intelligence. I am sorry I had to be closed to you, but it was necessary."

She had to be closed to everyone, Lana added.

"You could have told me what was coming."

You will be better prepared for the next birthing.

"What do we do now?"

"We will start the hatchling's education after second feeding. Are you comfortable with everyone in this colony?" Amber said.

"Yes, of course I am. Is there something I should be aware of?"

"After a hatchling has achieved sentience and the birth mother has opened the intellect pathways, females will educate the hatchling while it is in the egg. I know you are comfortable with my touch, but to educate the hatchling, several females will have to place their heads on you for several hours, when they will open their minds for the hatchling to learn. Your education will start as well, but I do not expect you to be able to keep up with the speed of the hatchling's education. You will have nine more opportunities to learn from them."

"Would it be more comfortable for you if I was not lying on the ground when you place your head on me?"

I suddenly found myself in the workspace with Amber beside me.

Please show me what you would like to do.

We worked with a plan for a recliner. Eventually, she chose a design that allowed me to sit at an angle, high enough off the ground so she could shuffle her legs under me as she squatted and placed her head over the egg. I made sure it was thickly padded and covered with an awning, because I would have to lay in it for hours.

I will give this construction to one who will have it ready after second feeding.

When we arrived at the bathing pool, I had to ask about an inconsistency I perceived.

Is a birthing animal male or female?

They are all females. Male birthing animals are used only to fertilize the eggs of the female.

So, no birth mother will tolerate any male near her eggs.

Yes.

I am a male, and I have an egg growing inside me. Would you say a male is near your eggs? I said, rubbing both hands on my stomach.

Lana suddenly rocketed out of the water and stood partly between Amber and me. I felt she was prepared to protect me while other females stood nearby, closely watching us.

He has an interesting question. How will you answer him? Lana said.

He is my bonded pairing. When we bonded, we gave ourselves to each other and became one. I do not distrust myself, so why would I distrust him? Amber said, and I felt Lana relax.

I can see you are truly one with your surrogate, Lana said, and jumped back into the pool while Amber and I eased into the water.

Your mother was going to protect me from something. Do you know what that was about?

No one will damage you while I am here, Amber said.

No female will allow any male to approach a birthing animal while an egg is in growth. That is why she has been guiding you away from nearby males, Lana said.

Amber helped me onto her back and started swimming toward the scrubbing ledge. As she swam, my hand slipped and I landed on my stomach. I heard, or more accurately, I felt something grunt. Amber looked over her shoulder at me, but continued swimming. When we arrived at the scrubbing ledge, she helped me onto the ledge and pressed her head over the egg. Suddenly, she bounced backward as if she had been kicked between the eyes.

Do not squash me. I do not have any room.

Amber and I looked at each other in surprise.

I am not comfortable.

Is the hatchling speaking already? Lana said as she surfaced beside us.

My name is Kaa.

He learned from my surrogate, Amber said.

Amber smiled and placed her forehead on mine, and I briefly felt pressure inside my head.

Kaa said, *She gave us an ability we did not have before. We can think without everyone hearing us, unless we want them to.*

How can you be speaking already? I said.

My mother guided me, and she says I should learn from you.

I found myself looking forward to the education experience, and I would not be surprised if I was being influenced again.

Everyone in the colony is encouraging both of you to learn, Amber said.

I thought Kaa and I were having a private conversation, I replied, confused and a bit miffed.

You must remember we are one, all twelve of us.

All twelve of us?

You, my ten eggs, and I are bonded as a family. The hatchlings will learn from you as well, and that gives them an advantage.

When I eased into the water to rinse, Amber surfaced under me. I was lying on my stomach as she swam for the clothing dome.

You are squashing me, Kaa complained, and I sat upright to keep him comfortable.

On our way to the clothing dome, Kaa complained about my bouncing when I walked, so I lifted my swelled stomach with my interlaced fingers to try to ease it.

You are bending my nose.

His complaining had me biting my lip to keep a civil tongue behind my teeth and civil thoughts in my head.

After I fitted my shorts, Kaa said it was too tight, and I had to pull the cloth down from my waist.

I am not comfortable.

Amber picked me up and carried me to the feeding table.

Amber sampled the first item and set off the usual flurry of claws, tongues, and flying food. Kaa wanted me to get some of this and some of that, not having a clue what he was asking for. When I got what he wanted, I wondered how he could taste anything.

I can taste things through you, he said in anticipation of new sensations, and speaking of sensations, I got the impression he was drooling.

I do not drool.

Yes, you do. You are in there, drooling all over yourself right now.

You stop, or I will —

Stuff a cork in it. This is why I did not like children on my home world. Complaining, curtain-climbing, ankle-biting, crumb-snatching, rug rats are suitable only for barbecuing and eating.

Mother, does his species eat their hatchlings?

Do not tempt me.

Mother!

Stop it! Amber said sharply.

I felt Kaa was happy because he had gotten me in trouble, and I was about to say something else, but a grumble from Amber was enough to keep me quiet.

After the feeding, Amber placed me in the recliner when an elderly female arrived.

"Are you ready to begin?" she asked.

"Kaa is the student, so if he is ready, so am I. What can I do to make this easier?"

"I suggest that you sleep. We shall begin."

She squatted, shuffled her legs under the recliner, and placed her forehead on my swelled stomach. Not knowing what to expect, I watched and listened. Kaa had gone to sleep, and after a few moments, I found myself in the workspace with the puppet again. A string dropped from above, attached to the puppet, and I promptly went to sleep.

***

Twenty-two females educated Kaa and me during his six days of education, and after it was done for each suns, we would wake up and go to sleep again until morning. At least I was well rested.

It would be impossible to write about everything I learned during our education. Suffice it to say I was considered to be an educated Draasen male, but I had the feeling several things had been left out, perhaps deliberately.

***

Lana's prediction was right. Over the past six suns, Amber had to carry me everywhere, mostly because Kaa complained about everything. I appreciated that all he could do was complain, but he had been quiet all morning, which was a welcome relief.

When we finished bathing and adjusted our clothing, Kaa made an announcement.

I am ready.

Amber picked me up and ran to the hospital. As we entered, several females were preparing equipment. I did not want to miss anything, so with my new ability to think privately, I had been planning my next moves before the surgery started.

"I will be awake, and I will watch everything from beginning to end," I stated as I settled on the table, covering my forehead with my hands to keep Lana from placing the sleep device she was fond of using on me.

Open your mouth. Lana squirted some thick, pain relieving liquid under my tongue.

"I want Elder here." A flash of surprised glances went around the room.

That is not permitted, Lana said.

"Is that a protocol, or are these big, strong females afraid of one, tired old male?"

Amber gave me a narrow eyed look that suggested there was going to be a discussion about this after the birthing.

Because this is a male birthing, I will let him enter and watch. More surprised glances went around the room.

Elder looked nervously at the females when he entered.

"Old man, I need you to support my head and shoulders, so I can watch."

Oracle, start the sterile field, Lana commanded.

From Oracle came a faint light that washed over the area and produced a pleasant smell, like after a thunderstorm. Amber, Lana, and two assistants extended their claws, spread their fingers, and turned their hands over several times in the light. With Elder supporting me, I watched as Lana took one of her instruments and carefully cut into my right side. I felt the pressure of the cut, but no pain, and I could not help thinking the cut was very long. One assistant used her fingers to hold the incision open while Lana used another instrument to cut into the egg. She made two incisions, leaving a strip in the middle holding Kaa in, until Lana extended a finger, carefully slipped her claw behind the strip, and pulled. When it snapped, Kaa spilled out of the egg into Amber's waiting hands. After being quiet all morning, the first thing he did was complain.

I am hungry! I am cold! I am hungry!

Kaa was vocalizing well, but it made no sense. It was like a baby crying, and I quickly buried the thought because he did not need any more reasons to complain. He was doing enough of that on his own. Amber carried him to a large pot of warm water and placed him in it, where she bathed him and helped him exercise his arms and legs. When she finished with him, he quietly lounged in the water with his chin over the edge of the pot. I had to admit he was cute.

While Amber was attending to Kaa, Lana placed one of her instruments in the egg casing and pressed a trigger to send a shock into me.

"Hey! What are you doing?"

No sooner than I'd spoken, she moved the instrument and shocked me again.

It is necessary to signal all three filaments to release.

She moved the instrument around and zapped me a third time, sending a shock across my stomach.

The two support filaments and the nourishment filament must release from you, and this is how it is done. When they have released, I will remove the egg casing from you, and then seal the incision.

"You could have said something before you zapped me."

You should consider sleeping through a birthing.

While we waited for the filaments to release, I watched Kaa as he tried to move around in his pot of water. I almost laughed when he discovered his tail. He was stumbling all over himself as he ran around the pot, trying to get away from the thing following him, screaming for his mother. Amber had to convince him everyone had a tail, except me.

Lana reached inside my incision and gently pulled on the egg casing. I felt the filaments briefly resist as she pulled it out. Then she tossed it near the dome wall where the grass tendrils rose from the floor and quickly consumed it. Lana pumped a clear fluid into the incision and closed it with a device that sealed the skin together.

The magnetic bindings will hold the incision closed only if you move slowly and carefully. I will expect you to do so.

117

She mounted a healing accelerator on her hand, and passed it over the incision and all around my midsection.

Make yourself useful and carry him to the High One's dome, Lana told Elder.

He gently picked me up and carried me out of the hospital. When we arrived at the dome, he gently placed me on my feet and squatted in front of me with his palms up. As I pressed my palms down on his, he started a private conversation.

Thank you for asking me to be with you for this birthing. All of the males linked through me and saw it as well. We are all very privileged to have you as Surrogate to the High One.

Thank you for being my friend, I replied.

He helped settle me into the bed, handed my journal to me, and left. After I had been writing for a while, Amber entered, bringing a feeling of happiness with her, gently carrying the sleeping Kaa in one hand. She squatted on the bed and pulled the edge of the circular bed that opened into an oval depression. It filled with a blue gel that quickly hardened in the air, and then she carefully placed Kaa in the oval and with a gentle tongue, touched him on the head and neck.

"Thank you for him. He is perfect in every way. There was a time I thought I would lose all my eggs, but from the moment I touched your mind, I knew you would be the one. By saving my eggs, you have saved me, and I can remain High One."

Kaa woke and started squawking. Amber suddenly grunted, holding her chest.

Lana, something is wrong, I said.

Do not be concerned. What you are going to see is something no mature male is ever allowed to see, not even pairings.

Amber struggled to slide the top of her clothing down to her stomach. To my surprise, a large area of skin across her chest had changed from the usual dark gray to nearly white.

From near her left arm, a thick flap of skin curled forward, and she gently pulled it across her chest, exposing an area that swelled. From the bottom of the single, wide breast, a nipple elongated and seemed to have a life of its own, acting almost like an elephant's trunk as it moved around. She reached for Kaa, who was squawking and struggling to get to his mother. She picked him up and he opened his mouth. The nipple that had grown to over a foot long found Kaa's open mouth and slipped down his throat. Amber sighed while Kaa fed open mouthed. When he was full, he wrapped his tongue around the nipple and squeezed it, shutting off the flow. The nipple slipped through Kaa's curled tongue and shrank back into her breast. Kaa was ready for another nap and was almost asleep when Amber gently placed him back on his bed. She pulled her cloth back up and carefully settled it around her newly exposed skin.

"That looked painful."

"It was at first, but feeding him was a wonderful experience." She seemed to glow as she watched Kaa sleep.

"Do you have to pull the skin off every time you feed him?"

"Not for Kaa, but I will for each new hatchling. Your species is fortunate to have permanent glands that fill for each birthing."

"Speaking of feedings, we missed ours. Can I get something for you?"

The door opened and two females walked in with trays of food.

"My mother has taken care of that."

***

Kaa's demands for feeding woke us several times during the night, and when he woke us after suns rise, I thought my sleepy eyes were fooling me. Kaa was noticeably larger, and he had a full set of small teeth. At this rate, he would be as tall as I was in just a few days. It was then I realized I had never seen a Draasen child. The thought had never occurred to me that there were no children in our birthing colony. The obvious reason was they grew so fast.

"Are there any opportunities for him to grow beyond being just a colony member?"

"Only the future will show us." I felt she gave me a guarded answer, and I was about to pursue that thought when she said, "Kaa will start walking this suns. Would you like to help?"

"Sure, what can I do?"

"You can support him while he takes his first steps." She picked Kaa up and went outside.

When I started to get up, I felt a tight discomfort across my stomach that made me roll on my side. "Maybe I should get clearance from your mother before I do anything."

I will come to examine you. Do not move until I arrive.

Despite Lana's advice, I struggled to the door. I was surprised at how much effort it took just to get outside the dome, and it made me wonder how human females made birthing look so easy.

Lana arrived and used her arm-mounted equipment to examine me.

I will release the magnetic bindings from your incision. It has healed deeply enough to hold on its own. You are healing well, but you must go slowly for another suns before you can resume your activities.

She detached an instrument from the side of her arm-mounted equipment and passed it over the incision. I felt a release of pressure but no pain. When she finished, she squirted some pain medicine under my tongue and left.

I tried not to laugh as I watched Amber trying to get Kaa to walk. He had an ear-to-ear smile while he was supported by his mother. He was laughing, looking around, wobbling and stepping on his own feet until he squatted and opened his mouth. He was ready to be fed again, so Amber carried him inside. I was not about to move around, so I relaxed in the shade of the awning until Oracle appeared off the end of my nose.

"What do you want?"

The Most High One is interested in you.

"Why?"

You have birthed one of her people, and she demands to experience the birthing. She wants to know if your species can be used as birthing animals.

Amber came out of the dome at the same time Lana arrived at a run.

"Did you hear that? The Most High One must have lost her mind. If she thinks I will become a birthing animal for her, she is crazy! Send that to her highness!"

Amber put her hand on my shoulder and said, *Silence! Say nothing more!*

I felt Amber was frightened and in one unguarded moment, I felt many things suddenly spike across our link. There were plans in motion, and the Most High One had acted against many of the long established protocols.

We may have to accelerate our –, Lana started to say when Amber interrupted her.

Oracle, can the delivery of birthing experiences be stopped?

There was a long delay before it spoke again.

Central reports that Core sends assurances the current birthing visual will be forgotten by the Most High One. Core will not notify the Most High One of future arrivals. Core cautions your surrogate against negative outbursts. The Most High One has sent many males on the long walk for less.

I did not like the whole situation with Core, Central, and Oracles. It was all sentient, and that worried me because Core made its own decisions. Being sentient, who did it serve?

Amber was looking at me with the stone face that told me I was out of place again. Then she locked eyes with her mother. I felt communication between the two, but I was not allowed to hear it.

"What is going on?"

It is for you to answer him, Lana said, and walked away.

Amber placed our foreheads together in a private conversation.

Any comments about the Most High One are not permitted. In the future, you will keep your comments to yourself. I understand the Most High One offended you, but we will handle future situations without your comments. If you wish to make something known, speak privately with me first.

Yes, High One.

She went into the dome to see what Kaa was squawking about.

I was hurt and angry, so I put up my shield and tried to relax under the shade of the awning, until I was hit on my chest hard enough to knock the wind out of me. My reaction was simple and automatic…attack the attacker. I got my feet under me and sprang at the retreating fist. I caught Lana by surprise when I tackled her chest high as she squatted near me. We tumbled to the ground, and I was about to club her with my fist until I realized where I was. My hesitation allowed Amber to lift me off Lana, and I dropped my shield while I struggled in Amber's grip.

"What are you doing?" I shouted at Lana.

My scan showed no life signs, and I thought you were on the long walk. I remembered a technique from your memories, and I hit you on your chest to get your heart started again.

"I had my shield up to get some peace and quiet."

Lana passed her equipment over me and looked at the readouts. *Use your shield again.* When she passed her medical equipment over me, she touched me with her bare hand and a private conversation link formed. She looked at me, and then her equipment.

Can you hear me?

"Yes, clearly."

She released me and passed her equipment over me several times, alternately touching me, then not. She looked at the readouts, and then turned her arm toward Amber, who examined the readings. I dropped the shield and she passed her equipment over me again.

Interesting, there were no life signs at all, even when I touched you. She went into a private conversation with Amber for several minutes.

"Why did you use your shield? You know it stops our link," Amber said.

"I needed some space."

"Do not do that. You are a male, and you will remain open for all to see and hear. Do not use your shield again unless I tell you to."

Being myself was getting me in trouble again, just like it had done most of my life. Still, the Most High One had no business wanting to use humans as birthing animals, and that annoyed me to no end.

When Amber gave me another stone-faced look, I stopped thinking about the situation, and thought happy thoughts.

Chapter 9
RAGE

Kaa grew fast during his first month. Even though he ate constantly, I was afraid he might die from malnutrition because he grew into a walking stick figure. I was frequently assured it was normal, but I still worried about him. After all, he was my first-born, or more accurately, my first hatched. In two months, he grew from a wonderfully cute little handful into a tall energetic male who was much more muscular than anyone else in our colony. He frequently acted like a body builder at a competition, flexing his muscles and showing off his physique at every opportunity. I was not sure if it was a stage he was going through or what the story was, but no one seemed to object.

***

The sentience of our second egg was much different. After twenty-two suns, everyone had been expecting the telepathic screech common when a hatchling achieved sentience. Amber was nervous because it was late in coming. Toward the end of the suns, I thought I heard a soft whisper deep inside my head.

"It is time, I think. Can you check to be sure?" I said.

Instead of checking, Amber swept me up in her arms, ran to our dome, deposited me in the recliner, and placed her forehead on my stomach, over the egg. Lana came and stood beside her.

You were correct. It is time, she said, and placed a sleep device on my forehead.

***

When I was allowed to wake, I was aware of a new presence.

I am Dee. Mother says you are the birthing surrogate that carries me. Mother says you are a good male, and I have learned from you as Mother showed me.

Dee's attitude was a welcome change from all the complaints Kaa had right from the start.

It is late and we need to rest, Amber said.

When we settled into our bed, I had a thought I had not considered before, and Amber tiredly sighed in anticipation of being kept awake again.

Dee and Kaa do not have long names like the others do. They should have the Draasen long names.

Dee said, *I like the name I have selected for myself.*

Dee and Kaa are happy with their names, and the symbols for their names have been recorded by Oracle. There is no need for concern. Please, go to sleep.

***

In the afternoon of the thirty-first day after Dee's egg was released, we had just sat down to have second feeding when I noticed every female was watching Amber.

"What?" I said, and as if on cue, everyone was looking at anything but her.

"They were not looking at me. They were, but they were not. She is late. It is time for Dee to be birthed. Very late," she stammered.

"Do I have any control of the time she is birthed?"

"Yes. No! She is late in asking."

I started getting confusing signals across our bonded link when Dee suddenly announced, *I am ready.*

125

Lana ran around the table, scooped me in her arms, and took me to the hospital while Amber lagged behind. When Amber entered and looked at me, I received a confused jolt across our link that said, *That is a male.*

Lana said, *You should sleep during this birthing.*

"Next time, I promise."

Oracle provided the sterile field over the area, and this time a female supported me. After Kaa's birthing, Amber had made it abundantly clear no male would ever attend another birthing. When she told me that, I wondered where I would be.

I watched as Lana performed her skills, and when she snapped the strip of the egg to release Dee, Amber caught her and Dee started vocalizing.

I am hungry! I am cold and wet! I am hungry!

"Dee, look at me," I said.

I am hungry! I cannot move. I am cold! I am hungry!

"Dee. Dee! Amber, please bring her to me."

Amber turned with Dee in her hands and I gently lifted her head.

"You are as beautiful as your mother," I said, stroking her tiny head with my thumb.

As Dee calmed down, Amber pulled back from me. Suddenly, I felt confusion and hatred across our link, and Amber's eyes changed to a yellowish tint.

"Lana, what is happening?"

Silence! I am going to send the signals for the filaments to release.

I braced and she sent the shocks through the filaments. While we waited for them to release, more females were entering the dome. In fact, it was getting crowded with them.

When the birthing was completed, I was carried out of the hospital to Kaa, who was waiting to take me to the dome. It was the first time he had carried me, and he was strong; much stronger than Amber.

Did you peek in, through me, at the birthing?

Yes. Please do not tell Mother. She will be angry with me.

Kaa helped me settle into the bed, and he left in a hurry. Amber walked in and I felt something was not right. She did not appear to see me as she squatted on the bed and yanked at the edge, making the bed for Dee. When she dropped Dee in it, I saw Amber's eyes were swirling with yellows and reds, and our link was very active with conflicting feelings and messages. Knowing how sensitive females were about their eggs and hatchlings, I decided I had better leave, and as I struggled toward the door, Lana arrived, picked me up, and ran to Kaa's dome.

Kaa, stay here with him until this passes, Lana said, and squatted in the doorway.

"Kaa, what is happening?"

"Something is wrong with Mother, but no one will tell me what it is. I want to run and hide, but they will not let me out."

I went to the door and saw Amber pacing in front of our dome with her claws extended. I felt her confusion and anger sparking at every male she thought of, even me. I heard Dee squawking from inside the dome, but Amber continued to pace.

Use your shield, Lana said.

When I raised my shield, Amber stopped pacing and started crying out in bagpipes-like tones, and though I could not understand exactly what was going on, it broke my heart to hear her.

Lana grabbed my arm and said, *Leave your shield in place until I tell you to stop.*

Dee started squawking with more insistence and Amber went inside to feed her. I could do nothing while the minutes passed like hours.

Eventually, Amber came out of the dome and started crying out again. When I asked Kaa what she was saying, he told me aloud she was mourning because I had gone on the long walk and her eggs were gone. When I heard that, I pounded my fists on Lana's back as she squatted in the doorway. I was angry at not being able to go to Amber when she needed me. Knowing why she was crying was tearing me apart.

I slipped past Lana and painfully struggled toward Amber. Lana picked me up and carried me to her, where she set me on my feet, intently watching her daughter's actions. She told me to drop my shield, and as I did, Amber raised her head and looked around. Our link reconnected and I felt joy replace loss. Love replaced despair, and the mixed messages were quickly fading. When Amber started toward me, Lana picked me up and started to run.

"She is okay! Put me down!" I commanded.

Amber took me in her arms and I was rewarded with one of her smothering, breathtaking hugs.

You require an explanation, Oracle said as it floated nearby.

I was not interested in what it had to say, but I had no choice because I was not going to break our joy-filled unity just to get rid of Oracle.

What you experienced goes back in Draasen history to the time of the First Most High One. You know part of the history when the females took control of their species. During that time, vengeful males sent many of the birthing animals on the long walk. In response, a violent rage took over the females, and they sent any male they could find on the long walk. With no males to fertilize the eggs, no birthings occurred and the population dwindled to less than two hundred thousand females. The First Most High One ordered a relentless search to find the males and bring them back. They were to be protected from harm. Ultimately, four hundred seventy-eight elderly males were found, and the Draasen species was preserved. The rage now occurs only among birthing females, and occurs most frequently when a new female is birthed. Awareness and discipline is carefully practiced. Most birthing females know when the rage is about to surface, and can successfully suppress it. When Ssurlanaseethesess recognized the rage surfacing in High One Ambrisseethsss, she carried out a successful distraction to shorten the length of the High One's rage.

As I listened, I became uncomfortable being in Amber's arms because I was vulnerable if she lost control again.

I am sorry. I was overwhelmed. I have never felt such rage. I wanted to send you on the long walk, and would have but for my mother. What would I have done without you? I am very sorry. I felt the sadness well up in her as she begged forgiveness.

My answer took no thought because I responded from my heart. *You are my life, and I live for you. You controlled yourself, and this is proof of your strength as High One and your love for me. Your control protected your eggs and me. I forgive you. There is nothing you can do I could not forgive you for.*

Lana approached us and said, *High One, I need to examine your surrogate.*

I held up my hand to Lana, asking her to wait just a moment. Above all, I wanted Amber to be happy again, so I decided a bit of silliness was in order. When she placed me on my feet, I reached up towards her. She bent down and I put my hands on each side of her chin.

"Where are the pretty colors? I know they are there somewhere," I said in a squeaky high voice, pulling her chin from side to side to look at each eye. "Where are they? Where is the green? Where is the blue? Uh, uh, oh look here, look at this, here comes the green. I see it, here it comes. Tada! There it is!"

I felt her smile in my hands as I nuzzled her snout.

You make it hard for me to be unhappy, she said with a deep sigh.

Once in a while, you just have to play the fool.

Chapter 10
RESCUE

A month after Dee was birthed, she had grown to her full height, over eleven feet tall. I really liked her a lot, and not just because she was my first daughter. She had become a gracious young lady who always had a smile and a kind word, and not just for me, but for everyone, including the males in our colony. I hoped this would never change. On the other hand, I wondered if she was gearing up for the time when she would want to take a mate and fertilize her eggs. No matter. Just like any other human father, the boys would have to come through me first.

***

With the success we had so far, I was looking forward to releasing and birthing another egg, but unexpected events changed our plans.

The suns were just rising when our door opened. The lights came up and Amber woke with a startled snort as Oracle soared in.

High One, my intrusion is necessary. A dangerous situation requires your attention. A large fragment of the Baleoran transport will enter the atmosphere and impact the water just before suns rise. A large wave will be created, and colonies closest to the projected impact area are being evacuated. I will update information as it becomes available.

"Oracle, wake and notify the colony. We may be needed to help evacuate colonies lower to the water than we are," Amber said.

"This is my fault," I said as we walked outside our dome.

"Why is it your fault?"

"If I had not ordered Oracle to clear the wreckage from orbit, this would not be happening."

"You did not order it. I approved your request."

"I am sorry for disappointing you."

"You are not a disappointment to me. Whenever you have tried to make decisions on your own, your intent was to act in the best interests of our people, and because of that, I usually agree with what you want to do."

"Oracle, where will the wreckage land?" I said.

Look toward the suns rise. You will not be able to see the impact due to the curvature of the planet.

"Can a defense platform destroy the wreckage before it enters the atmosphere?"

The defense platforms are stationed at the planet's poles. The fragment is out of their range.

"We should be able to see it as it comes through the atmosphere."

Amber squatted outside our dome, placed me in her lap, and we sat, waiting for the impact. A few minutes later, we saw a streak appear low on the horizon, which grew into an orange fireball that ended in a flash, briefly lighting the horizon.

High One, probes report the debris has impacted an evacuated island. The island fractured and slid into the water, creating pressure waves radiating outward beneath the surface. Probes report a wave height of one hundred ninety feet crossed an island near the point of impact. The pressure wave will attenuate as it approaches this location, with an anticipated wave height of sixty feet as it passes this area. No evacuation of this colony will be necessary.

"What about the humans? They do not know it is coming!"

"What do you need to save them?" Amber responded immediately.

"I need all three transports, three pilots, and ten males. I want to take Kaa and a healer with us."

I will go, Lana stated.

"You should stay here. Your skill would be better used with all your equipment available to you. I need someone who is skilled in first aid."

I will go, Elder said as he limped toward the hospital with Lana.

Looking around, my volunteers were standing a respectful distance from Amber and me as the transports filed out of the maintenance cave.

Please join me in the workspace. When we had all gathered there, I began. *Here is the plan. This is the building we will be going to.* I created an image of the bank and the surrounding area using the bank's fire evacuation plan I remembered as my example. *This is the second floor layout. We will begin the evacuation on the second floor, where I expect the humans will be sleeping. Silence is important. When we arrive, pull the transports close the structure. Pilots will remain with the transports. Kaa and I will jump to this outside extension. Kaa will join you four and wait outside this door for me to open it. You will take up positions at these points in the hallway. If the humans are alerted, your presence should be enough to send them to this room, where Kaa and I will be waiting. The remaining six will act as guides between this outside door and the largest transport, where the humans will be loaded on. Your priority is the safety of the humans. Are there any questions?*

What will you do if they do not want to leave? Amber said.

I will make them see that it will be in their interest to leave willingly. Those who resist will be carried out. Do not speak aloud in English. It will confuse them. If the situation changes, we may have to change these plans, so be ready. Board your transports.

I dissolved the workspace and my volunteers got on their transports.

Can you arrange for a large dome to be set up with a table and seats for our guests? I said to Amber.

I will have a table and seats moved into the birthing animal dome. Oracle told me it will not be safe for them to return to their island until next suns.

If the wave is high enough, their building will probably be destroyed, so we will have to figure out what to do with them after they are here.

Be careful and return quickly to me.

We were ready to go, but we had to wait while Elder limped to the transports, carrying medical equipment.

"Come on, old man! Time is wasting!" My tone betrayed my impatience.

Patience! Old bones do not move fast, he said as he trundled aboard.

Go to the human's island as fast as possible, I said to the pilots when our door closed.

The three transports lifted together and soared over the cliff with a pod leading us. Kaa had to snatch me from the air while we were briefly weightless during the sudden drop toward the water.

Oracle, how much time is left before the wave hits the island?

A probe reports you have twenty minutes before the first wave will arrive. You will arrive in five minutes.

I do not hear any coherent thoughts from anyone in the structure, Kaa said.

What coherent thoughts? I said.

When you sleep, your thoughts are confused and shift to different subjects.

Good. It means they are all asleep and dreaming.

When the transport touched down, I ran across the ground toward the drive-through lanes with Kaa at my side. At my direction, he picked me up and easily hopped the fifteen feet onto the roof extension, then he hopped back down. I opened an unlocked window and crawled inside, quietly moving through the hallways, and down the back stairs to open the back door.

Get in position, I said, and the four streamed up the stairs in front of me.

Thump!

Quiet. Watch your head, I said, looking at the one who held his head as I walked by him.

At a signal from Kaa, they dropped to all fours, reducing their height significantly as they squeezed through doorways.

We are ready, the males said in unison.

"Kaa, wake them up. Shout in the Draasen language."

After he shouted in the Draasen bagpipes-like tones, he told me almost everyone was awake.

"Hey everyone, listen to me! Come to the lending area! Quickly, people, quickly! We do not have much time!" I shouted.

Oracle, send the pod in here and have it turn on the light.

In the early morning light of the two suns, I saw the water was already pulling back from the shore. We were running out of time. Suddenly, I heard screams and yelling from the hall.

They have discovered us blocking the passage.

I needed their cooperation, so I asked the Draasen to send a calming influence. When several people rushed into the room, they tried to stop but stumbled over one another when they saw Kaa and me. Some screamed when they saw Kaa squatting beside me, causing more panic.

"Everyone calm down! Listen to me! We do not have much time. These people are called Draasen. They will not hurt you." A quick count showed some were missing.

Locate anyone who is not in the room with me and send them this way.

"Ray!" Ann shouted as she ran to me, ducking from Kaa, who leaned over me to watch her.

"Ann, we do not have much time." I heard more screaming from the hallway.

We found five humans who were hiding, and they are moving in your direction. One female will not wake, but does not appear to be damaged. What should I do with this female?

"Ann, is anyone hurt?"

"Cherie has been sick for a couple of days."

Take her to the transport. I want the others to take up positions in the hallway here, here, and here, I said as I sent an image of the floor plan to reposition them.

"Everyone, listen to me! These people will not hurt you. They are here to help. There is a tsunami heading this way and it will destroy this building. Everyone will be transported to safety, but we must leave now! I want everyone to go out the back door. There will be more of these people to guide you to the transport. They will not hurt you!"

Tonya shouted, "Nobody move! There's no wave coming! What do you want?"

"I do not have time for a debate! Do you want proof? Just look out the window! Look! What do you see?"

"Where's the water? Where'd the water go?" Ann exclaimed.

Except for several large pools, the water had disappeared, and I saw the wave rising in the distance.

"What was the first thing people saw when the tsunami hit Indonesia?" I said.

"The water pulled back from the shore, just like that," Ann said.

"If you want to live, get out now! Ann, go!"

"No! I want to stay with you!"

Kaa said, *I will protect both of you.*

Almost everyone rushed from the room, except Tonya and Rico.

"You are not leaving?" I said.

135

"I always thought you were full of crap. Now I'm sure of it," Tonya said.

Everyone is moving out of the structure except those with you.

I need two of you to come in here and take these two to the transport.

"Suit yourselves. Ann, we can leave," I said, and we climbed out the window.

Ann and I crawled out the window. Kaa broke through the window and squeezed out, picked us up, one under each arm, and dropped to the ground. I looked up when I heard the defiant pair shouting and struggling in the arms of the males, who also came out the window and dropped to the ground. Suddenly, the two males fell on the ground, screaming in pain as Tonya and Rico were running away. They were immediately captured and carried to the transport. I went to the injured pair and saw they had been knifed. Elder began treating them where they lay.

Get them into the transport! Everybody, move!

When the injured Draasen were loaded onto the largest transport with the humans, I told the pilot to leave. The transport lifted and sped away, static sparking all over my body. While the last of the males were running to the small transport, Kaa picked Ann and me up and ran to ours. I started to relax until a water creature rose from a deep pool in front of the small transport. The transport hit the creature, turned sideways, and plowed into the sand. It recovered quickly and slowly rose.

Is everybody all right? Can you fly?

The magcoils are heating. I cannot get enough speed to escape the wave. We are prepared to go on the long walk.

No, no, this is not happening. Turn us around! We have to save them!

Amber said, *NO! Do not turn around. They are prepared to go on the long walk.*

Turn us around and get above the wave, I calmly told our pilot. I felt she was torn between obeying the High One and obeying me. *I will not let them go on the long walk. Turn us around, please.* Our pilot reluctantly complied.

Amber was about to say something until I said, *No one goes on the long walk, not on my watch! Do not worry about the magcoils. Turn your transport around and go back to the structure as fast as you can.*

I cannot get high enough to get above the wave. It will catch us, and we will go on the long walk, the pilot said.

You will go on the long walk, but not this suns. Get as much speed as you can, and fly over the structure to a hill behind it. When you reach it, drop the grappling hook. When it hooks, reel it in and land. Hurry, you do not have much time.

Our transport rose above the crest of the wave so I could watch the damaged transport.

You must move faster.

The magcoils will burn out.

Burn them out! You do not have far to go!

The wave was almost on them when the pilot accelerated, trailing smoke as they gained space in front of the wave. The grappling hook dropped and dug into the side of the hill as the wave broke over the transport. I lost sight of it as our pilot pulled back, and banked into a tight orbit. When we circled closer, I felt one male in pain, then another. Finally, I felt all four as they regained consciousness. When the wave passed, the transport had landed on its side. The grappling hook had prevented them from being tumbled by the wave and buried in debris after it was swept away.

Another wave is sure to come. We have to get down there and get them out, I said.

I am sorry, Surrogate to the High One. The High One insists on your immediate return, our pilot said, turning away from the island.

Where are you going? We are not leaving them!

I will assist you, a voice stated from an approaching transport.

Consort to High One Sialisannsee, we need help.

I have been listening. I will retrieve the four in the transport and bring them to your High One's colony. I was relieved when the other transport landed, but unhappy that we were speeding away from them.

Ann was looking up at Kaa while she was held in his lap.

"Are you okay?" I said.

"Look where I am. Look!"

"Is there a problem?"

"This thing will not let me go!"

"His name is Kaa. He is a young Draasen male, and you are being held for your protection. There are no seats or seat belts, so Kaa has to hold you until we arrive at our colony."

Her fear is resisting the calming influence I am sending to her.

"Ann, listen. The Draasen would never hurt you, so do not be afraid of them. When we arrive at our colony, you will learn about them, and I know you will be pleasantly surprised."

"We'll see."

Despite my assurances, Ann kept staring at Kaa as if her glare would compel him to release her.

"Ann, what do you feel?"

"What do you mean?"

"You have your hand on his arm. What do you feel?" Ann crossed her arms, trying not to touch him. "Oh, come on, he will not hurt you. Give me your hand."

With a little tugging, she unfolded her arms and allowed me to put her hand back on Kaa's arm. "Now, what do you feel?"

"It's warm."

"Yes, he is. What else can you tell me?"

"It's very strong," she said, squirming to leave his grip.

"His name is Kaa, and he is like you in many ways."

"He's not like me at all."

"I have lived with them for a while and I know a few things about them. They are intelligent, like you are. They feel fear and pain, like you do. They have hope, desire, and love, like you do. Where is the difference?"

She appeared to relax slightly as she said, "They won't hurt me?"

"Well, maybe if they step on your foot. They are a bit heavy."

She gave me a tiny smile, and then looked up a Kaa again, and he smiled back.

"That was a smile," I said, just in case his toothy grin frightened her.

"Okay," she said, and Kaa set her on her feet.

"That was not so bad, was it? We are approaching the island so Kaa will have to hold you again." I straddled Kaa's leg and he wrapped his arm around me.

"You don't seem to have any problem touching him."

"Of course not. I trust him a lot more than most humans."

Kaa, be ready to catch her when the transport climbs.

The transport pulled up and Ann screamed as she fell backward. Kaa caught her and placed her on his leg. When we landed, the survivors were being guided to the dome. Some were being held off their feet at arms length, kicking and swinging their fists at the Draasen.

Kaa, take Ann to the dome with the others.

My mother is unhappy.

I thought she might be. I had disobeyed Amber's orders, and asked others to do the same. I was sure the consequences would not be pleasant.

When we left the transport, Kaa picked Ann up and started toward the dome.

"Put me down! Ray! I want to stay with you! Ray!"

"Kaa, wait a minute. Ann, my queen is unhappy with what I did, and I have to face her."

"I can tell her what happened. I can help you!"

Kaa, take her to the others! Amber said.

When I arrived at a circle of females, our pilot was kneeling with her arms behind her back in front of Amber in a subordinate position. There was no accurate way to describe what I received across our bonded link, but if I had to choose a word, seething might fit. The yellow and red shifts in her eyes told me I was in deep trouble, and I quickly knelt as well.

The transport with the four rescued from the damaged transport arrived. The pilot was the least injured, but she had several deep cuts. The rest were in bad shape. As the group made their way toward us, a male collapsed behind me.

Stay in your place! Amber commanded when I started to go to him.

Three of the injured moved between Amber and me. The injured male wrapped his arms around me from behind and lost consciousness.

"Lana! This one needs help." She did not move. I looked at Amber, who returned a stone-faced glare at me.

"So, you will not help him. What kind of High One are you? I thought I knew you, but obviously, I did not. I do not know you anymore." I raised my shield, cutting all telepathic contact with everyone.

While I applied first aid, Lana signaled for me to drop my shield.

I will continue his treatment.

What about the others?

This one needs my attention now.

Please save him. He deserves better than to die like this.

It is not his time. I will keep him from the long walk.

I went to the two males who had been pulled away from the gathering and were being treated.

How are you doing?

Surrogate to the High One, my leg is broken in two places and my tail is stretched. He placed his hand on my chest and said, *Thank you for saving me from the long walk.*

You are welcome. I would never leave any of you behind.

I felt all conversations stop, and when I looked around, every eye was on me.

Are you going to be all right? I asked the other injured male.

Surrogate to the High One, I have a broken arm, a few cuts, and my tail is stretched. He placed his undamaged hand on my chest. *Thank you for saving me from the long walk.*

You are welcome.

I looked for the third injured male, but he was gone.

He is with me in my dome, Lana said.

I ran to the hospital, and when I entered, Lana and an assistant were operating on him.

His damage is severe, but he will live. The High One is unhappy with you, but most of the females support you. A High One unhappy with a birthing animal. A female disobeying the orders of a High One. Females supporting a male. This is all extremely unusual.

"What do you mean? This whole situation is 'extremely unusual'. It has been 'unusual' since I was taken from Earth."

The High One wants to speak to you, Lana said.

"I am not interested in talking to her." I felt Lana's surprise when she looked at me.

I suggest you talk to her very soon.

When I left the hospital, I felt very alone. I was reminded that I still had to settle the human survivors as they shouted at me when I walked by. I had to face my queen's anger, and that scared me. I began wondering who I was. Who were my people? I did not know anymore. I wandered around the colony, thinking, until I arrived at the bathing pool and sat down.

"As I understand it, you are in quite a pickle," Elder said.

"Where did you get that?" I said, laughing at his comment.

"A smile during difficulties helps one feel better."

"I did not get a chance to see the two that were stabbed. How are they?"

"I repaired them on the transport, and they will have recovered by suns rise."

"What am I supposed to do, old man? Six were injured, and one almost went on the long walk. The High One is angry with me. I have to settle the humans. What am I supposed to do?"

"I would not be as concerned by the High One as I would be by the Council of Five. You have been summoned before them, and they will decide what is to be done with you."

"Something else to worry about. What is the Council of Five?"

"You might call the Council of Five...an inquisition."

"An inquisition? You mean a trial, for saving their lives?"

"Males are guilty until proven innocent."

"That is ridiculous!" I exclaimed, and for the first time, I worried about having been accepted into Draasen society.

"Protocols from human society do not apply here. You are in a unique position, but you are not above our protocols. You know this."

"Yes, I know."

"You are unlike many males because you do not take advantage of your position. Everyone knows you think of others before yourself. I am disappointed you are not speaking with your pairing. Your words hurt her, and she thinks you are separate from her."

"I had a point to make."

"I understand you were angry because no one would help the injured, but you must understand that protocols control our actions, and everyone was acting within them."

"I know."

"When are you going to talk to the High One?"

"I am not sure if I am going to. I am on the edge of a decision to rejoin my people."

"Your people? You do not consider yourself Draasen?" The disappointment in his voice was obvious.

"I do not know. I do not know!" I said, frustrated and undecided, kicking water into the air.

"Everyone knows you accept responsibility for your actions. Consider accepting this: The High One is responsible for you, and avoiding her only delays what must be decided."

"I know."

"Go to the High One. An apology will repair the damage your words caused. You must face the Council of Five and answer for your disobedience. You will have the opportunity to explain your actions. When you do, remember, your actions saved the lives of several people. It is very important you remember this."

"Thanks, old man," I said, getting to my feet.

"Kneel before the Council, and remember your actions saved lives."

"I will."

I may have been a little out of line, but I also felt completely justified for what I did. Repeatedly, I was told to be myself, but that was not working out at all.

As I approached the Council of Five, I was guided to stand before a quintet of females squatting in a semicircle. The Council leader was an elderly female sitting in the center, with slightly younger females flanking her. Amber was standing behind them with Oracle hovering beside her head. If this was an inquisition as Elder suggested, I was in deep trouble because the word inquisition conjured up several historical facts, not one being pleasant.

I felt very alone and wished I had not ignored my link with Amber. I looked at Amber, and then eased down on my knees. The Council leader spoke first.

Male, you have violated three protocols.

First: Disobedience of an order of the High One.

Second: Encouragement of others to disobey an order of the High One.

Third: Taking initiative without consulting the High One.

These violations are not in dispute. You are guilty. You have been summarily removed from your positions as Escort and Consort to the High One. You will now respond.

I had not been told I would be removed from my positions. That hurt more than anything else. I was going to let them have their way and accept whatever punishment they judged as appropriate, until I remembered what Elder said. It must have been important, or he would not have insisted I remember it.

"There is a saying on my home world: the end justifies the means. This means, any action is acceptable if it leads to a successful result. When the High One asked me what I needed to save the humans, I was provided everything I wanted without question. I believed I was authorized to do whatever was necessary. I acted immediately on plans I was making at that moment, and I did not have time to consult with the High One. I did not have time to do anything except to react and save the lives of the four on the transport. I did not willfully disobey the High One or deliberately ignore the protocols. I took action to save the lives of the High One's people, and the humans."

During the rescue of the four in the damaged transport, what did you mean when you said 'No one goes on the long walk. Not on my watch'? the Council leader said.

"I was responsible for everyone's safe return. Those on the damaged transport claimed they were prepared to go on the long walk, but I would not allow that to happen when there was a chance to save them."

Did you place yourself in danger of going on the long walk at any time?

"I told my pilot I had no intention of going on the long walk, and she kept me safe by getting above the wave where I could safely observe what was happening to the transport. On behalf of the pilot of my transport, I request she be excused for her actions because she acted under my instructions to save lives. I am the only one who must answer for what I have done. I feel completely justified with everything I have done, except one. High One, I apologize for my angry words. I was wrong for ignoring you."

Forgiveness, love, and happiness flooded across our link and overwhelmed me. I desperately hoped there were no more questions because in my current condition, I could not have given a coherent answer.

We will deliberate.

The five stood, made a circle, and put their heads together. Amber hopped over them, landed in front of me, and took me in her arms. I did not think I would ever get used to her breathtaking hugs, but I would not stop her from doing it. Especially at times like this.

I am sorry for everything that happened. I am sorry for what I said to you. I promise I will never do it again, I said, holding her close with my arms around her.

One thing remains before we can move past this. The Council of Five is deciding what to do about your violations of protocols. Whatever they decide, we will always be together.

Despite the comfort I always found in Amber's arms, I had an uneasy feeling. The Council of Five had separated and took up a semi-circle position again.

Amber stood beside me when I knelt before the Council again.

We have completed our deliberations and have come to the following decision. The male is guilty of violating protocols as stated, the Council leader said dispassionately.

My heart fell into my stomach.

Each violation will be stated with our conclusions.

First: Disobedience of a High One's orders. We have considered the male is human by hatching and has been free from Draasen protocols before his acceptance into Draasen society. The statements

145

of the male concerning the need to act quickly were correct. The information provided by Oracle's pod confirms this. The actions by the male saved lives.

Second: Encouraging others to disobey the order of a High One. The transport sent from the colony of High One Sialisannsee was slow to arrive and was a factor in the decisions made by the male.

Third: Taking initiative without consulting the High One. The High One gave the male permission to act independently, leaving the male to act as required to save lives.

Our conclusions for punishment: The statements from the High One, the visuals provided by Oracle, and the statements of the guilty male have swayed the decision for punishment, to favor the male. It is our decision the male be reinstated to the positions of Escort and Consort to the High One. It is our decision the male be educated in protocols. It is our decision the High One will punish her consort as she considers appropriate. The pilot of the transport acted in the best interests of Draasen society, and she will not be required to answer to this Council.

As I fished my heart out of my stomach, the Council leader stood and said, *Surrogate to the High One, in the future, consider your actions, and your words, carefully before you act on them. The Council thanks you for preserving the lives of our people, and the lives of the humans.*

"It is an honor to serve," I said, and saw Elder squatting a respectful distance from us. "Hey Old Man! Did you hear it?" I said as I ran to him.

"Everyone was required to hear the decisions. You were very fortunate the High One gave you permission to act on your own. Other things worked in your favor, not the least of which you are Surrogate to the High One and carry her eggs."

"Your advice was absolutely correct. It swayed their decision."

"You delivered the facts in a way that left no option for any other decision."

"May I have my surrogate back?" Amber said.

"Of course, High One."

"Thanks, old man, for everything."

I saw Amber smiling after him as he limped away. She took my hand in hers.

"You have a good relationship with him. Sometimes I wish I did not have the duties I have. I miss being able to interact freely with the others."

"You still have me. Uh, wait a minute. You have to punish me. What do you have in mind?"

After a moment of thought, she smiled. "Punishment can wait. We must see to our guests. They are not happy about their situation."

"I would much rather see to your needs."

"Our guests need your attention. The males watching them say they are afraid."

"Yes, High One."

I was reluctant to release her hand, but her smile encouraged me to follow her instructions.

The trial was over, and better than anything else, I had been forgiven. I had a smile on my face and bounce in my step while I walked to the dome where the humans were being held.

"Everyone, take a seat. I have a lot of information to put out."

Most of them continued to shout questions and demands.

I addressed the guards inside the dome. *After I cover my ears, everyone in here shout "silence" in the Draasen language.*

After a deafening, bagpipes-like burst, I uncovered my ears and it was quiet.

"Much better. Everyone, please take a seat and your questions will be answered. None of you will be hurt, so relax. Those of you who are being held, listen to me. They will let you go if you behave."

Release them, but watch them. They may try to run.

The humans hurried away from the males, but did not try to leave the dome.

"Please take a seat." Some started shouting questions again, but when I covered my ears, it got quiet. I smiled and put my hands on the table. "Thank you. The people you see here are called Draasen. They are gentle and peaceful. They will not hurt you. It is important you understand they are people, not animals. They are intelligent, far above any of us. The High One of this colony will welcome you, and you will respect her position. Please remain quiet while she speaks to you."

When Amber entered the dome, she was in her robes with her scepter wrapped in her tail held over her right shoulder, and the blue gem of her circlet sparkling on her forehead. I offered the Gesture of Respect for everyone to see. She returned my gesture, and then stood at her full stature, looking very regal.

I turned and said, "The High One, Ambrisseethsss, will now speak to you."

"Welcome to my colony. Your removal from your colony was necessary for your protection. I am disappointed by your violence where two of my males were injured. Their injuries have been healed and the incident will not be spoken of again. When the one called Cherie arrived here, she was very sick and she is being treated by our healer. I encourage each of you to visit our healer for an examination. My Consort, Raymond, will explain the very few rules that exist for guests of my colony. Please be comfortable, because you are safe here."

There were hushed conversations, and many suspicious glances toward me that I ignored as Amber left the dome.

"As you can see, she is a gracious lady, and she is very special to all of us. Before we begin, is anyone hungry?"

Almost everyone was nodding when the males brought a steaming tray of scrambled eggs and the green bacon bars. Plates and spoons were brought and passed around.

"Can someone toss one of those green bars to me, please?" I said, expecting a toss that never came; no one was taking anything from the trays. "Is something wrong?"

"What if they're trying to poison us?" Tonya said.

"Why would they bother doing that? It would have been much easier just to leave you on your island instead of risking their lives to save you. Tonya, take some eggs from the tray for me. Pick from any part of the tray you want, and get one of those green bars for me."

When she made her selections, I took the plate and sat back down. I took a mouthful and made a show of enjoying it. "The eggs are delicious, with just a hint of butter."

I was not surprised that Ann was the first to try them. "They really are eggs. They're good too!" she exclaimed.

Initially, there were tentative samplings, and from their comments, most were enjoying them as well. Some sampled the green bacon bars, but not everyone trusted the color.

"I can start answering your questions while we eat. Since everyone has many questions, ask your questions in a round robin fashion, one question at a time please. We will start with Ann. What is your question?"

"Why didn't you tell us they speak English?"

"I wanted to keep confusion to a minimum, so I asked them to remain quiet. They all understand and speak English, some better than others. Next question."

"What do they want from us?"

"Nothing. You were saved because you needed saving. Please, talk to these people, learn from them, and they will learn from you. Next."

"Are we prisoners or slaves?"

"Neither. You are guests of the High One, but there are certain rules—"

"If we're not prisoners, why can't we leave this place?"

"Tonya, please wait for your turn."

"No! I will not wait! I'm in charge of these people, and you'll answer my questions now!" she stood and shouted, beating her fist on the table.

"Tonya, do you know what you need? You need a time out." I turned to one of the Draasen males who stood behind me. "Take her to their sleeping dome and close the door. Please keep her there until she decides to calm down."

She was picked up and carried, kicking and screaming, to their sleeping dome. Everyone could hear her muffled, angry screams and pounding on the door.

"You only get one chance to make a first impression, and some of you have not done very well. If any of you cannot set an example of a civilized human being, please leave the table, and join Tonya in the sleeping dome." I waited for anyone to leave, but no one did. "If any of you want to leave before we have finished, please feel free to do so. You will be escorted to the sleeping dome, and there you will stay. You will not be harmed, but you will be restricted for the safety and comfort of everyone else. Now, getting back to the question; you are neither prisoners nor slaves. You are guests, but there are rules to follow. First, and foremost, this is a female-dominated society, so follow the instructions of any female you meet. Be in the sleeping dome before dark. There are no lights outside of the domes, and if you wander too close to the cliffs…well, it is a very long fall. There are four caves. You can go in any of them, but be careful if you do. My people want to meet you, and speak with you if you give them the chance." Several of our guests gave me looks I could not interpret. "Now, I want all of you to pay careful attention to this, because this is my rule: be polite to my people."

Amber had changed from her robes and returned to the dome. She looked toward the sleeping dome as she squatted beside me. I stood and offered the Gesture of Respect; she accepted and said, "It sounds as if one of the females became unmanageable."

"Yes, High One. I sent Tonya to their sleeping dome so everyone else could hear the rules and ask questions."

"I understand. Please continue."

"Thank you, High One. Rico, you are next."

"If we're not prisoners, why can't we leave?"

"Where would you go? The only way off this island is on the transport that brought you here. In this colony, there is nothing to fear except ignorance. Next question."

We were interrupted by screaming from the hospital.

Amber said, *Cherie has been allowed to wake. She sounds as if she is healthy.*

"Everyone, please wait here and enjoy breakfast. I think Cherie has discovered the Draasen."

When I entered the hospital, Lana did not say anything, but she had her ears tightly-folded against her head. In the next dome, Cherie was standing on the table, screaming.

You should have kept her asleep until I arrived, I said to one of Lana's assistants.

Surrogate to the High One, I did not expect this reaction.

Can she leave?

Yes. The toxins that damaged her have been removed.

"Cherie. Listen to me! Cherie! Oh, for Pete's sake. Everyone, please leave!"

She finally stopped screaming as she watched the departure of the Draasen, and said, "What are those things? Where is everyone? And what are you doing here?"

"They are called Draasen. You were unconscious when we evacuated everyone off the island you were on before a tsunami flooded it. The others are fine. We will join them shortly. These people are friendly, and they will not hurt you. This island is where I was taken when the silver pod forced me to leave, and I have been living here with these people since then. Please, sit down. How do you feel?"

She sat, or rather wilted, onto the table. "Weak, tired, but better than yesterday. I think it was yesterday. How long was I out?"

"I am not sure, but I was told two days. Everyone is having breakfast. Would you like some?"

"Can I have some water?" she said.

"We will have water, and if you want to eat something, you can. You will like the Draasen. They are different from us, but they are very friendly."

"They won't hurt me?"

"Absolutely not. From what I heard, it sounds like you poisoned yourself. Did you eat something you should not have?"

Cherie's brow furrowed as she thought about something, but I was unable to hear her thoughts.

Lana said, *She thinks Tonya gave her something to cause her damage.*

"Cherie, what are you thinking about?"

"Nothing. Don't worry about it."

"Did you accidentally eat something, or did someone poison you?"

"I don't know. I'll have to think about it." She scowled and gave a sideways look.

"Let me help you off the table."

When we left the room, I felt her hesitate.

"Ohhh, there's more of them." She started to panic again when she saw Lana and her assistant, who were just finishing with their patient.

"Relax. This is Lana, and she is our doctor."

"Hello, Cherie. Welcome to our colony. Drink as much water as you can and you will feel better. Please return here...tomorrow. I would like to check the progress of your healing." Lana squatted and extended her palms up toward Cherie.

"Cherie, this is a Draasen greeting. You respond by placing your palms down on hers. Are you going to accept her greeting?" When she did not move, I said, "Here, let me help you."

I stood behind her, reached under her arms, and lifted them by supporting her elbows. Lana turned Cherie's hands over and raised her palms under them.

"How is your patient doing?" I said.

"His damage was extensive but the surgery was successful."

"I want to be here when he wakes up."

"I will call for you."

"Thank you," I said as I helped Cherie walk away.

"See? They are very gentle."

"They speak English."

"Yes, they learned from me."

Kaa approached slowly and said, "She is not walking very well. Can I carry her?"

"This is Kaa. He would like to carry you to the others."

"I don't think so!" She let out a shriek when Kaa picked her up.

"Thank you, Kaa," I said, walking beside him.

When we arrived, the astonished looks when Cherie was carried into the dome made me smile. Most were concerned about how she felt, but others were not.

When a pot of water was brought, I gave the dipper to Cherie.

"Slowly, Cherie, slowly. Too much, too fast will make you sick."

"I'm thirsty," she said, breathless between gulps of water.

"How about something to eat?"

"Later."

I saw Dave examining the wall under the watchful eyes of the guarding males.

"Dave, what do you think?"

"I've never seen anything like this. The wall is as thin as paper, but it's solid, and I don't think it's metal. Just how advanced are these people?"

"They were exploring the galaxy long before our species dropped out of the trees."

"Can these people take us home? Can they take us back to Earth?" Cherie asked.

I had everyone's undivided attention.

"There are many hard truths in our lives, and that answer is the hardest truth you will ever hear. High One, can we have Oracle join us?"

When Oracle floated into the dome, there were startled gasps and mumbled conversations.

"This is Oracle. To keep things simple for the time being, think of it as a voice interactive computer that floats around. Oracle, greet our guests."

"Welcome. You are safe in this colony. You will not be harmed." Oracle responded in a computer-like voice. It was the first time I had heard Oracle speak aloud.

"Before we continue, I would like Tonya to hear this. Excuse me for a minute."

I walked to their sleeping dome and said, "Tonya, if you can you behave yourself, I will let you out."

"Okay."

Be ready. She may run when the door opens, I said to the female guard who had brought Tonya to the dome.

When the door opened, Tonya strode out and stopped in front of me with her fists defiantly on her hips.

"You will not lecture me. I will not listen to you."

"I have no intention of lecturing you. I want you to be quiet while questions are being answered. You cannot hear the answers if you are running your mouth. Shall we join them?"

Tonya pushed me out of the way and started toward the dome, but the guard stepped in front of her, got in her face, and with bared teeth, growled at her.

"You said they wouldn't hurt me."

"If you lose the attitude, they will not. Are you going to behave?"

"Only if I want to," she snapped back at me.

"She needs to hear what is happening, so I am placing you in charge of her actions." I said to the guard. "If she gets loud again, put her in your lap and hold her there. If you have to, wrap your tail around her mouth to keep her quiet. Can you do that?" I said to the guard.

"Yes, I will do that," she said, glaring at Tonya.

When we rejoined the others, some were glad to have her back, greeting her with high fives and congratulating her for her defiance. The solidarity troubled me, because there would never be cooperation if they continued to follow her lead.

"Now, I will answer the question, can they take us home? The short answer is yes, but there is more. I want all of you to pay attention to what Oracle is going to show you, but I warn you, there is nothing good in what you are about to see. Oracle, close the doors, dim the lights, and display the images from the probe."

Chapter 11

THEFT AND PUNISHMENT

In the semi-darkness of the room, Oracle's display floated above the table. Nearby, Cherie touched Ann on the arm and nodded her head toward us when Amber picked me up and placed me in her lap.

Ann and Cherie like you. There may be a competition for your attention, Amber said.

There is no competition because I am yours.

I wonder who would win.

You are not going to let this go, are you?

I am only commenting that it would be interesting.

I wrapped my arms around her long face and tickled the sensitive skin under her chin with my nose.

Stop it. You will have me laughing. Stop! she said, squirming and snorting.

Cherie and Ann were staring at us when I let Amber go. I pointed to the display, but they started whispering to each other and glancing at Amber and me.

When the date was displayed from the desktop calendar and the dialog about the freezing temperatures was completed, the display was closed, and the doorways opened. I heard weeping and whispered discussions.

I stood and spoke as gently as possible. "As you saw, Earth was destroyed over seven hundred years ago. The government we trusted to defend us used nuclear weapons and destroyed the whole planet while defending it against the Baleorans. The Draasen will not take you there; it is a frozen, radioactive wasteland that will kill them and you."

"There's no hope for us," Ann said.

"There is always hope. Not for what you knew in the past, but for your future. If you would open your minds to new possibilities, you would find a new direction, like I have. You have a lot to think about, and I am sure you have many questions to be answered, but for now, feel free to explore the colony. Ask your questions, and we will help you in any way we can."

Everyone left the dome in small groups, except for Amber, Kaa, Cherie, and me.

"Cherie, you seem to be taking this very well," I said.

"Your little movie only confirmed what I already suspected. I'd been telling myself my family is dead, and I'll never see them again. I miss them a lot, and I've had my time to cry."

"You are a lot stronger than I was when I was shown what happened."

"Can I ask a personal question?"

"Sure."

"What's your relationship with her?"

"If I answered that question, it would open other questions I cannot answer, at least not yet. I can say I have been accepted as a member of Draasen society, and having joined with them is one of the best decisions I have ever made."

"Since you won't answer that question, I'll tell you what I see. The tattoos on your legs match some of hers, and you've taken off your wedding ring. When you look at her, you do it with obvious affection. She picks you up, and you don't object. You were tickling her, and I think she enjoyed it. What's going on?"

While I considered my answer, Kaa said, *Can I have her?*

Why do you want her? I said, intrigued by his question.

I like her. She likes you, and she wants to take you from my mother.

I felt Amber tense, and I immediately said, *I am yours and I will not change that for anyone.*

I will keep my tail around you while she is here, Amber said.

Mother, I can distract her, and keep her away from you.

Very well. Kaa, you may have her.

I heard Cherie's quick intake of breath. "They're telepathic, aren't they?" Cherie said, surprising me with the question.

"What makes you think that?" I said hesitantly.

"Their ears quivered when you looked at them, and I felt a faint buzzing in my head that has stopped. You're telepathic too, aren't you?"

Surprising. She is unusually observant and intuitive, Amber said.

"She just talked to you again, didn't she?"

"Cherie, I need you to keep a secret. Can you do that?"

"You know you can trust me."

"You are right. They are telepathic. They have given me this ability to help integrate me into their society, but it works only with them. I cannot hear your thoughts, but they can. I want to keep it a secret because I am not sure how everyone else would react to it. Eventually, they will know about it, but not right now. They need time to adapt, and process what they have seen."

"You say they can hear my thoughts. Okay, what am I thinking?" she said looking at me.

"It's impossible to hear the thoughts of others," Kaa repeated.

"Well? Is that what you were thinking?" I said.

Kaa continued repeating her thoughts, "Yes. How does he do that? Does he have to keep doing it? Stop it — "

"Stop it. Stop it! Okay, they can read minds." She looked up at Kaa as he smiled at her.

"They do not read minds. They hear the thoughts you are about to speak, but they do not listen to your thoughts all the time. It is similar to what you might hear in a crowded room with everyone talking, and then you hear your name. You tune out everything except what is being said about you. Most of the time, they are very selective about who, or what, they want to hear, but you can bet that every one of the guests, including you, has the undivided attention of every Draasen in this colony. Until everyone becomes comfortable with my people, I want to keep their telepathy a secret. Kaa, take Cherie on a tour of our colony."

"I want you to take me," Cherie said, looking at me.

"Ah-ha. I will let that one go, and have Kaa show you the colony. He would be a far better choice, and he will not let anything happen to you."

He took Cherie's reluctant hand, and they left the dome together.

Amber, I apologize for them. You wanted to release an egg, but we cannot do that now.

We have to decide what to do with them. Unless they want to become members of our society, they cannot stay here, or in any birthing colony.

Is there another island where they can start their own colony?

There are several unoccupied islands suitable for colonies. I will speak to Oracle before I decide what will be done with them.

We should walk around the colony. Would you like to walk with me?

Of course I would. She picked me up and walked out of the dome.

Being carried is not what I had in mind when I said we should walk.

I enjoy carrying you. She pressed her muzzle into my stomach, tickling me.

"Ray, if she's their leader, why does she carry you like that?" Dave said as we walked by him.

"The answer is complicated. Can you ask me later?"

I will see Oracle and decide what we can do with them, she said, putting me on my feet.

I tried to keep our fingers touching as long as possible as we separated, then I watched her walk toward Oracle's dome until Cherie tapped my shoulder.

"She loves you, doesn't she?"

"She loves all her people."

"Have you taken her to bed yet?"

"That is a bit blunt, even for you."

"Well, have you?"

Kaa, you are not distracting her, I said.

I am enjoying this.

KAA!

"You have not seen the preparation cave. It is what you call the kitchen," Kaa said to Cherie.

"I don't want to see the kitchen."

"It is very interesting." He picked her up and walked away with her, saving me from an awkward answer I was sure she would not understand yet.

She leaned back in Kaa's arms and shot an irritated look at me.

"Sorry about that," I said.

I watched many of our guests carefully avoid any Draasen they came close to. I suppose if the situation was different and I had been taken from the island like they had, I might be fearful of them as well. They needed to walk a mile or two in my shoes.

"I can hear something bothers you," Elder said.

"They are the same, self-absorbed mob they have always been. They cannot begin to understand us unless they are open to new possibilities."

"There are two who may be acceptable."

"Who?"

"Ann is the most accepting among our guests. Cherie is interesting, but be careful with her. She has a duality."

"What do you mean?"

"She wants you because you have an important position. She would accept our society only if she can possess you."

"Kaa said Cherie wants to take me from the High One."

"That will not happen. She will never be allowed to have you."

"Why is that?"

"You and the High One are bonded until the long walk. The High One cannot lend you to any of our females because you are not Draasen-hatched."

"What do you mean by lend?"

"A bonded female can lend her male to fertilize an egg, but he cannot bond with the new female. The lending of males must occur because we have one male for every eight females."

"Very interesting. I did not know that."

"Even if she could, I doubt the High One would lend you to another female. She loves you very much, and she will not let anything happen to you."

"Would you say the High One possesses me?"

"It was the same when my pairing possessed me. In a different way, I am possessed by every female who wants me to fertilize an egg."

"Yes, indeed my friend; we are possessed."

***

Just before second bathing, I noticed Tonya and Rico were missing. I was going to look for them when Amber returned from Oracle's dome, and told me we would discuss the resettlement options for our guests after bathing.

While I relaxed on my ledge in the bathing pool, I felt a sprinkle of water hit my face, then another. Glancing around, I saw Cherie squatting, her hand moving gently in the water. I leaned my head back against the rocks and felt another sprinkle. When I looked again, Cherie stood and slowly removed her blouse, casually dropping it on the rocks. She removed her slacks and dropped them. When she stretched up on her toes, arms high in the air, I found her desirable, something I thought I had lost for a human female. She certainly had a spectacular figure.

Cherie screamed when Amber suddenly surfaced beside me and cleared her nostrils at Cherie. Still half in the water with her arms supporting her, she leaned toward Cherie.

"You cannot have him. I will not give him to you," she said with a deep growl.

Do not hurt her, I said.

Silence! You have no say in this.

"You can't own him like a toy. He needs to be with his own kind. Not with some alien who wants him as a pet."

That was definitely a wrong answer. Before I could move, Kaa shot out of the water and swept Cherie up in his arms just as Amber snarled and took a snap at her. He sprang into the air and landed in the pool.

Wait! Stay Here. You gave her to him, I said, pulling on Amber's arm.

She was very angry as she looked over her shoulder at Cherie and Kaa, sweeping her tail back and forth underwater.

You should have made me stay here, and let them all go on the long walk.

My statement had the effect I hoped for. For the first time since Amber had surfaced, she looked at me, and I felt her start to relax.

I should set an example and be more tolerant of their different ways.

We could tell Cherie what I am doing for you. What do you think?

Kaa, bring Cherie to Oracle's dome after bathing.

Can I stay with her? Kaa said.

I want you to stay and watch her.

Come on, we need to get scrubbed, I said, and Amber helped me onto her back.

When we passed Kaa and Cherie, I was surprised to see her smiling at him.

"Be careful, Cherie. You could get lost in those eyes."

"We need to talk," she said to me.

"It has already been arranged. We will get together after bathing."

While Amber and I bathed, Cherie watched us. Afterward, we fitted our clothes, and waited for Cherie and Kaa, who were fussing with each other on the scrubbing ledge. Kaa wanted to wash her, but she kept pushing his hands away. When she dove into the pool, she let out a surprised screech as Kaa surfaced under her. At the edge of the pool, I helped Cherie off Kaa's back and when she got to her feet, she tried to cover herself with her hands.

"You do not have anything to be embarrassed about. Besides, if you were meant to cover, you would have been given three hands. Come on, we will get you some clothes."

When I finished fitting a cloth around her, I asked her to spread her legs.

"I most certainly will not."

"You amaze me. You were as naked as a jay bird for all to see in the bathing pool, but you will not spread your legs to finish dressing. I will stand way over here. Now, go ahead, spread them."

After giving me a look that could melt iron, she carefully spread her legs. The cloth unzipped between her legs and stopped at the top, creating shorts. The look on her face made me laugh. "You should learn to trust my people. They would not hurt you."

"No way. You saw her. She tried to bite me."

"Trust me; if she wanted to bite you, you would have been bitten. It was just a warning snap in your direction."

"Where are my clothes? I mean the ones I came here with."

"They have been recycled. You look good in that."

"It doesn't leave much to the imagination," she said, twisting to look at her form-fitting outfit.

While we walked toward Oracle's dome, I found myself agreeing with Amber: our guests must leave. The moment I decided, I felt a subtle tugging in my head suddenly stop.

You were doing the influence thing on me again. Why are you so uncomfortable with them? I asked Amber.

I do not like her. She knows what she wants, and she will keep trying to get it.

"Welcome to my center," Oracle said when we entered.

"Cherie, Oracle will show you what has happened to me since I have been here. Please, make an effort to understand what is going on, okay?" I waited until she nodded acceptance. "Oracle, you may begin."

The light dimmed and Kaa placed Cherie in his lap. Oracle showed my arrival at the colony and the many things I had been subjected to. It explained what had happened to Amber, the surgery to save her life, the implanting that saved her eggs, and briefly showed my birthing surgeries.

"Well, what do you think?" I said when the light came up.

"That could've been another movie; a made-up story this time."

I pulled my waistband down to fully reveal the two scars on my side.

"Oracle, I need Dee to be here."

When the door opened, Dee arrived with her hands full of food as she chewed on her latest mouthful.

"Kaa is our first hatchling, and he is about two months old. This is Dee, and she is about a month old."

She is confused. She does not accept what she has seen as real, Kaa said.

"What proof can I offer to help you understand this is all real?"

Cherie scowled up at Kaa when she realized he had relayed her thoughts to me.

"You are catching on. I thought telepathy would have convinced you."

"No, it's not that. I had hoped you would've wanted me, but you're having her children. That's so strange. Men don't have children, women do."

"I always thought I did not need children to make my life complete. Since I have had these two wonderful hatchlings, I cannot imagine life anywhere else. I am very glad Amber chose me to come to her."

"I wouldn't want those eggs in me. It's disgusting just thinking about it."

Kaa grunted, put Cherie on her feet, and left with Dee.

"It helps if you are willing to accept the situation. I decided to join with these people, and I have no regrets that I am bonded with her."

"Bonded? You mean you are married to it? I can't believe I'm hearing this."

Amber was becoming more annoyed by the second.

"Truth is truth. You saw it for yourself. What you decide is now up to you."

What is she thinking? I said.

She is not convinced about our situation. It is past feeding and I am hungry.

You could have gone to feed at any time.

I am not leaving you alone with that female.

"I can see you are comfortable with her. Maybe there's nothing here for me," Cherie said.

"We should go eat," I said.

"Where'd Kaa go?"

"You kind of…offended him."

"I did not."

"Actually, you did. When you said their eggs were disgusting, that did it."

"They seem to be overly-sensitive."

"They are not animals. They are people, very much like us, and if you consider their feelings, things will become a lot easier."

***

As the plates were being passed around the feeding table, a ground-shaking thud shook everything.

Our guests are trying to pilot the High One's transport.

Bring them to me, Amber commanded as several females arrived at a run and stood in the doorways.

"What's happening?" Ann said.

"Someone is trying to steal a transport. Everyone stay here until we can sort it out," I said.

There was another thud and several screams echoed from the cave. Six wayward guests were brought from the cave and dropped in front of Amber.

Amber spoke directly to me, tense with anger. *They will leave my colony at next suns. I will not punish them. They are guests, so I will leave this to you.*

Thank you, High One, but what can I do?

Bring order back to my colony.

Can I do what I want?

Only within protocols.

I addressed the six standing before us. "What is wrong with you? These people saved your lives, and this is how you thank them? The High One is very disappointed by your actions."

"You said they won't hurt us, so what do you think they'll do? Nothing!" Tonya said.

"Yes, it would be very unusual for the High One to authorize punishment because, unlike you, they are gentle people. Obviously, they are more civilized than you are."

"See? I told you," Tonya said to her companions.

"But, what about me? The day I left, some of you wanted to kill me. Should I return the favor and have you tossed over the cliffs?"

You will not send them on the long walk, Amber reminded me.

"Fortunately for you, I am a member of Draasen society and being such, I cannot punish you as I would like." Tonya and Rico exchanged smiles.

Suddenly, Kaa ran to Tonya, dropped to all fours, and got in her face.

Kaa! What are you doing?

She poisoned Cherie. He looked at Rico. *This one almost sent the one called Dave on the long walk, and she approved of it.*

"Dave, what happened to you after I left?" I said.

"When the silver thing flew off, I started to follow you, but Rico knifed me in the back and left me on the beach to die. Cherie and Ann helped me back to the building and kept me alive." He lifted his shirt to show me a puckered scar. "He used me as an example, and said he'd kill anyone who got out of line."

"That is useful. Thank you. I want our doctor to have a look at you, just in case. Lana, can you check his damage?"

"Yes. Dave, please come with me."

"Tonya, what am I going to do with you? I have been informed that you tried to kill Dave and Cherie. This is completely unacceptable, even for you," I said.

"I didn't do anything," Tonya said.

"I...heard you are the one who poisoned Cherie."

"No, I didn't."

Kaa pressed his snout against Tonya's cheek and rumbled a deep growl.

"Kaa thinks you did, and I trust him more than you. You may as well admit it."

"I didn't do anything."

"Are you sure? Okay. Kaa, go ahead and eat her."

Kaa snarled as he bared his teeth, and with a growl he opened his jaws wide.

"No! No! I did it! I did it! Please, don't let him kill me, please!"

"Kaa, that is enough. Thank you. Tonya, I would like to know why you did it."

"She was working behind my back, trying to get Ann to take over. If you hadn't showed up, she would be dead, and so would Ann."

"Take these two and lock them in a dome. Let the others go. Shall we go back inside?"

"Ray, would you have killed her?" Ann said.

"As you saw, she was not killed by the evil creatures," I said sarcastically.

We are not evil creatures, Amber said.

Of course not, dear one. No one knows that better than I.

"Your superior numbers could have easily overthrown their little dictatorship, and you should have punished them accordingly, but you did nothing. Now, what are you going to do with them?" I said.

"I'm not going anywhere they go. They'll try to kill me again," Cherie said.

"That is a possibility. Now that Tonya and Rico are under control, someone has to take charge." I was not surprised to feel a gentle tugging in my head again. This time, it was an influence encouraging a female to lead.

"We have a lot to talk about. Can we have some privacy while we discuss our options?" Ann said.

"Sure, take all the time you need. Why not discuss it over dinner that is getting cold?"

As Amber and I left, Cherie gave me a knowing smile. She knew there would not be any privacy.

***

While Amber and I relaxed outside our dome, she kept me informed of the discussions. It was almost dark when we were called back, and Ann stood when we entered.

"What have you decided?" I said.

"By a majority vote, I'm now in charge. I want to thank your High One for her hospitality, but we have decided we want to leave. But I saw the tsunami destroy our building, so I don't know where we can go."

"We will help you. In the morning, we will take you to an island that is safer, and has more resources."

"What can we expect from these people?"

"I have arranged for you to have whatever you need."

"Will you be coming with us?"

"I will go with you to help set up your colony, but I will not stay because I have...obligations I need to complete. I will return here with my people."

"What about Tonya and Rico?" Cherie said.

"Ann, I would like your group to give us a decision by first suns concerning those two. We will wake you at suns rise so we can all bathe and have first feeding. A transport will be provided after that. It is getting dark, so we will all go to your dome."

When we entered, I said, "This is the bed. It may look like a big, blue dinner plate in the ground, but it is very comfortable. It is covered in a material similar to our clothing, and there are blankets of the same material if you think you need them. Someone will be outside if you need anything. Good night, everyone."

"Where are you going to sleep?" Ann said.

"I will be sleeping with my queen, like I always do."

169

"Are you really going to sleep with her?" Ann said.

"Yes, he is," Amber said and carried me out of the dome.

When we settled in our bed, Kaa said, *Ann and Cherie want to talk to you.*

Can it wait until next suns? I said.

The appointed High One wants to ask private questions. Kaa, tell them we will see them here. Bring them to us, Amber said.

When they arrived, I said, "Come in and have a seat. You have something on your mind that could not wait until tomorrow." Cherie looked disappointed as Amber and I lay together.

"Cherie told me these people are telepathic. Is it true?" Ann said.

"Yes. They have been for thousands of years. How many others know about that?"

"Just me. Why didn't you tell everyone about it when we arrived?"

"How do you think they would have reacted if I came out and said my people are telepathic, pointed a finger at Tonya and Rico, and said they were guilty of poisoning Cherie and nearly killing Dave? Would anyone have believed me?"

"I see what you're saying."

"Cherie did not believe it either, but now she understands. She was in contact with Kaa until she insulted him."

"You insulted them?" Ann said.

"I didn't mean to. I'm sorry for what I said," Cherie said to me.

"Kaa is outside, and you could apologize to him. They are great listeners."

When Cherie left, Ann said, "No one thought you were alive. Why did you wait so long to contact us?"

"I was not welcome. Rico wanted to cut my throat, and you saw Tonya push me at the silver pod. She was hoping it would kill me."

"How do you know that?"

"Amber was listening and she told me."

"If you would've come back sooner, you could've taken over from Tonya and Rico with our help."

"And what would I have done with them? Send them away so they could come back and kill me? Or, maybe I could have killed them. No, I think what has happened was for the best. I was not there and everyone is alive."

"How long would you have left us there?"

"The truth is, you would still be there if the tsunami had not arrived."

There was an uncomfortable pause before Ann said, "I see. May I ask you a very personal question?"

"It depends on the question."

"Everyone sees how you act with her. We see the smiles and knowing looks, and how gently she treats you. Some want to know if you sleep with her. Well, I see you sleep with her, but do you really sleep with her?"

"I sleep with her every night."

She wants to know if we have fertilized eggs together.

I know, but I want her to ask the question.

"I can see that, but, you know, do you, you know, do it?"

"We do many things together. Which 'it' do you want to know about?"

"You know, have sex?"

"Oh. No, we are forbidden to do that. We find love and intimacy in ways you have never experienced." It took a supreme effort not to laugh at her furiously blushing cheeks.

Kaa and Cherie came back in. He squatted and she let him put her in his lap.

"Can I assume you have made up?" I said.

"Yes, we have," Cherie said, smiling up at him.

I was feeling the same accepting influence I felt when I arrived.

She will leave despite his efforts to keep her, Amber said.

171

He might want to go with her.

I was left in telepathic silence as Kaa and Amber spoke to each other.

"Ray, what's happening?" Cherie said.

"A private mother and son discussion. Ann, is there anything else you want to ask?"

"You said they would help us. What can I expect?"

"We can fully support your colony and give you everything you need. There will be a Draasen presence providing training, communications, and medical assistance. With the training they provide and the resources found on your island, you will be able to trade with other colonies. Then, as your situation improves, you can reduce their support and eventually eliminate it. That may not happen in the short term, but it is an option I would consider."

"Who'd be in charge, them or us?"

"As far as the Draasen are concerned, you are the appointed High One of your colony, with all the power and privileges necessary to run a colony. At first, a senior female will be in charge, and you will work closely with her. As your colony becomes established, you would take responsibilities from her. Eventually, they would become observers, consultants, and assistants. Having said that, I must give you a warning; do not expect them to become servants. That will not happen. Everyone is going to have to pull their own weight. They will help, but they will not do it all."

"I see."

"I have something else for you to consider. If we happen to find other humans who were taken from Earth like we were, would you take them into your colony?"

"I have a lot of decisions to make. Can we discuss that later?"

"I am really hopeful we will find more people, and if we do, we need to help them as well."

During my conversation with Ann, I felt Amber was unhappy when Kaa and Cherie left together.

What is wrong?

My hatchling is leaving. He will follow that female to their colony.

Why are you unhappy about that?

He wants to bond with her, but I will not allow it.

Why not?

She is not good enough for him.

Cherie is pleasant and thoughtful. She has always been kind to me, but if she has something she wants to do, she gets it done.

"Cherie told me when they talk telepathically, their ears quiver. I could tell you were talking to her, just now."

"I am sorry. You should not have been left out."

"What's it like, reading minds?"

"They do not read minds, they hear thoughts. It can be intimidating, and it is hard to keep secrets from them. You saw what happened between Kaa and Tonya when he heard her thoughts. There are no lies, or reading between the lines here. I would like you to keep their telepathy a secret until everyone becomes comfortable with my people."

"I've heard you say 'my people' several times. What do you mean by that?"

"I have been accepted by Draasen society as one of their own. My loyalty, dedication, and love all belong to my queen."

"Are you human?"

"If you are asking if I consider myself human, no. I am Draasen, and happy to be so."

"When you offer to help us, are you thinking about our interests, or your own?"

"Do you know what it means to be extinct? It means no more, ended, finished, and the human race is almost extinct. If you are asking if I have another agenda, yes. I am not looking out for just your interests, or your colony's interests; I am looking to the survival of the human species. I am in a position to see that happen, and that is my interest. The Draasen have an interest in humans because I do. Accept them and they will accept you because they are peaceful people. They are not perfect, but they are a whole lot better than most of the human race ever was." I could see Ann was surprised by my answer.

Eventually, they will have to be moved from this planet and placed on another that is not occupied for them to develop naturally, Amber said.

They would be in danger from the Baleorans and their own failure.

Their numbers would be too small to be of any interest to the Baleorans for thousands of years. As for their failure, we all must walk within the Great Ring in our own way.

"Ann, there is something else to consider. For the human race to redevelop as it should, they will have to be returned to Earth after it has recovered. It will not happen in our lifetimes, so I want you to keep the thought of returning to Earth in the minds of your colony members. Make sure it not forgotten. Earth was home to the human race, and it can be again."

"I have a lot to think about. I'll take what I've heard and let them know about it, some of it anyway. I'd like to go back now."

"Someone is outside who will take you back to your dome. Tomorrow will be a long day, so try to get some rest."

"I'll try. Good night."

"Amber, where is Kaa?"

"He has gone to his dome. That female went with him."

"I am not surprised," I said.

"I am proud of you."

"Why?"

"I asked you to be yourself, and you did that with Ann. I think she will be a good High One."

"I am sure she will, but not as good as you." I snuggled against her and went to sleep.

Chapter 12
ACCEPTANCE

Wake up. You wanted to be with the injured male when he woke. Join me at the bathing pool when you have finished with him, Amber said.

As we parted, our hands slipped apart but our fingers lingered together. She looked back at me and smiled as she walked to the bathing pool. Kaa and Cherie came out of his dome. She looked around and saw me as I walked to the hospital. She ran to me, spun me around, and hugged me.

"Good morning. Do I need to ask if you are in a good mood this morning?"

"I'm happier than I've been in a long time. Kaa and I had an amazing time last night. We talked for hours, and he showed me so many things I can't sort it all out. He wants me to be his Escort, or something like that. He likes me and with him protecting me, I'll be safe from everyone and everything."

"Cherie, walk with me. I completely understand what you are saying because I have experienced it on a more intimate level than you have, but I have to tell you about Kaa and his life as a Draasen. These people live an average of three hundred years, and despite his size, Kaa is still a baby. They bond for life in what they call a pairing, and if one dies,

176

the other will not bond again. What I mean is, unlike us, they will not get remarried. If you take the Second Step of Acceptance with Kaa, you will give him, maybe, thirty years of happiness, and I have no doubt they will be the happiest years you can imagine. Then, when you die, you will condemn him to two hundred seventy years of loneliness. Is this what you want to wake up to in the morning?"

"You really know how to ruin a good thing, don't you?"

"Did you want me to lie and tell you what you wanted to hear?"

"No, you wouldn't do that. What am I supposed to do now?"

"Well, there is another possibility. What I described is called Consort and is the Second Step of Acceptance; a permanent position in Draasen society. You can still enjoy the First Step of Acceptance called Escort. It is like dating taken to a different level. If you can control the situation, and yourself, you can be Kaa's Escort for a very long time, even until you die. Did Kaa tell you Escort was temporary?"

"Not exactly, but I had the feeling it was."

"I have found feelings say a lot more than actual words around here. I notice a lot more, now that I know what to feel for. I want you to know I am privileged to have been chosen by Amber."

"Hey, wait a minute. You're married to her, right? You're much older than I am."

"Oh, thank you very much for your observation."

"Sorry. That didn't come out like I wanted."

"I know what you meant, and you are right. I have about ten or so years I can give to her, and I have told her that, but she is not concerned. I enjoy being with her and being apart, like we are now, makes me uncomfortable. Having her in my thoughts is a very peaceful feeling, but it cannot compare to when we touch. There is certain...something, impossible to describe. It can only be felt."

"Why are we here?" she said when we arrived at the hospital dome.

"A male was severely injured while everyone was being rescued, and is recovering here. I wanted to be here when he wakes up. Lana, how is he?"

He is healing as expected. I will keep him here until next suns to be sure he is ready to return to us.

"Lana said he is —"

"I heard what she said. I don't know how, but I did."

Lana looked down at Cherie, her eyes narrowing.

This is Kaa's doing. How far has he gone with you? Lana said.

"He hasn't gone anywhere with me. We spent the night together, that's all."

Did you take the First Step of Acceptance with him? she said, growling as she dropped to all fours and leaned toward Cherie.

"Lana, stop it!" I shouted.

Is he your Escort? Lana said, nose to nose with Cherie.

"I want him to be."

With blazing speed, Lana closed her jaws over Cherie's head down to her chest. If she clamped down, she would easily bite Cherie in half. I could hear Cherie's muffled screams as her arms waved uselessly on both sides of Lana's jaws.

"Let go! Open up! Let her go!" I shouted, pounding my fist on her snout and trying to pry her jaws apart.

Mother! Release her! Amber commanded when she arrived with Kaa.

Cherie staggered backward against Amber, and when she looked up at her, she fainted.

"Eww, she is all slobbery. Kaa, take her to the bathing pool and clean her up. Lana, would you have sent her on the long walk?"

No.

"Then, why —?"

She is not the correct choice for Kaa.

"Oh, so you make the decisions around here. I thought the High One is in charge."

Without looking at me, Amber guided me with one hand toward the door, and then used her tail to push me gently out of the dome.

I went to the bathing pool and felt Kaa was very unhappy as he held the unconscious Cherie in his lap.

She will not wake. Is she damaged?

No. She fainted. Pick her up and follow me.

I led them to a cool water drainpipe, brought handfuls of water, and cooled her forehead and face. Slowly, she began to rouse.

"What happened? Where am I?"

"Take it easy. You are lucky to be in one piece."

"She tried to eat me!"

When she saw Kaa, she let out an ear-piercing scream and jumped on me for protection.

She is afraid of me, Kaa said.

She is confused. Please leave, and I will try to calm her, I said, trying to pry her arms from my neck without much success.

"Cherie, there are no more Draasen near us. See? They are all gone. I need to breathe, okay?"

After she settled close beside me, I had to stifle a laugh at the memory of Cherie inside Lana's mouth.

"It's not funny. You said they wouldn't hurt us."

"They would never intentionally hurt you."

"How do you explain what happened to me?"

"Simple. Are you hurt?"

"Yes! No. I don't know."

"Do you have any injuries? Are you bleeding anywhere?"

"No," she said after a quick examination.

"Well, there you are, undamaged by the vicious creatures who you thought were trying to eat you." Unable to stifle my amusement any longer, I burst out laughing.

"It's not funny! How would you like to be eaten by them?"

"I think I will pass on that. Someone is very concerned about you."

"You mean Kaa?"

"Absolutely. After you fainted, he carried you here. He cleaned you up and protected you."

"Why did I need cleaning?"

"You were a little slobbery after Lana let you go."

"Oh, yuck."

"He is anxious to be with you again, but he will not come to you unless you say it is okay. See if your telepathic link still works."

Cherie hesitated but she called to him. Kaa squatted and offered the Gesture of Respect. I went to him and accepted his gesture.

"Thank you, Kaa. Cherie, he wants your friendship and your trust. You accept by placing your chin on your chest and press your palms down on his, like I did."

Cherie nervously shifted her weight from one foot to the other. Then, she hesitantly walked to him, pressed her palms down on Kaa's, and quickly pulled them back.

"Kaa, be gentle with her. She has been through a terrifying experience. Shall we bathe?"

Kaa and I jumped in, and he offered his hand to Cherie.

"Well, are you going to take a bath?" I said.

"Is that...doctor here?"

"Lana knows what frightens you, but you will not be bothered by her again. She will not disobey the High One. Please, come in and let Kaa show you how gentle and how strong he can be for you. Do you remember how you felt this morning?"

Kaa was a pitiful sight with his sad face looking up at Cherie, his hand extended to her. It took a while, but she finally took Kaa's hand and allowed him to help her into the water. She had been through a lot, and I was not so sure I would have been as trusting as she was. After a while, I was surprised to hear Cherie's laugh as she sat on his stomach as they floated together. I smiled when I remembered how I'd felt when I arrived. Amber brought me to her perfectly. Now, I was hers, and I would not have it any other way.

When I thought about it, it seemed odd to me that Lana had asked Cherie if he was her Escort. She would have known, considering how closely these people were linked to each other.

Our people, Amber gently corrected me when she arrived. *My mother deliberately held Cherie because she disapproves of those two being together. I am disappointed with Kaa, but I would tolerate the two of them together. I am glad you told Cherie the truth about the Steps of Acceptance.*

Cherie brought up a point I want to check with you again. You know humans do not live as long as Draasen, and I can only give you about ten years before I go on the long walk. What are you going to do then? I know you will not pair again, and I am unhappy our bonding has condemned you to a life of loneliness, but there is nothing I can do about it unless Lana knows how to extend my life, which I think is doubtful. Amber lifted me out of the water and held me close. There was so much joy in her touch and in my mind, it was nearly unbearable.

My decision to accept you was correct, and I would not change my decision. You gave your life to me, and we will make it a happy time together.

She believed in me, so I should not question it. I wanted the best for her, but I could not give her as much as I would like. I just did not have the time.

You do not need to give me more than you are. Be yourself, and you will go beyond my highest expectations. I do not need to ask for more.

She sprang into the air and we splashed in the pool together. When we bobbed up, she floated on her back, holding me close on her chest while she gently swept her tail under the water, leisurely moving us toward the scrubbing ledge. It was times like this I hoped would never end.

A pair of females scrubbed Amber's back while I gently scrubbed behind her ears. She was always appreciative of everyone's attention, but she especially liked mine. I looked around and found most of the humans in the pool area except for our two detainees.

They will be given the opportunity to bathe and have a feeding. They will be watched so there will be no trouble from them.

I looked for Kaa and Cherie. It was obvious they were going to be a while longer while he scrubbed her. We finished bathing and went to the large dome where the humans would gather to eat.

"Do you have to be with our people at every feeding?" I said.

"It is expected of me. I will let them start, and return to you for first feeding."

When I entered the dome a few were already there, waiting in their tattered earth clothes. As the rest started arriving from the clothing dome, I complimented those wearing the Draasen clothing, with hopes that everyone would eventually wear them.

Amber returned from the Draasen feeding table and squatted beside me as the trays arrived. Knowing our guests would not know protocols, I quickly spooned a plate of eggs for Amber and offered it to her. She took the first tongue full from the plate as the others started digging in on the trays.

I will be glad to see the humans gone, Amber said.

You are not being very gracious.

I understand you want to see them survive, but having looked into your memories and seeing how the human species is, I have serious doubts about their survival. Do not feel sad about what I said. I know you will do everything you can for them.

My first duty is to you and your eggs. I have never lost sight of that, and I will never change toward you. My love and devotion are yours, and when it is my time to go on the long walk, I will do it with your love in my heart.

Sometimes it made me sad I would never know what it would be like to be truly and completely Draasen. It was one thing to say I was Draasen, another to actually be one. It was like being a member of an exclusive club, but not having the jacket.

Amber suddenly left the table, calling for her mother and the two most senior females to meet her at Oracle's dome.

"What's going on?" Cherie said.

"I do not know. She did not tell me."

"I heard her call for Lana and two others."

"You heard that?"

"Yes. Are you in trouble?"

"I hope not. I have not done anything I know of."

I could tell Amber had arrived at Oracle's dome because our link stopped. I felt calming reassurances from our colony members, because they knew separation from Amber made me uncomfortable. I wondered if it would ever pass. I hoped not.

When everyone had finished eating, they filtered out of the dome. Cherie and Kaa lingered for a while, but they were more interested in each other, and when they left, I sat alone and waited for Amber. When our link reconnected, Amber was very happy about something.

"I have a gift for you, but I cannot give it to you now."

"You have given me too much already."

"It will complete your entry into our society. I know you will like it because I will enjoy it as much as you will. Long ago, the love of a High One created the situation for the gift to her surrogate, and I cannot wait until I can give it to you, but I must. It has been given only once in all of Draasen history."

Whatever the gift was had her excited and I wondered what it could be. She placed me in her lap and held me close. We received the strangest looks when our guests began returning from exploring the colony. Let them stare. I had the greatest love in the universe, and I would show it at every opportunity. When Ann arrived, Oracle floated in and stationed itself at the top of the dome. Kaa ran in and slid to a stop, carrying Cherie.

"Ann, have you made a decision concerning your two prisoners?"

"Yes, we voted on our decision last night. It's my duty to tell them what their punishment is."

"I will have them brought in."

When Tonya and Rico arrived, they were struggling in the grips of their guards.

"Ann, as the new leader of your colony, has a decision been made concerning these two?"

"By a majority vote, we have decided you will be banished. I don't know where you will go, but it won't be with us."

Tonya and Rico started shouting and pleading with anyone who would listen.

"They will be taken in a separate transport to the island they came from. I will see to it they get a couple of domes and access to food and water. Take them back to their dome. Ann, you should look in on them from time to time to monitor their progress, because they should be considered for re-entry to your colony."

"I'll discuss it with them later."

Sometimes, it is hard being a High One, Amber said.

"Okay. Have you considered our offer of support for your colony?" I said.

"Yes, we like your offer of full support. When can it be arranged?"

"They are already working on your island."

"How do they know where to go?"

"I...anticipated you would want to be supported and had Oracle alert the other colonies. You will have an Oracle in your colony as well."

"Do we really need one?"

"Yes. The Draasen need an Oracle for support away from their colonies. We can leave whenever you are ready."

"We're ready now. Let's get going."

On orders from Amber, three transports filed out of the maintenance cave, and when the smallest transport moved to where Tonya and Rico were being held, I realized we were setting up a prison colony.

In our very distant past, we had such places, Amber said.

What do you do if someone gets out of control or refuses to comply with protocols?

We make a detention dome where females are kept until a Council of Five makes a decision. There are Councils available in every colony, but there has been little need for them. Did you know your judgment was the first time a Council of Five had been brought together on this planet in five hundred years?

I still have a lot to learn.

Tonya and Rico were loaded onto the small transport and left the island. When everyone had boarded the largest transport, I jumped on to let them know what to expect.

"As the transport leaves, it will fly over the cliffs and drop toward the sea. It is similar to a roller coaster on the first drop, so I want everyone to sit and hold onto one of the posts in the floor. If you feel comfortable being held by the Draasen, let them hold you. Please hold onto something before we leave," I said, and joined Amber on her transport.

When Amber gave the order, the transports lifted and dropped over the cliffs. Flying quickly, it was not long before we saw the island looming in the distance.

When we landed, there was a lot of noise as heavy equipment was being used to dig out the bathing pool and cut caves into the cliffs. Other Draasen carried what appeared to be long rolls of carpet. Amber said it was grass from their home world that kept natural vegetation from reclaiming the colony area, and kept the colony clean. When they finished rolling out a section, it began digging roots into the ground, heaving and rolling along the entire length until it leveled out, quickly grew a couple of inches, and changed into the bluish green color we were used to seeing.

People are talking about you, Cherie said.

Really? What do you think?

When they talk about you, they look at me. They don't trust me, but they don't say anything to my face. I think they're afraid of Kaa, Cherie said.

Why are they afraid of me? Kaa said.

You are much bigger and stronger than they are. They do not trust you because of what happened with Rico and Tonya. I am glad they did not see the incident in the hospital, I said.

While we waited, Amber became quiet and withdrawn. I felt something had her on edge.

"What is wrong?"

"I am not comfortable."

"Do you need Lana?"

"No. It is these people."

"What about them?"

"It is nothing for you to be concerned about."

"Come on, I want to hear it."

"They are a disruptive influence," she said with a snap in her voice.

"No, that is not it. Unless I know what the problem is, I cannot fix it."

I suddenly received an angry flash across our link. It lasted only a second, but it took a minute for me to figure out what I felt.

"It is not just these people, it is Cherie. She wanted me, but could not have me, so she took something else...Kaa. Yes, if you separate Kaa from her, she may try to come at me again. I hope you are not jealous."

She took my head in her hands and bumped our foreheads together hard enough for me to see stars. It became quiet, and in my peripheral vision, I saw all heads were turned toward us, watching. It was vaguely amusing to see only the heads of males peeking over the edge of the unfinished bathing pool.

I am not jealous!

You sure act like it.

You changed when they arrived. You are almost as you were when you first came to me. I have been afraid of this since they arrived.

To help them, I have to think like them. You do not have any need for concern because I will always be yours. It will take time for them to know your people.

Our people. Do you see one of the changes?

I am sorry. They will soon be on their own, and you will have me all to yourself again.

When we separated, the area became full of noises and activity again. The working males carefully avoided Amber when she walked away.

"What was that about?" Ann said.

"I came close to breaking one of our protocols, and my High One reminded me about it."

"I was watching them when the two of you were head to head, and I think they were scared. If we break these protocols, what happens to us?"

"Do not worry about their protocols. They do not apply to you or your colony. Like I said before, I am a member of Draasen society. In my unique position, I am expected to know and uphold our protocols."

"What would have happened if you broke a protocol?"

"It would depend on what I did, but the maximum penalty would have sent me on the long walk."

"What's the long walk?"

"It means I would have been killed."

My answer started murmurings from the group around me.

"If I stayed with Kaa, and I broke one of these protocols, would I be killed?" Cherie said.

"It would depend on what you did, but females are far less likely to be punished than males are."

"I've heard you mention your unique position a couple of times. What is this unique position?" Ann said.

You should tell them about being my surrogate, Amber said.

Can we have the feeding table and a dome set up? I also need access to Oracle.

I will tell the males to set them up immediately. I have told Oracle you are allowed access through the pod sent with us.

"Ann, I will answer your question when the feeding table is set up. I want you to know I kept two secrets from all of you. These secrets can cause a lot of suspicion and mistrust if you do not try to understand what is happening. Please be patient until we are ready."

A table and stools were quickly set up. While a large dome was being set over the area, I told Oracle through the pod how to display what I wanted them to see.

"We are ready, so please take your seats. What you are about to experience will be easier to see if you close your eyes. I know it sounds confusing, but trust me with this. What you are about to see is one of the secrets I kept from you."

The pod displayed Kaa's birthing directly into everyone's mind amid muffled comments as they watched. When it ended, the supervising females, who experienced the birthings as only they could, approached me, offered the Gesture of Respect, and thanked me. The males, who had stopped their activities to watch, wanted to thank me as well, but with Amber nearby, they would not get near me.

"Now you know one of my secrets. I did not want you to know about this until you were ready. What are your thoughts about it?"

"Why can't they have their own children? Are we here to be baby makers for them?" Ann said, causing fear to grow like a wildfire.

"No! Definitely not. Everyone, please, calm down. Ann has an excellent question, and you need to understand the answer. What you saw is my choice. My position in Draasen society is called Surrogate to the High One. They cannot birth their own because an engineered virus destroyed their ability to give birth. They have to place their eggs in host animals to birth them."

"Why you?" Ann said.

"The birthing animal in our colony died and I was asked to birth the High One's eggs, and I agreed. If you were asked, you would make your own decision, and your decision would be respected. You would never be forced to do anything like that."

"There must be other colonies with those animals."

"There are, but none were available at the time and my queen was about to lose her eggs. When I agreed to do this, I gave myself to my queen and the Draasen people."

Ann was shaking her head when she said, "I am not so sure about all this. If we tell them to leave, will they go?"

"Yes, but it is not a good idea. You cannot make it on your own."

Ann left the dome and walked to one of the males who carried a folded dome.

"What are you doing here?"

"High One, I am here to help set up your colony," he said, quickly putting down his burden, squatting, and offering the gesture of respect.

"Ann, do like this," I said, putting my hands in front of me, palms down.

"Are you going to stay here, after the others leave?"

"High One. I will return to my colony when my duties have been completed."

"Make sure you do. Go!" she said with a wave of her hand.

"Thank you, High One."

Ann then went to one of the females, who offered her gesture.

"What do you do here?"

"High One, I am supervising the males."

"Are you going to leave when the setup is finished?"

"Ann!" I put my hands in front of me, palms down.

"High One, I will remain with three other females and ten males as the support you requested."

"I see. Where is the...senior female of this group?"

"High One, she will not arrive until first suns."

"I want her here now. There are some rules I am going to establish. We are humans, not Draasen. We'll have our own laws, and we will not tolerate any interference," Ann said, and walked back to the dome. "Cherie, you'll get rid of that male you have been fooling around with, or you can leave with him."

Ann surprised me when she stood up to the Draasen and their adherence to protocols, but there were some things needing discussion.

"Ann, walk with me." She looked at me as if I had told her to chew her arm off. "Please, walk with me."

"I know you like Cherie, but there's nothing you can say that'll change my mind about her."

"It could cost you another member of your colony."

"If she wants to leave, it's her choice."

"What I wanted to say is, by refusing to return the gesture of respect, you have lost some credibility among the Draasen. You will still be respected because of your position as High One, but it was rude not to return the gesture to a female. In the minds of the Draasen, you have reinforced yourself as the leader of this colony, but it could have been done with a bit more tact. You can get away with that kind of behavior with the support people, but do not even consider refusing the gesture to any High One, under any circumstances. It would be very bad. It is your choice, but I suggest you lighten up a bit. You are not bound by any of their protocols, but it would not hurt you to be a little more polite. These are gentle people, and they do not need to see the abusive side of human society. They already know about it from me."

"I'll consider it."

"Thank you. You could...something is wrong."

Cherie told them we are telepathic, Kaa said.

"What's happening?"

"Come on. Cherie told everyone the Draasen are telepathic, and we may have a riot on our hands." We heard yelling as chaos spread in the dome.

Kaa, shout "silence."

Kaa's bagpipes-like shout stunned everyone into silence.

"What is going on?" I said.

"I'll handle this," Ann responded. Amber growled when Ann moved me out of her way with her arm. "I know you've just found out they are telepathic. I learned about it last night. Cherie's been able to speak with them since she's been with the one you've seen her with. It's something they can give that we can do without."

"What if they go telling everybody what they hear?" Dave said.

"What do you have on your mind you do not want anyone to know about?" I said.

"I'm not telling you!"

"And they will not tell me either. Their telepathy is the second secret I kept from you. Yes, they can hear your thoughts, but they would never tell anyone. They understand private thoughts are just that, private, but they would hear your thoughts and act on them if you were going to hurt them. Otherwise, they could not care less about what you are thinking."

"Can you hear what I'm thinking?" Dave said.

"No. It works differently on us. My situation is different because my queen has given me a more intimate form reaching much deeper into my mind. Cherie has been given a limited and temporary ability to speak with Kaa. Today, I can hear what Cherie is thinking, if she lets me, and she can hear me, but neither of us can hear any of you. Tomorrow, if she does not renew the ability with Kaa, it will disappear. High One Ann, I am sorry I had to cut you off like that, but I knew how to handle the answer."

"You know more about the Draasen than any of us, so why don't you stick around for a while? You can calm everyone with explanations I can't," Ann said.

"When my queen leaves, I must go with her because I am carrying eight of her eggs." I felt calming influences at work, but I would not tell anyone about it. There was no need to create more mistrust.

"I don't think I've made a good impression with them. When the senior female arrives, does she have to be told about it?" Ann said.

"She already knows."

"How can she know already?"

"Telepathic communication is instantaneous. You might consider an apology to the female you did not return the gesture to. She would be happy to accept an apology and not tell anyone about it."

"What can I do to make it right?"

"Females have priority with everything, even apologies, so we will find her. When she accepts your apology, the senior female will be informed and the transition should be smoother."

I led her to the correct female, but she did not offer the gesture of respect. She was not being rude, because Ann made it clear there would be no adherence to Draasen protocols.

"I want to apologize for my behavior. I was rude, and it was unnecessary." Ann offered the gesture.

"High One, thank you for your apology. We are pleased you will consider learning some of our protocols."

"Thank you for understanding," I said to the female, and offered my gesture.

"Now, we need to find the male."

"An apology to a male in a matriarchy like this might be misinterpreted. I will take care of it."

"I'll go back and see what's happening."

"Cherie is answering questions about her experiences with Kaa. I will see you when the senior female arrives."

"How are things going with you and Cherie?" I said when Kaa joined me.

"She is not certain what she will do. She cannot come with me if I have to leave. My mother will not allow that."

"I am sorry. I should have kept you two apart."

"We will know something after the senior female arrives."

"I am going to the bathing pool to greet the males. They experienced your birthing, and wanted to thank me, but your mother was too close for them to do it."

"I will go with you. These males are not like the ones in our colony. They are different."

When we arrived at the edge of the new bathing pool, several males were operating what resembled a large drill on the bottom. Kaa picked me up, and when we dropped in, the noise and activity stopped. They immediately squatted and offered the gesture of respect. I greeted each one and they thanked me for allowing them to see Kaa's birthing. After talking with them for a while, they became more at ease.

Suddenly, all of them squatted with their hands behind their backs. Amber and two females were looking down at us.

Sorry, guys, I have to go.

Kaa picked me up, bounded out of the bathing pool, and stood me in front of Amber.

You should not be with them. They are different from our colony males.

Kaa said the same thing. I do not see how they are different.

They are not your males to represent, and you gave them a privilege they must never have. You allowed them to touch you, a birthing animal carrying eggs.

Kaa does. Elder does. What makes them different?

These males are different. You should not be with them.

High One, I think if I can be with males, like those working here, it brings acceptance to you.

I do not require male acceptance.

I do. Judging by the way her eyes narrowed, I was not sure if I was in trouble or not.

I will inform the females they were obeying your commands, and I will suggest they should not be punished for their lack of activity.

I was glad they agreed with her, and the drilling restarted. I looked into the bathing pool and caught the eye of one who was watching the rim. I nodded to him, and he sent what I could only describe as a telepathic nod back to me.

Amber made me walk behind her, holding my wrist wrapped by her tail, as we walked back to the dome.

"High One Ann, the senior female is arriving. Please follow me," Amber said. *Wait here,* she said to me.

Cherie said, "It looks like you don't have the same position you had before you came here."

"I know you have been listening, so what is your point?"

"Oh, nothing; it just looks like you've been knocked down a notch, that's all."

"What about you and Kaa?"

"We've decided it's best for everyone if he leaves with you. It was tempting to have him stay, but we couldn't be happy with all the pressure we were getting."

"If I may speak frankly; Amber does not like you, and your relationship with Kaa caused a break between them. If it is any consolation, I think you did the right thing. You have experienced something none of this group will ever know, and I am happy you had the chance to experience some of what I enjoy."

Ann, Amber, and the senior female entered the dome.

"You will call me Teal, which is a shortened version of my name I will allow you to use. High One Ann will be my primary student, and I will train her in the operation of your colony. I understand you want to retain as much of your society as possible, and I anticipate it will be a difficult transition for everyone. I request you accept patience. As your education and experience progress, we will take a less active part in your society as you apply what you learn to your colony. Put away any fear and doubt you have. If you have an open mind, we will learn from each other."

I wondered where Teal had learned to speak English. She was not from our colony.

"High One Ann, are you ready to install Oracle?" Teal said.

"I don't know how."

"You will learn. Follow me."

"Come on, we can watch this. It is something you will never forget," I said.

When everyone gathered around an area that would become Oracle's dome, there were surprised mumbles when a shaft of light rose from the ground. Teal opened a purse and handed a black sphere to Ann.

"Place this on the top of the Oracle interface."

I had to smile because Ann was surprised by the weight of it, as I once was. There were more surprised mutterings when the sphere stayed where she put it. The orb changed from a black ball to a swirling, multicolor Oracle. Then it rose, and resettled on the shaft. When Ann turned, her hand brushed through the light shaft and she hopped sideways, shaking her hand.

"High One, are you damaged?" Teal said, examining Ann's hand.

"No, but it tingles. It felt like an electric shock."

"High One, it is for you to tell the males to enclose Oracle."

"Males, enclose the Oracle!"

"High One, it is time to feed. As I understand human behavior, you allow your males to talk during a feeding. This would be a good time to answer their questions. Please gather your colony in the feeding dome."

"Everyone, it's time to eat, so let's get back to the big dome. High One, will you be joining us?"

"Thank you for your offer, but I must return to my colony. I will take my surrogate and Kaa with me," Amber said.

"I'll walk you to your transport."

I saw Cherie was following, and I hung back to talk with her.

"I wanted to say goodbye," Cherie said, taking my hand.

"I will stop in for a visit when my queen allows me to. You have a unique perspective into Draasen society. It will serve you well as you learn with my people."

"She owns you, you know that?"

"You still do not get it, do you? I have given my life and everything I am to her. If things were different, and you could have bonded with Kaa, you would understand why I have no objections to, as you put it, being owned, so consider me bought and paid for."

"It's called love," Ann said when we stopped at the transport.

"Of that, I have no doubt," I said.

"It's obvious, seeing how you act around her. Do me a favor? When you're pregnant again, come back. I'd like to see that."

"Good idea. I'd like to see it too," Cherie said.

"You just want something to laugh at."

"No, really? How many men get pregnant?" Cherie said.

"As High One of your colony, you can request I visit at any time, with the understanding my queen will have the final decision."

"High One, can I say goodbye to Kaa?" Cherie said.

"Yes."

Kaa swept Cherie up in his arms and hopped a short distance away with her. I felt them enter a private conversation, which was just as well because I was tempted to listen in. Amber grumbled as she looked at them, and I put my hand on her thigh for our own conversation.

Soon we will be gone, and Cherie will stay here.

The sooner we can leave the better it will be.

"Maybe, some day, I'll have the opportunity to speak to them like you do," Ann said, looking at Amber's ears.

Amber waited patiently while Cherie and Kaa said their goodbyes. When Kaa finally put Cherie on her feet, they were reluctant to separate, their fingers touching as long as possible.

I know we act like that.

Yes, and I have missed it. I had to act differently around members of the other colonies. I will be happy to get back to my colony.

"Ann, we must leave. I wish you luck with your colony. If you need anything, have Oracle contact me, but before you do, try to resolve any concerns with Teal first. She will be able to answer most of your questions." I offered the gesture of respect, palms up, to Ann, the High One of her colony. She accepted my gesture, and then she hugged me.

"I know; hugging is not part of Draasen greetings. High One, thank you for your patience and support. Please return at any time, and we will welcome you as best we can."

Amber considered something for a moment then placed her palms facing Ann.

"Ann, this gesture is offered only between High Ones of equal rank."

"Thank you, High One," she said, matching palms with Amber.

"Ann, you had better step back. Transports create some nasty static charges when they fly."

"Ray…thanks, for everything."

When we left the island, I closed my eyes and settled back in the comfort of Amber's arms. Deep in my thoughts, I was vaguely aware of the flight home. The word home came with mixed feelings. I had been set on a path by the Baleorans, and I continued the path when Amber accepted me. For a while, I thought I was comfortable with my former work mates, but, like Amber, I was happy to be away from them. What I was feeling led me to something I missed at the time. When Kaa and I dropped into the bathing pool, I was comfortable being with the males, and when I was sent a telepathic nod, I had been accepted by them. I had been accepted by everyone and when it happened, I changed, lost my humanity. No, not lost, but gave it up for something better, and I wondered how much of my humanity followed me to my new state of being.

You cannot shed what you were like cloth at a bathing pool. I could not help you with any decisions because they had to be your decisions.

You led me with a silken bridle of love and affection. You knew all along I would follow the path you guided me on.

I knew it at first, but when the humans arrived, I was not sure which decision you would make. I did not want to influence you in any way, so I allowed you to make whatever decisions you felt comfortable with. I am happy you have decided to stay with me.

Our link opened unlike any other time I had felt before. I felt as if I had been lost, and was suddenly found, stripped of what I had been, and became something different. I was Draasen and having felt that, my humanity seemed to be little more than a footnote in my life. How could that be? I had been human for fifty-eight years, and after only a few weeks, I had become a Draasen. I had said I was Draasen before, but it seemed like I never meant it; never really felt it. Now, in my heart, I knew I was Draasen.

Amber was ecstatically happy as she tossed me into the air and spun me around to face her as she caught me. She gave me a breathtaking hug and affectionately stroked her long chin on top of my head. After we landed at our colony, we sat together in the transport for a long time before Lana interrupted us.

High One, the colony has gathered to greet our new Draasen male.

"I thought I was already a member of the colony."

"You are being accepted as a Draasen male, not as a human who was my surrogate."

"Was your surrogate?"

"You are my Draasen surrogate now."

She had me precede her out of the transport. Everyone had gathered in two columns, males on one side, and females on the other. I offered the gesture of respect to Amber, which was more of a thank you to my queen than anything else. I was tempted to greet the males first, but protocols demanded females had priority. I greeted each female, who gave me words of welcome and encouragement. I then greeted each male, who said nothing to me. Instead, I was given a telepathic nod.

As we walked to the bathing pool, Lana stopped us.

When you arrived at our colony I had my doubts about you, and for a long time I still had them, but not any more. Enjoy your bathing, my hatchlings.

She knows I do not like being called hatchling, Amber said.

What about me? I am not her hatchling, so I accept it as a term of affection from her.

In the future you will be tested, and there will be times you will question your actions. If you continue to be yourself, you will succeed, and make me very proud.

She gave me a gentle nuzzle across the back of my neck, tickling and raising goose bumps all over me.

That one affectionate nuzzle became the most endearing and enduring memory I have.

Chapter 13

TRAINING

It has been a while since I wrote in this journal, and I had to remember how many birthings we have had to figure out how much time has passed. We birthed six more eggs, so it has been over a year, a human year. Other than the birthings, not many things have happened. There was one thing I did not want to write about because the smallest reminder of it brings me to tears, but Amber insisted I write about the birthing of our sixth egg. She thinks writing about it will ease my pain.

Twenty-three suns into the release of our sixth egg there were no signs of sentience. Amber was worried because she could not hear anything when she placed her forehead on my stomach. Lana said we should let the egg continue to develop in the hope it would achieve a late sentience, but it never did. It could have been called a stillbirth, although by the exact human definition, it was not. The hatchling had a beating heart, but not intellect, and no chance of achieving one.

After the birthing, Lana kept me asleep while my little Draasen, a female, was disposed of. It sounds harsh, but it is the only way to describe what they did. There were no graveyards or memorials in Draasen society, and they euphemistically said the bodies of those who had gone on the long walk were "taken home." The body of my little girl was taken home to an uninhabited island where there was a vast carpet of the home world grass. The grass had been grown in an aggressive state, and her body was gently left there to be consumed by it. I did not know why it affected me so much. It still does.

***

Thirty suns after our eighth birthing, I was all set to release our ninth egg, but Amber said we would wait and would not say why.

There were a lot of transports coming and going, and when I started looking around, I discovered our massive storage cave was being emptied. When I asked one of the supervising females why, I was politely told to ask my High One. When I pressed her for an answer, Amber came and said they must not be disturbed.

After that, Kaa and Dee became my constant companions. They guided me wherever I went, which did not always coincide with where I wanted to go. They were like a pair of sphinxes when it came to certain information about the colony, which annoyed me to no end.

Amber bathed and ate separately from me and everyone else. I would see her running around the colony, usually with a senior female, long into the night. When she returned to our dome, she was always tense and very tired. Our affection for each other was as strong as ever, and I would encourage her to stretch out and relax on our bed while I scratched her in all the places she enjoyed. She would sigh and rumble with enjoyment, and during some of those unguarded moments, I would hear snippets of information, but not enough to put anything together. When she caught me listening, I felt a flicker of fear from her, and she would guard her thoughts.

***

After several days of observing the activity, I was relaxing in the bathing pool when two females launched themselves out of the water and hit the ground running. They sped away, turning and weaving to avoid domes and each other. As I watched, they turned back, tumbled together, and rolled to a stop. At first they wrestled, employing kicks, clawed slashes, and tails sweeping around to trip and grapple. When one bit into the shoulder at the base of the neck, the other went limp and fell to the ground. Another female rushed in and had some difficulty getting the victor to release her bite.

Dee surfaced beside me and said, "Do not be concerned. This is part of the training we will be doing, and some will be damaged."

"What happens if someone goes on the long walk?"

"It should be expected," Dee said casually.

"Is there a reason for this?" I was appalled by her answer.

"Be alert and be careful."

When the injured female was helped up, five more females ran from around a dome near the cliffs and turned toward the caves. I thought they would run into one of the entrances, until they jumped into the air where they landed on the rock face and clawed their way straight up the side. The males did not participate in the training and went about their routines, some bowled over by running females when they did not move out of the way fast enough.

It is my time for training, Amber said when I left the clothing dome.

Kaa took me to an open area where a tall, burly female arrived by transport. I could feel her confidence when she offered the gesture of respect to Amber, and then came to me. She was as muscular as Kaa, and had several scars on her body. She had the look of a fighter, and I had the impression she was trying to intimidate me. She was being successful.

So, this is the surrogate I have heard so much about.

Yes, I am the one.

You will call me Tikanseecallesths. You will not shorten my name, she said as she slowly walked around me.

It had not crossed my mind.

You are not a very impressive creature.

She suddenly dropped to all fours, then wrapped her hand around my throat. Kaa rushed toward us, and when she looked at him, I reached up, pulled a finger loose, and bit it. She let out a short bark as I jumped up, wrapped my legs around her long snout, and slapped my hands against her ears. Kaa saved me from a painful landing when she jerked her head up and tossed me head over heels. Several males quickly gathered and squatted.

High One, your surrogate surprises me. He has a warrior's instincts, she said, rubbing her ears as she walked toward us. *Males, move aside,* she said to the squatting wall between us. *Move aside!* She attempted to push through them, but they pressed tightly together. *What does this say about you, little surrogate? Would you let these weakling males fight for you?*

As one, every male stood and growled at her, and she backed up in surprise.

What does this say about you, Tikan? Is the big, bad Tikan afraid of a few males?

This is interesting. I have never seen complete acceptance from males for one of their own. Surrogate to High One Ambrisseethsss, step forward, please.

I had some difficulty moving between the standing males. When I reached the front, Kaa stepped between Tikan and me, and she laughed at him. She squatted and offered the greeting of respect to me. I accepted when Kaa let me move around him.

High One, are you ready to begin? Tikan said.

I am ready. Kaa, keep him safe.

Amber rushed Tikan, who stepped nimbly out of the way, striking Amber on the back of her head, knocking her down. I tried to squirm out of Kaa's grasp to help her, but she jumped up, and they squared off. Amber rushed again, anticipating Tikan would turn, but Tikan sprang into the air and kicked Amber on the shoulder, knocking her down again. Tikan seemed to anticipate every move Amber made, but she would tell Amber what she was doing wrong, and how to correct it.

The training session seemed interminable, and I was glad when Tikan called a break for second bathing. I had to call for Amber, and when she surfaced beside me, I started private conversation with her.

We are protected here. Why do you need to fight? I said.

Danger comes from many sources.

You are not going to tell me why you are training, are you? Her enigmatic stare said no. *Can Tikan hear your thoughts?*

Possibly. I will guard my thoughts.

Before you do, turn it to your advantage.

How?

If she can hear your thoughts, let her listen. Let her hear your thoughts when you start an attack, then change the attack without thinking about it. After that, you should guard your thoughts to keep her guessing.

I can do that.

After bathing and a light feeding, Tikan was waiting to continue the training. Amber made a straightforward charge at Tikan, who hopped sideways and kicked Amber on the shoulder as she passed. She stumbled, but did not go down. She started another attack, and as Tikan started a side step, Amber angled into her and punched her in the neck. Tikan staggered backward, clutching her throat. Kaa told me the hit was final claws. He explained if they were not training, Amber's fingers and claws would have been extended, and they would have gone through Tikan's throat.

After Tikan recovered, she attacked with a flurry of feet and fists. An overhead tail strike glanced off Amber's shoulder. Tikan jumped when Amber started a tail sweep. She stopped the sweep, quickly reared back on her tail, and kicked Tikan solidly in the chest with both feet. Tikan landed hard and slid to a stop several feet away. Tikan was down, struggling to breathe. Lana rushed in and was attending to her when Amber walked toward them. Tikan suddenly rolled and kicked Amber in the side, knocking her off her feet.

When the combatants slowly struggled to their feet, Tikan said *High One, your training is completed. You have learned well. There is one important lesson you must remember. Can you tell me what it is?* When Amber did not answer, Tikan said *Surrogate to the High One, you know what it is.*

If an enemy is down, never assume they are out of action. They could still attack, even from a position of weakness.

Correct. High One, you must be certain they have gone on the long walk before you approach. If you are not completely certain, expect an attack you are prepared to defend against. High One, with your permission, I need your healer's assistance.

***

For the rest of the suns, we quietly lounged in front of our dome until Lana arrived.

"How is Tikan?" I said.

She is recovering.

I felt something else needed to be said as we sat, looking at each other.

High One, your surrogate does not like surprises.

I know. Next suns, we will travel to our home world. My mother will test your shield and give you instructions to follow. I have only one instruction for you: be yourself.

Raise your shield, Lana said.

She gave me hand signals to raise and lower my shield as she used equipment to monitor me.

You must raise it faster when you see my signal.

"It might be better if you just said shield when you want me to raise it. I may not be in a position to see your signal."

Shield!

I snapped the shield up, and then, on signal, dropped it again.

Much better. Expect my order for your shield at any time, and leave it in place until I signal otherwise.

I felt Lana was nervous about something, and her thoughts were guarded when she left.

"With all the activity, it looks like everyone is training for war," I said.

It is time to rest.

When we settled in bed, Amber wrapped her arm around me and held me a little tighter.

Chapter 14

LONG LIVE THE QUEEN

Just before high suns, Elder arrived at our dome with a large bag for Amber and a smaller one for me. She placed her robes, scepter, and circlet in her bag. My bag was just large enough for my journal and my snow globe ring holder. When I picked up the globe, my mind was filled with the memory of my human wife. Briefly, she seemed like a stranger, but it was quickly replaced with the joy and sadness of her memory. Amber waited until I found the courage to put the globe in my bag.

"Is it possible she is still alive? In stasis somewhere, waiting to be eaten?"

I do not know. Do you want to ask Oracle?

"No. It is unlikely she is still alive after seven hundred years."

When we walked to the transports, I was a mixed bag of emotions until Lana stopped me, holding a small bulb of liquid in her fingers.

"What is this?"

A fluid to settle your stomach.

"My stomach is not upset."

One of the effects of weightlessness on humans is an upset stomach. Open and swallow.

"Weightless? Are we are going to be weightless?"

Yes. Open. Now, get on the transport.

After the transports lifted and soared over the cliffs, ours banked toward the human's colony and landed.

"What are we doing here?"

I felt you would want to say goodbye to them.

"Thank you," I said, turning to hug her around her neck.

I ran out and greeted Ann as High One.

"Ray, welcome to my...our colony."

"I am sorry for not giving you any notice, but I have some news."

"Teal said you were coming."

"Of course she did."

When Cherie arrived, I had her step back to give me a profile.

"Oracle said you are one of the new pregnancies. How far along are you?"

"About five months."

"Do you know what sex the baby is?"

"I'm having a boy."

"Congratulations. What will you name him?"

"Jake James, the middle names of my two boys. I will call him JJ."

"An excellent name and a fine tribute to the memory of your family. Ann, I wanted to stop and say I am leaving for the Draasen home world. Our colony has been shut down and I have not been told anything about it, or the trip. I am not sure if I will return, but if I am needed, you can always contact me through Oracle."

I took Cherie's hand and pulled her to their healer.

Keep a close medical eye on this one. I want her to have a successful hatching.

I have studied human hatchings from the memories of the colony members who allowed Oracle to download them. I will do my best for this female.

"I asked—"

"I heard what you both said. It's the first time I've heard telepathy since Kaa left."

"It is possible you heard us because we are holding hands. I wonder if your telepathic contacts will have an effect on your baby."

The birthing of the male will allow us to test for telepathy. Be quick, we must leave, Amber said from the transport.

"Already?" Cherie said.

"High One, I must leave. My queen was very gracious in allowing me to stop and give the news myself," I said, offering the gesture of respect.

Ann accepted my gesture and then hugged me.

"I'm sorry to see you go. Return when you can, and we'll have a party."

"I am going to hold you to the party offer. We have a huge project in front of us: The survival of the human species. After all, we are in the best position to do it. Cherie, your baby is the future of the human race. Take care of him." We embraced each other.

"I'll miss you," she said, with tears welling in her eyes.

"There is no need for tears. You have been an excellent friend, and I cannot say that about many people." I squatted in front of her and gently placed my hand on her stomach.

"Hey, JJ. Take care of your mother for me. Cherie, take care." I gently touched her cheek and returned to the transport.

"They may be the last humans I will ever know."

That is a possibility.

After a short flight, I could see the shuttle on an island ahead. When we approached it towered over us like an office building, and I thought we were going crash into it, but we passed through the outer shell and landed inside. I squirmed off Amber's lap to look out through the sides of our transport. I marveled at the technology as the transport rose and stopped near several large cylinders set into the wall. The door opened and I looked down several stories to the ground. I could see no floor, but Amber picked me up and casually stepped out, bouncing as she walked on nothing, and climbed into one of the spacious transport tubes. I watched Dee and Kaa get into theirs and settle into relaxed positions.

The pilot announced we were lifting, and I felt the air pressure change when the entrance to our tube was sealed. The sides of the transport became transparent, and we rose straight up. Soon, we approached another transport, not much larger than ours, in orbit.

"How are we going to get to the other ship?"

We will join with the void transport and become part of it.

I watched as we collided and blended in with it. When everything spread out and settled, the pilot said to prepare for tunneling. When I settled with Amber in the weightlessness, I felt the air pressure change again. I became stiff, unable to move. Then I felt like I was being crushed and I could not breathe. My last memory was trying to scream when my link to Amber stopped.

***

My next memories were of screaming and breathing deeply. I was trembling uncontrollably as Amber held me and sent a calming influence across our link.

Tell me what happened.

"Our link stopped. I could not breathe. I was being crushed. I could not move. I could not breathe."

Your consort experienced the beginning of stasis without being affected by the vapor used to begin rest. I should have been informed your consort would not be affected by the vapor. The voice had a distinct, powerful presence.

He is a new species. We do not know everything about him yet, Lana said.

After the unfolding has started, bring him to my center.

"Who was that?"

Core, Amber said.

Core does not speak directly to anyone except the Most High One, Lana said.

"What is the unfolding?"

We will meet the Most High One when we are called to her. Remember to be yourself. Look, there is our home world, Amber said, and I was not sure if it was an answer or a distraction.

I could see oceans and landmasses, and many objects in orbit, sparking like diamonds. One of them caught my attention as we approached it.

"What is that? It is huge."

It is a defense platform, Amber said.

I wondered how long we had slept, and how far we had traveled.

We were in the magnetic tunnel for thirteen suns, and traveled thirteen hundred light years.

I thought I should guard my thoughts, but Amber said, *Do not do that. You are a new species on our home world, and you are to be open for everyone to see and hear. You have nothing to hide. Just be yourself.*

"You keep saying that, but is it what you really want? You know how I can get when I am being myself."

Yes, I know.

The side of the void transport became opaque and the cylinders began moving into groups. When our group had gathered together, we bubbled out into the smaller shuttle and began to descend. When we broke through the clouds, white domes could be seen everywhere. The scene almost looked like a pot of boiling milk.

As we descended toward an open area busy with activity, several strings of transports moved over domes, stretching into the distance. Some dropped from a string while others joined in a very orderly fashion. When we landed, several small transports entered at the base of the shuttle and were rising toward us. One stopped at our level just as our cylinder opened with a soft hiss. Amber carried me aboard, but there was no pilot, or even a space for one. On the control console was a pea-sized version of Oracle on a straw of light, but there were none of the controls I was used to seeing. We floated out of the shuttle and rose toward a string of other transports where a space opened for us, and we smoothly joined the traffic flow.

There were several females walking alone below us, but no males. Every male I did see was being pulled along by a female, with a wrist wrapped by their tails.

When we dropped out of traffic and landed between two domes, Amber said, *Follow me, and keep your hand on my tail.*

When I touched her tail, she wrapped it around my wrist and towed me along. I listened for any thoughts, but little was being said. Fear suddenly swamped my mind when everyone quickly hopped aside as three females walked by. They were looking at the symbols of position on everyone they passed, until one took a look at me and stopped. She grabbed my arm and turned me sideways to study my symbols of position.

"Hey! Knock it off!" I shouted, and wrenched my arm out of her grasp as Amber positioned herself between us.

Do not touch my surrogate, Amber said with a deep growl as she stood to her full stature, towering over the three females who had suddenly squatted. *You read his symbols of position and you see he is restrained, and in submission. Does your position allow you to handle every birthing animal you see? Leave us!*

Yes, High One.

I saw the nearest male looking at me, and when I nodded my head to him, he perked up. His female shook her tail as she held his wrist, and he assumed his submissive posture again. He gave me a telepathic nod as he was pulled away. Amber looked at me, gave her tail a shake, and pulled me behind her.

We soon entered a large dome with Elder pulled by Lana, and Kaa pulled by Dee. When the door closed, everyone was released.

Set up the dampening aura, Amber said. Elder unpacked one of his bags and attached a device to the dome.

"What is going on?"

You showed disrespect to the Most High One's guards, Amber said.

"No, I did not."

You complained when they touched you.

"You said to be myself."

The guards know we are here, and they must have reported it to the Most High One by now, Lana said.

An orb, significantly larger than an Oracle, passed through the dome wall just as a post of light rose from the floor, and the orb settled on it.

"Do we know this?" I said.

High One Ambrisseethsss, the dampening aura caused a loss of link to you. The powerful presence I had felt on the transport had returned.

I needed to shield our thoughts and protect us from influences.

I will not report your presence to the Most High One until suns rise. You have that much time to prepare. I will send an Oracle to you at first suns. The orb rose and disappeared through the wall while the light shaft disappeared into the floor, leaving no trace of its passing.

Mother, Dee, locate the others and tell them everyone must be in place by suns rise.

Amber picked me up and carried me to the bed. When she settled with me, I found myself in the workspace where the puppet was floating again. A string dropped, and I fell asleep.

***

When I woke, there was a faint light glowing from the walls and everyone was sleeping. I got up and cracked the door open just to look around, and I saw three males approach and squat in front of me. I opened the door just enough to squeeze out, and as one, they offered the gesture of respect. The first one I placed my palms on grabbed my hands and started a private conversation.

No female must ever know about this meeting, or we will be sent on the long walk. We feel we can trust you. What kind of High One is she? he said, while the others looked around.

My High One has been fair with everyone in our colony. I am the only male who was ever punished when I was called to the Council of Five.

You were called to a Council of Five and you were not sent on the long walk? He looked at me as if I might disappear at any moment.

Being a birthing animal may have influenced their decisions.

How are the males in your colony treated?

We are well treated, and they follow my High One, just as I do.

They follow you. You have the acceptance of the males in your colony, and the acceptance has followed you here. Will you help us?

I do not know if I can.

The door flew open and Amber growled as the males froze in fear.

High One, we were just talking. Amber leaned toward the male as he placed his head between his knees. *Please do not hurt him.*

I pushed on her stomach, but my feet slipped backward as she moved to him, turned her head, and bit his neck, but she did not clamp down on it.

Do not approach my surrogate again. Leave us.

When he was released, they ran off. I was yanked off my feet and dropped inside the dome.

What did you say to him? Amber said.

"He wanted to know what you are like as High One, and how the males feel about you. They need someone to help them, but I thought the Most High One's consort was supposed to do that."

The Most High One does not have a consort. She does not trust any males near her.

"And you want me to meet her? In case you have forgotten, she wants to turn humans into birthing animals. From what I have seen of this place, it makes me want to run and hide, preferably on another planet. When can we leave?"

We do not leave; we stay, Amber said.

"All right, we will meet her, and then we can go home."

We are home.

An Oracle passed through the door and said, *I am a messenger from Core. The Most High One demands your surrogate be brought to her immediately. The Most High One's guards are waiting to take him to her.*

The door opened and three guards stood outside. When I started for the door, Amber stepped in front of me, wrapped her tail around my wrist, and pulled me outside.

High One, you are not to accompany the alien male.

He is my surrogate. While he carries my eggs, I will stay with him. Even the Most High One cannot change that protocol. You will guide us to the transport now.

When the guards glanced at each other, Amber leaned into the face of the leader and snarled. They were quick to lead us to the transport.

When we arrived at the transport, a guard tried to enter but Amber pushed her aside while Dee, Kaa, Lana, and Elder entered.

High One, we must accompany you.

You will take the next transport.

The door closed, and the transport rose to join the string of traffic.

"Will you tell me what is going on now?"

The unfolding will be over soon. Listen to what my mother tells you.

Amber was no longer the gentle High One I thought I knew. She had become a female with a purpose, and I had no idea what the purpose was.

216

The flight was silent while everyone, except me, guarded their thoughts as we flew over domes and bathing pools. I noticed Elder had his head cocked to one side. At first I thought he had a stiff neck, until I looked down and saw every male at a bathing pool was looking up at us.

We landed in an open area in front of a huge complex of attached domes with a center dome much larger than the rest. Guards approached us when we stepped out of our transport.

High One, your males will remain here.

Good! I did not want to go in anyway, I said.

Surrogate to the High One, you will accompany me. When she reached for me, Amber growled and pressed her claws under the guard's chin, standing her up on her toes.

No one touches my surrogate!

An orb floated to the two females and said, *I am a messenger from Core. The Most High One is impatient with the delay. The High One will accompany the surrogate.*

Amber towed me toward the entrance, with Dee and Lana close behind.

I have one regret about our relationship, Amber said.

What is that?

We could not be a mated pairing. You would have been exceptionally exciting as my mated pairing.

Her confession bothered me, a lot, and I wanted to question it, but we entered what was called The Place of the Most High One, under an arch of decomposed Drassen skulls.

As we weaved our way through corridors lined with guards, I thought I recognized some of them as members of our colony. Amber flicked her tail and painfully twisted my wrist, but it did not stop me from looking at each guard we passed.

When we entered an antechamber, we were told to wait as the guard went into the main dome. I could hear the Most High One inside talking calmly until she suddenly shrieked something unintelligible. After a sudden commotion, I could hear her calmly speaking again. Then she screamed and called for a healer. There was another commotion when she screamed again because the healer did not respond quickly enough. I heard her kick the healer against a wall, and the painful cries of the healer as she was carried from the dome.

Open, Lana said, holding a small bulb of liquid in her fingers.

"What is it this time?"

Pain fluid. Put this on. She handed me a vest of thin, gray cloth she pulled from one of her bags. The weight of it nearly pulled me over.

"What is this? It weighs a ton."

Close it in the front by overlapping it. When we enter the Chamber of the Most High One, keep your mind open and offer the gesture of respect. Do not look the Most High One in the eyes. Wait for my signal to use your shield, and remember to be yourself.

Core announced the alien surrogate was waiting, but the Most High One did not seem to hear it. She kept shifting between unrelated subjects, becoming angry at something and flying into a tirade, then calming, seeming to be in control of herself. During a lull, Core again announced that the alien surrogate was waiting. I felt confusion before she shouted for us to leave.

"Good. I did not want to be here in the first place." I turned to look for the way out, but Amber put her hand on my shoulder.

Alien surrogate? What is an alien surrogate?

It is the surrogate to High One Ambrisseethsss from one of our colony planets. It is a new species called human. He is carrying the High One's eggs.

He? A male? Send it away, now!

"We are out of here," I said, but Amber kept her hand on me. Her sharp claws were partially extended, but they did not penetrate the vest.

The Most High One started ranting about the colony planets, complaining about supporting them. Then, she suddenly calmed, which was more unnerving than her ranting.

Core, where is the alien surrogate I sent for? Why is the alien thing not here? I want it here, now!

The door opened and Amber pulled me inside by her tail. There were at least twenty pairs of guards stationed around the perimeter. Some of them stepped forward, creating a path leading to the Most High One, reading our symbols of position as we walked by.

The Most High One wore tattered robes and a circlet without a gem. She was twirling her scepter by her tail as she stood on a raised dais, carefully watching us. We stopped short of the platform and Amber offered the gesture of respect.

Who are you?

Most High One. I am Ambrisseethsss, High One of my birthing colony, Amber stated respectfully, still offering the gesture of respect.

Why are you here?

Most High One, you called me to your presence.

I do not remember. You are not wanted. Return to your colony.

Most High One, you called for High One Ambrisseethsss. You are interested in her alien surrogate carrying the eggs of High One Ambrisseethsss, Core stated.

Yes. Yes! Where is your animal? I need a birthing animal, she said, suddenly having a remembered interest in me.

Amber pulled me from behind her, and I stood before the Most High One. Her eyes swirled with colors, each eye different. I offered the gesture of respect and stood very still.

What are you?

Most High One, I am Raymond, Surrogate to High One Ambrisseethsss.

Alien birthing animal! Yes, I remember. I remember a species called human. Yes, yes. She stepped off the dais and came to me.

When she squatted in front of me, I thought she was going to accept my gesture. Instead, she wrapped her hand around my neck and lifted me off the floor. I held on to her wrist to keep from being hung.

Male, I am the Most High One. You will not touch me! Despite the warning, I continued to cling to her wrist.

Most High One, he is not as durable as we are. You will damage my eggs, Amber said.

Eggs? I will have them removed. Where is my healer?

Most High One, if you damage him, he...will not be able to birth your eggs.

She stared at Amber like she had not seen her before. I worked one of her fingers loose and bit it, hard. She dropped me and looked at her finger, whining like a child.

Listen to me, you crazy cow! I will go on the long walk before I allow your rotten eggs inside me! I shouted, and charged her barehanded.

Walk, male! She reared back on her tail and kicked me in the chest with one foot, sending me flying backward. When I landed with a resounding thud, Lana telepathically shouted *Shield!* as I slid to a stop on my side. There was a grinding sensation in my chest when I tried to breathe.

Lana quickly positioned herself between the Most High One and me. She held my arm and said, *Close your eyes and try not to breathe.* Then she announced, *Most High One. High One Ambrisseethsss' birthing animal has gone on the long walk.*

Where is my healer? You, examine that thing and tell me if it has walked.

When the healer used her arm-mounted equipment to scan me, her hand brushed against my arm and a private conversation link formed. I said nothing, but it was too late. She knew I was alive.

Most High One, my equipment shows this birthing animal has gone on the long walk.

Good! One less male to feed. She was laughing until Amber hopped to the dais.

You have sent my birthing animal, carrying my eggs, on the long walk. Protocols forbid anyone from damaging a birthing animal, even Most High Ones. Step down quietly.

I am the Most High One! I do what I want!

Step down quietly, Amber calmly repeated.

Guards! Remove this female from my sight!

Females from our colony, who were posing as guards, quickly immobilized the Most High One's guards by pressing claws against their throats.

Take her! The Most High One screamed. *I will send all of you on the walk! Take her!*

Several former guards were being escorted into the dome and gathered together. Someone behind me shouted, *High One Ambrisseethsss! The Place of the Most High One has been secured and the guards have been neutralized!*

There is no one left to help you. Step down quietly, Amber said.

Never, the Most High One hissed.

Despite Lana's warning, I watched wide eyed as the outcome of the challenge played out.

The two carefully removed and neatly folded their robes, placing their circlets on top. When Amber placed her scepter beside her robes, the Most High One flicked her tail and her scepter flew over her shoulder. She caught it and spikes sprang out from the head.

I will display your head for all to see what happens to anyone who challenges me. She charged the platform, swinging the scepter at Amber's head.

Amber ducked, and then lifted a knee to her midsection, doubling her over. Amber spun around and drove her foot, claws extended, deep into the Most High One's side, then hopped backward. The Most High One collapsed, quivering as she laid on the platform as Amber patiently waited for another attack. I thought the fight was over when Amber approached the prostrate Most High One, until she sprang to her knees and swung her scepter. Amber was prepared and blocked the swing at the wrist, but momentum carried the scepter out of her hand and lodged it in Amber's side. She did not seem to notice it when she kicked the Most High One in the stomach, rolling her onto her back. Amber quickly wrapped her tail around the Most High One's legs and tail, pinning them together. She stood on the Most High One's arms, extended her claws, and drew back, prepared to send her on the long walk.

Lana frantically grabbed my arm and said, *Ask her to stop! Make her stop!*

I dropped my shield. *My queen; do not send her on the long walk,* I pleaded as Amber stood over the Most High One, arm cocked, ready to give final claws.

Surrogate, you have no say in this! Maintain your place!

As your surrogate and consort, it is my place to offer suggestions. If you send a helpless female on the long walk, you will be no better than she is.

What do you suggest I do with this female if I do not send her on the long walk?

She could be banished to a colony that had been taken by the Baleorans.

She will be a threat through her followers that are here.

You could send her followers there as well.

It is possible her followers will send her on the long walk.

Yes, but her blood will be on their hands, not yours.

Core! Who is the Most High One? Amber said.

In accordance with protocols, I recognize and obey Ambrisseethsss as the Most High One.

Amber pulled the scepter from her side. I felt she was not in any pain when she casually tossed it across the dome, where it clanged and clattered its way across the floor, screeching to a halt in front of the restrained guards.

Detain this female and heal her. Take her guards, and all who would be loyal to her, and detain them as well. I will decide what to do with them later. Core, set links for communications to all Drassen.

Most High One, I established communication links when you entered. All Draasen have been watching your challenge and your establishment as the Most High One.

Amber squatted beside me and started a private conversation.

You are damaged.

It is nothing. Please, let your mother heal you, I said, looking at the blood flowing down her side.

Not yet, there is something I must do. She stepped up to the dais.

Lana, give me something to stop her bleeding.

Not yet.

Lana gently helped me up the dais and Amber indicated that I should stand beside her. I wanted to place my hand on her wound to slow her bleeding, but I could not raise my arm.

People of Draasen, I am the Most High One Ambrisseethsss. This is my surrogate, Raymond. The former Most High One's reign of cruelty and fear is ended. My first duty as Most High One will be to return the right of song to the Draasen people. Song will be heard in domes and passageways again. Song will be heard on all colony worlds again. Song will be given to all hatchlings as part of their education again. I will be the first to bring song back to my people.

Amber's voice resounded in the acoustics of the dome as she sang in clear, bagpipes-like tones. The Draasen home world and all colony planets listened to singing that had not been heard since the former queen had outlawed it.

The right of song has been restored. Sing to your hatchlings. Sing to your bonded pairings. Sing to anyone for any reason at all. That is my command.

Command accepted, Core said.

My next duty as Most High One will be to remove the damage the former Most High One has caused. Then, I will hear from all who want to speak with me. Core will establish links after two suns.

When Core closed the communication links, Amber staggered and fell. Lana and several females jumped to the platform and carried her out of the dome. I was slow to follow with my broken ribs grinding with every step. They did not hurt much, but the bones grinding together were nauseating as I sat down on the back of the dais. My link with Amber suddenly stopped, and when it did, I realized I had been used. Amber had used me to birth her eggs. She had used me to gain the Draasen throne. Now, she had abandoned me on the throne, in a castle of domes, empty of everything and everyone. I loved her, but she had used me. They had all used me, every one of them. I felt betrayed and wanted to go back with the humans, if they would have me, but I was unable to move. I was hurt and alone.

"You are never alone. You are heard and loved by many more than you realize." Elder's voice echoed in the empty dome when he walked toward me with a female following him.

"She used me, old man. All this time she has been planning this, and she used me. My purpose has been served. When will I be returned to the rest of the humans?"

"Consider accepting this. Our queen needs you more than ever before. If she no longer needed you, you would not have been introduced to all Draasen as her surrogate, and you would not have stood at her side; a male in a place of trust."

"She abandoned me."

"No, she did not. She loves you too much to do that. Will you agree to stay here so we can protect you?"

"Obviously, I am not going anywhere."

The young healer scanned me and said, *There are four broken ribs. This will be easy and quick to repair.*

"Ssurlanaseethesess is excited by your availability. She has always cared for you as one of her own, and I am sure she will treat you gently."

"Gently? What do you mean gently?"

Chapter 15

THREAT

When I awoke, I wondered whose arm was over me. When Amber was asleep, I always felt a gentle, affectionate ripple across our bonded link, but there was nothing I could feel. I moved the arm, rolled over, and saw Lana sleeping. I was in bed with Amber's mother. I was in bed with my mother-in-law. What a horrible thought that was.

You have been accepted as a Draasen male, and you must follow Draasen ways. You are the representative of all males to the Most High One. Your acceptance by the males has been spreading since your disobedience of two Most High Ones, Elder said.

What did I do?

No male was ever allowed to speak to the former Most High One, or even be in this structure. You shouted at her and she kicked you with final claws. You disobeyed Most High One Ambrisseethsss by giving your suggestions. You survived, Elder said with unconcealed awe.

She said to be myself.

Yes, that is to be considered, but you must become the consort she needs so she can effectively rule all of Draasen. You can no longer be concerned just for your bonded pairing.

When can I see her? I said, concerned for Amber.

She has lost a lot of blood, and she will be slow to recover. She has been fitted with fluid accelerators, which increases her ability to create more blood inside her. She must remain asleep for them to operate efficiently.

When can I see her?

Ask our healer when she wakes. She is very happy with your availability. Even though you could not be a mated pairing, the two of you were very loud for a long time, and she is worn-out from the activity.

Do you mean we bonded?

Not exactly.

I wish I could remember what I did.

There was too much activity for me to remember in detail. I can say she is a very satisfied female, as is every female who telepathically linked to you.

Leave it to him to compound my embarrassment. I was flattered that I, somehow, managed to satisfy several females, but I did not need everyone to know I was sleeping with my mother-in-law, even if it was an accepted activity in Draasen society.

Your very loud availability with her has helped you gain female acceptance. The females who came with us have been telling everyone about you, and you are quickly gaining acceptance through them. The males have already accepted you, and they are your greatest supporters.

If he was trying to help me feel better, he was not doing very well. I needed Amber's touch and her presence inside me. I felt very empty without her.

Are you leaving me already? Lana said when I rose from the bed.

"I want to see Amber."

First, we will go to the Most High One's bathing pool, then we will have a feeding.

As I watched her rise and stretch, she reminded me so very much of Amber. In the early mornings we would talk, while I scratched her in all her favorite places, especially her chin. Sometimes, we would gently wrestle when I nuzzled her neck or nibbled her ears.

227

Thank you for allowing me to be the first to use your availability. I can feel you are uncomfortable, but you should not be. I am very glad I am able to protect you while your pairing is unavailable.

"Amber said she was going to give me to the crazy female."

When she said she would remove my hatchlings eggs from you, we waited until we saw what you would do. It worked well for us.

"So, the end justifies the means."

We learned it from you.

"How did she become the Most High One...I mean, the one before Amber?"

She attacked the previous Most High One without challenge, and sent her on the long walk. Initially, she was challenged several times in accordance with protocols, but her guards restrained the challengers, and she personally tortured them for all to see. When she was done, she bit their heads off and displayed them as an example to any who would challenge her. They were never taken home. Everyone agreed she must step down, but no one would dare challenge her again.

"Core must have weapons, like I discovered with Oracle."

Core had to obey its programming and accept the orders of the Most High One.

"Where is Amber?"

She must not be disturbed while she is healing.

"I am going to find her. If I have to search every dome on this planet, I will find her."

The door opened and Elder squatted in the opening.

You are not needed. Leave, Lana said.

He is the Most High One's surrogate, not yours, he said

"You two argue about it. I am leaving," I said.

Elder gave me just enough space to squeeze past him, and sent a map to Amber's location into my head as I trotted down the hall.

When I arrived at the hospital, two guards were standing beside an inner door they opened for me when I approached. Amber was on a high table with a sleep device on her forehead. She had several football shaped devices on her body, which I assumed were the fluid accelerators.

You are correct, Lana said when she entered.

"I hope you did not damage Elder getting out the door."

He loves you and he will protect you even to the long walk, but he knows not to stand in my way.

"When can she wake up?" I said, gently stroking the side of her face.

The accelerators are near the end of their cycle. I could wake her by the end of suns, but she needs to rest. When she wakes, I know she will want to assume her duties. Will you allow me to heal her completely so we can have a strong queen?

"Do you want to keep her asleep because she needs to heal, or because you want another chance at my availability?"

Both.

"At least you are honest. Okay, wake her at first suns, and I want to be here when you do. I think I need to bathe."

The Place of the Most High One was massive and confusing, with many interconnected hallways and domes, as Lana carried me to the bathing pool. Elder followed.

The Most High One's bathing pool was a smaller version of the colony pool. I jumped in and looked for my ledge, but it was not there.

Do you want a place to sit? Elder said.

"I got used to having one."

I will install it for you.

"We should ask Amber before we make changes."

The Most High One will want you to be comfortable, Elder said.

When he came back, he jumped in and installed a seat for me. Then, he set up his snorkel and dove to the hot water outlet. When Lana and I finished bathing, we left him to enjoy the pool alone. Possibly, for the first time in his life, he had something all to himself.

When we entered another dome, Kaa and Dee brought in trays of food and we all sat at the table.

"What are we waiting for?" I said.

You are the senior Draasen at this table. We wait for you, Lana said.

"Wait a minute. You are the senior here."

I am the senior female, but you are the senior Draasen. We wait for you.

Rather than argue, I loaded my plate with food and took the first bite. It was a small seating and there was no food flying around. Somehow, I missed that.

"Lana, how did you know the former queen was going to kick me?"

I did not know.

"You must have known something. You helped me put the vest on."

Our original plan was to cause confusion when you used your shield, neutralize the guards, and my hatchling would challenge the former queen in accordance with protocols. No one could have known you would attack the former queen, but the male you call Elder made the protective cloth and insisted it be brought for you. Her claws nearly penetrated it when she kicked you.

"Why did you want me to stop Amber from sending the former queen on the long walk?"

She had to demonstrate she would act in the best interests of our people, and she would hear everyone, even her male consort.

"What happens now?"

When she has healed, she will begin listening to the females, and you will stand with her as her consort and surrogate. At first, she will be very busy with many things to manage. If you obey our queen and show respect to our people, you will be accepted by everyone. The two of you could be the greatest pairing in many thousands of years.

"Core said I was to be brought to its center when the unfolding was complete."

Surrogate to the Most High One, you can come to my center now, Core said.

"Do you always listen to everyone's conversations?"

You are being evaluated, Core said.

"I will wait for the Most High One to wake before I come to you."

I await your arrival.

"I have a lot of questions I want to ask, but I do not trust it."

Why do you distrust Core? Lana said.

"You have not been zapped by it...I have."

You were trying to access restricted information.

"Without information, we may as well be brainless, but I picked up some clues along the way. For example, I know Core has been working with Amber to remove the former queen."

How do you know that?

"I figured it out when we arrived. You said Core does not speak with anyone except the Most High One. If it was not working with Amber, it would not have spoken to her in the shuttle before we landed. Core came to us in the dome and said it lost a link with her. If it can secretly work to remove a queen, what else does it have on its mind?"

I never got an answer.

***

After feeding, I really missed Amber. I wanted to find a sunny spot and lay in the suns with her, like we often did, but I knew it would not happen anymore because she ruled over eight billion people now. It looked like the fun was over, and I was certain her duties would keep us apart.

You must remain close to the Most High One while you attend to your duties, Core said.

"And what duties are those?"

The Most High One will determine what your duties will be.

"During the unfolding, someone said the guards have been neutralized. What does that mean?"

Anyone who resisted the unfolding was given the opportunity to accept Most High One Ambrisseethsss.

"What happened to those who did not?"

They were given final claws, Core stated dispassionately.

"How many Draasen went on the long walk as a result of the unfolding?"

Three hundred six thousand, four hundred seventy-three females loyal to the former Most High One. Nine hundred twenty-eight females loyal to Most High One Ambrisseethsss.

"How many males were sent on the long walk?"

None. You were the only male to sustain damage during the unfolding.

"How many are on the long walk on the colony planets?"

None. The former Most High One did not have any interest in the colony planets.

Hearing the numbers made my heart ache. The price of Amber's rise to the position of the Most High One was expensive in lives lost. Too many lives lost.

Why do you damage yourself with this information? Lana said.

"I wanted to know. Core, how many people still loyal to the former queen are still alive?"

Two hundred forty-one are currently being located.

"While the former queen lives, she will be a threat to my pairing. When can she be moved to another planet?"

Do not be concerned for the safety of your pairing. She is very well protected. The former queen made changes to this structure that make it very safe.

Hairs rose on the back of my neck.

What did you feel? Lana said.

"Core, what changes were made to this structure?" I said.

Should I display them?

"Yes. Display the Place of the Most High One before she became the Most High One, and display another as it is now."

What are you looking for? Lana said.

"The former queen could have put in a secret passage."

She was afraid to leave this structure. Why would she want a secret passage?

"Lana, you surprise me. It would allow her to escape in an emergency. Now, it could allow someone to sneak in from the outside and send all of us on the long walk while we slept, and the former queen would regain power."

Everyone had a great interest in the images Core created, but as we studied them, there were few differences between them.

"Core, did the former queen create any tunnels under this structure?" It did not answer. "Core, respond." It remained silent. "Core, how many males were sent on the long walk during the unfolding?"

None. You were the only male to sustain damage during the unfolding.

"Core has been ordered to remain silent about the tunnels. Double the guards inside, and place guards around the outside to keep anyone from cutting their way in. Make it happen. I am going to Amber."

When I ran from the feeding table, Kaa picked me up and ran to the hospital. He placed me on the table. Lana ran in and performed a scan.

She is still healing.

"I am not leaving her. We are going to be here a while, so we may as well get comfortable."

Lana settled near the wall and placed me in her lap. While I sat in her lap, bored and dozing off, I felt...a blank area. It was the only way to describe it. It was as annoying as it was curious, just on the edge of my telepathic ability. As I slowly looked around, I felt it moving, but when I concentrated on it, it disappeared. I dismissed it as my imagination and started to doze off again. It returned, closer than before, and seemed to be inside the wall beside me. I quietly got off Lana's lap and felt the wall. Lana suddenly picked me up and placed me in front of Amber's table. Then she directed Kaa to stand on one side of where I had been standing, and she stood on the other. The wall opened and a female rushed in with her claws extended. She was tackled by Kaa and Lana as the guards rushed in and helped restrain the female.

Who are you? Why are you here? Lana said.

"Lana, I am looking directly at this female, but she is a total blank to me."

Kaa pulled a floppy blue hat from her head, and I felt anger and hatred explode from her.

"Take this female and lock her up. Send two more guards back here."

When the guards left with their prisoner, two more entered and I posted one at the door, and told the other to go into the opening. When she went in, I followed her.

You are not going in there! Lana shouted.

"Lana, guard Amber. Kaa, follow me."

The passage was pitch black as I picked my way along. Kaa picked me up and moved quickly forward. When we reached the outside I saw someone lying on the ground. Kaa said it was one of our guards, and she was on the long walk.

We cannot leave her there.

I backed into Kaa when several shadows moved toward us from the darkness outside.

These females will take her home.

Kaa picked me up and carried me back into the passage, leaving the guard at the opening.

When we arrived at the hospital, I was thankful for the light when Kaa put me on my feet. Then, he blocked the passage by squatting in it.

You were wrong to go outside, Lana said.

"The assassin was here to send Amber on the long walk, and I have no doubt the former queen ordered it. I had to be sure there was no one else."

Through you, the guards experienced the telepathic blankness the head covering created, and they will watch for anyone wearing them. The guards are searching for more passages like this one.

"We need to close this tunnel."

We are sealing the passage from the outside. Two others need to enter from your side to bring what we need to finish, Dee said.

It was not long before Dee and another female emerged, carrying equipment on their backs. Another pair went in to finish filling the passage.

The guards are alert for any activity. It is time for you to rest, Lana said.

"I will have plenty of time to rest after I have gone on the long walk."

Before I could protest, Lana put me in her lap, placed one of her devices on my forehead, and put me to asleep.

Chapter 16

ARMED

I will wake the Most High One when you are ready, Lana said when she woke me.

Lana removed the sleep device from Amber and she slowly stirred. When she opened her eyes and sat up, our link established, and I felt whole again.

"Good morning, my queen. Or should I say, Most High One?"

I was not dreaming? Core, I must be updated.

Core floated through the wall of the dome and said, *Most High One, may I approach to perform the update?*

I am prepared.

Core floated to her forehead and linked with her. I felt our bonded link flow in and out of focus as Core gave Amber the updates. It took only a few seconds and when it was complete, Core disappeared through the wall.

I can feel you are unhappy. Why?

"I was used to the colony. I knew what to do, but this is all new. I am uncomfortable with the whole thing."

Do you want to know a secret? I am uncomfortable too, but do not tell anyone, she said, smiling at me.

"When you fought the former queen, she did not put up much of a fight. Do not take this the wrong way, but I expected more from her."

She depended on her guards to defend her. With her guards restrained, it was easy to remove her.

"Easy? You almost went on the long walk! When you pulled the scepter out, you did not feel any pain. How did you manage that?"

My mother placed one of her devices between my ears so no one could see it. You could not have one because you do not have enough hair, she said, ruffling my thinning hair.

I tried to hide the thought that she had wanted to give me to the former queen, but I could not keep it from her.

I am sorry, but it was necessary. When she kicked you, I knew our people would not tolerate anyone sending a birthing animal on the long walk. It allowed me to challenge her in accordance with protocols.

"But, everyone saw I was still alive."

Our people have suffered too long under her oppression, and they are happy she has been removed in accordance with protocols. We are very happy you did not go on the long walk.

Most High One, please come to my center. Bring your surrogate, Core said.

Amber carried me through the throne room and stopped in front of an unguarded door.

Wait. Open and swallow, Lana said, holding a small bulb in her hand.

"What is this?"

Pain fluid. Open and swallow.

"Why do I need it in there?"

Do not argue.

I swallowed it and followed Amber through the door before it sealed behind us.

Welcome to my center. Most High One Ambrisseethsss, what is your command?

I want to release all commands the former Most High One has installed.

The mass release of all commands without review will cause severe personal damage.

"Wait a minute. What do you mean by personal damage?"

A mass release will activate all defensive measures on protected inputs.

How many inputs did the former queen make? Amber said.

194,283 verbal inputs.

"We are going to be here a very long time," I said with a groan.

How many telepathic inputs did the former queen install? Amber said.

Seventy-three.

"We need a faster way to do this. Maybe we should get some help."

Most High One, if you use the directed input device, you can quickly review and release commands individually.

A shaft of light rose from the floor in front of her, and when it rose as high as Amber's forehead, it bent near the top toward her.

Most High One, please place your forehead on the directed input device.

Where do you suggest I start? Amber said to me.

"Well, most of the recent commands are probably useless to anyone but her. Maybe you should start with those and work backward."

I will begin at the end, she placed her forehead on the light shaft.

Our link disconnected when she began her review. I expected to feel reassurances, but felt nothing. Lana was just outside the door, but I could not contact her.

Surrogate to the Most High One, my center is designed to block telepathic contact.

"How can this dome block telepathy?"

Random electrical impulses sent through this dome scatters telepathic patterns. All Oracles and Centrals have it installed. Please approach the panel with the green illumination and place your feet on the illuminations in the floor.

When I stood on the lights, I was unable to move. After a few seconds, I felt an intense burning on both my thighs and calves and smelled burnt flesh. A few seconds later, I was released to hobble away from the panel.

Surrogate to the Most High One, I have made the necessary changes to your symbols of position.

"I wish you would say something before you do stuff like that!" I said, gingerly rubbing the areas where I was burned.

Core was becoming an annoyance. I wanted to leave its center but not without Amber.

"How much longer is she going to be?"

She is going to be the Most High One until the long walk, unless she surrenders her position to an acceptable replacement, or is challenged.

It took a moment for Core's answer to sink in. I did not ask the right question.

"Can you determine how much longer she will be evaluating and releasing commands?"

She has released 3507 commands. The rate of release has slowed.

"She might be getting tired. Tell her she needs to stop."

The light shaft pulled back and our link connected again.

"Are you all right?" I said.

Yes. Examining and releasing so many of the commands drains me. Some of the commands are still protected with dangerous results. Please do not attempt to access anything. Core, reset the device.

"Wait a minute. Core, are there any commands dangerous to her if she releases them?"

There is no danger to the Most High One when she releases verbal commands.

The hairs raised on the back of my neck again.

You felt something. What is it? Amber said.

"Core, is there any danger to the Most High One when she releases the programmed commands?"

Of the seventy-three telepathically programmed commands, twelve are protected in a unique way. Improper release of those commands will result in severe damage.

"Core, take those twelve commands and place them in an area where only the Most High One can access them. Place a warning on it informing the Most High One they are dangerous commands before she begins to access them."

Only the Most High One can make changes to the command structure.

Separate those commands as my surrogate has suggested. That is my command.

Command accepted.

I knew I chose correctly when I chose you.

***

It took several hours for Amber to finish releasing the verbal commands. When she was done, she was tired and I said she should rest before doing anything else. Lana was waiting for us when we walked out of Core's center.

"Lana, have any more passages been found?" I said.

Those revealed when you had Core display the two images have been sealed. The search continues for any others.

"Core, will you answer questions concerning changes made to this structure?"

That information has been released by the Most High One.

"How many tunnels have been created during the changes made by the former queen?"

One. The tunnel is under this structure. It splits into three openings. One is located under the Most High One's sleeping dome. One is located under the detention dome. One is located inside the nearest landing area.

"Has the tunnel been used recently?"

Yes.

"When and where was it used?"

It was used in the darkness after last suns. It was opened at the landing area and the detention dome.

"Most High One, I think the former queen has escaped."

Amber had Core ask the detention area guards if she was still there.

She is missing. I will send my guards to look for her.

"If you send your guards from here, you weaken your position here. You are safe, now that we have located the tunnels and doubled the guards. Since our people do not like her, let our people help look for her."

Core, send a message to everyone on the home world that the former queen has escaped detention. Anyone who sees her is to report her location.

Most High One, the message has been sent.

Come with me. We will relax in the suns until second bathing, Amber said.

In the center of the dome complex, we found a grassy area open to the sky. Amber lay on her side and I relaxed against her chest. It was quiet times like these I enjoyed most of all. We heard someone singing who was sure of the tune and sang it with confidence.

You are doing very well as my consort.

"It is only the beginning. I am sure I will make mistakes and when I do, I hope you will not bite my neck like you did the male outside our dome."

He was much more confident than he needed to be, and my discipline reminded him of his position. All males need discipline.

She flipped me onto my stomach and started to bite on my neck, and I screamed before I realized she would never hurt me. She was laughing when I squirmed out of her grasp, jumped on her, and blew a raspberry on the back of one of her ears. Her screams brought people from all directions.

Never do that to me! she said, frantically rubbing her ear.

"You started it."

Your activities had everyone in a panic, Lana said, after she dismissed everyone. *Do I have to keep my tail around both of you?*

"We were having fun."

Most High Ones do not have fun, Lana said.

"Is that what made the former queen lose her mind?"

It is possible her lack of trust, and detailed control of Draasen, left her damaged, Core said.

"How often does it happen?"

When a Most High One cannot rule effectively, a challenger will ask her to step down, Core said.

"I heard she sent all her challengers on the long walk. You have weapons. Why did you do nothing to remove her?"

I am programmed to obey the commands of the Most High One.

"Yet you helped my pairing remove the former queen."

The former queen did not command that I was not to assist others in her removal.

It seemed Core cared about the Draasen people, but I still had my doubts, and not just because it successfully manipulated the removal of the former queen.

Most High One, please send your surrogate to my center immediately, Core said.

Mother, take him to Core's center. When Core is finished with you, join me at second feeding.

"Lana, do you know why we are going to see Core?" I said.

I know my hatchling is to be closely guarded.

"Did she do something wrong?"

I do not know.

When we arrived at Core's door, it opened, and we started in.

Ssurlanaseethesess, you are not required to attend.

When the door closed, a panel opened on one side.

I have intercepted a message and learned there will be an attempt by the former queen to force the current Most High One from her position. Take the item from the open panel and place it on your wrist.

"What is it?"

It is a warrior's weapon. You must use it, because my programming forbids me from damaging a female in any way.

"So, you leave it to a male to take the responsibility for sending a female on the long walk."

The design of this weapon is intended to incapacitate by temporarily neutralizing the telepathic organ. It is ineffective on you because you lack the organ necessary for telepathy.

"How does it work?"

Place the weapon on your wrist.

I was confident as I slipped the wide armband over my hand and inserted two fingers into loops. It tightened on my wrist and a golf ball sized bubble on the top began to glow. Then, I felt an influence affecting me.

For you, an influence is as effective as a presentation.

"I could have refused."

You would not refuse because you want to protect your pairing. I know your human experiences as a warrior make you comfortable with weapons.

"How does it work?"

The loops around your fingers control the mechanism. Look at your target and bend your hand at the wrist.

I tried to target a panel on the wall, without success.

"Does it work?"

It is connected to your telepathic ability and will operate when you want it to. Since you require a demonstration, look behind you.

I turned to see the former Most High One coming at me with her claws extended. The weapon fired and she disappeared when a narrow beam of light struck her in the head.

"You said it would not kill anyone!" I said, with a perverse satisfaction that she was gone.

It was an image of the former queen. Did you feel the weapon's pulse as it passed through you?

"It went through me?" I said, feeling around myself.

Core provided a presentation. When the weapon fired, the beam went through my opposite arm. It was disturbing how easily it worked, and I tried to take it off.

Leave the weapon on your wrist.

"It is too dangerous. It fires too easily and I might accidentally use it," I said, struggling with it.

If you remove it, you will not be able to put it back on quickly enough.

"Okay, how do I get it off?" I said in frustration at my inability to remove it.

I will not allow the weapon to be removed until the attempt against the Most High One has been resolved.

"I need to bathe. Can I take it off then?"

Fluids have no effect on the weapon. You may leave.

When I left Core's center, Lana was waiting.

What is that?

"It is a gift from Core."

What does it do?

"Supposedly, it disables a Draasen's telepathic ability."

Is it a weapon? Did you learn nothing from your experience at the colony? She was suddenly wary of a weapon in the hands of a male.

"I did not ask for this thing. Core locked it on my wrist, and I cannot get it off. I am supposed to wear it until it allows me to remove it."

Only warriors are allowed to have weapons. Do you know why you have it?

"Core said there will be an attempt to remove Amber from her position."

When?

"Core did not say, but it might be soon."

I will have the guards examine everyone more closely.

I asked Amber where she was, and I was directed through the hallways to the feeding table.

What are you wearing?

"It is a weapon. Core thinks there will be an attempt to remove you from your position. Please, do not listen to our people, at least for a while. It will give us a chance to find the traitor before she can get to you."

We know someone will try to remove me, and now we are prepared for it.

She did not seem concerned by the possibility of being displaced, or that I was wearing a weapon.

With you protecting me, why should I be afraid? Eat, you will feel better.

When the feeding was over, we walked back to the chamber of the Most High One, where I stood beside my queen, weapon ready to defend her, while she listened to the concerns of our people.

***

The rest of the day passed without incident. After Amber heard the last request, a female casually walked in. Initially the guards stopped her, but she walked around them and approached the throne. None of the guards moved to stop her.

I have a message from the true Most High One. She squatted with her chin on her chest and arms at her sides. I saw what appeared to be a soap bubble form around her head.

"Get out of here!" I shouted, but Amber did not move.

I rushed in front of Amber as the bubble stretched toward us. I bent my wrist and the weapon fired just as the bubble reached me.

I remember falling backward before I blacked out.

Chapter 17
REVENGE

When I woke, I was being carried by someone who was running. Sharp claws dug painfully into my side when I tried to squirm into a more comfortable position.

Remain still and be silent.

When I tried to contact Amber, claws dug into my side again.

I said silence!

I was carried along narrow, little used passageways until we reached an open area and approached several females near a shuttle. I recognized the former queen standing inside a circle of females. The circle opened, and I was dumped in front of her.

I told you to bring him to me undamaged! she shouted in a fit of anger when she saw I was bleeding. She clawed the female, leaving deep gashes in the side of her face.

After a moment, she was apologetic and ordered a healer to repair the damage she had just done. Then she turned to me.

I can be very gentle if you will let me. Please, birth my eggs and I will give you anything you want.

Anything? Even my freedom to return to my queen?

I am your queen! I am the only queen you will ever know! she shouted with a snap of her jaw's just inches from my face. *Where is my sister?* she said, looking around.

Most High One, when I entered your chamber through the secret entrance, I saw this alien thing use this device on her, just as she started to use her ability. The female handed my weapon to her.

Did you send the hatchling on my throne on the long walk?

I could not. I had to leave quickly because many guards were entering. I had only enough time to get this alien thing for you.

Did you try to send the hatchling on the walk?

No, Most High One.

The former queen started quivering and her head spasmodically jerked around. She stepped over me, opened her jaws, and viciously beheaded the female. She squatted in front of me again, her jaws dripping with blood.

See? I can be gentle.

Gentle? You took her head off!

I was quick, and she did not suffer.

It was a lie. I had heard painful thoughts as life faded from the head beside me.

I understand, I said, deliberately not giving her any title, and offered the gesture of respect.

I will treat you gently. My skin crawled when she accepted my gesture.

Most High One, the males have arrived.

Males? Send them on the walk!

Most High One, you need the males to fertilize your eggs. This alien thing cannot do that for you.

Yes, yes I need them. No! Yes, I do.

When eleven males squatted outside the ring of guards, another group arrived and squatted between us and the transport. Many more were coming from every direction.

Most High One, there are too many males.

Send them on the walk! Make them all walk!

They quickly formed multiple rings around us and pressed inward. The guards plunged their claws into the throats and bodies of the closest males as they pressed tighter against us. Those in front were held up and pressed forward, their sacrificed bodies acting as shields for those pushing from behind. I felt many were dying as we were pressed together. I was trapped against the former queen's legs as she screamed and clawed at any male within reach.

Suddenly, my feet were pulled out from under me and I was dragged from the inner circle and handed off to other hands. When I found myself outside the circle, I was picked up and taken from the fight. I looked back and saw a few females jump into the air, but they were swarmed and taken down. More males jumped toward the center, standing on the heads and shoulders of others, plunging their clawed hands and feet into the center of the circle. I tried to call for Amber, but our link was silent.

Who are you? Where are you taking me?

I am taking you to the Place of the Most High One.

When we arrived, Lana was waiting near the entrance. He placed me on my feet and ran off before I could thank him. As he ran, his thoughts were guarded.

"Where is Amber?" I said as Lana began attending to my injuries.

She is safe inside Core's center. Now that the danger is passed, she will be let out.

My link was suddenly restored, and I was overwhelmed by the flood of concern, love, and affection coming from her. Amber's contact made me light headed.

What is wrong? Lana said when she caught me as my knees buckled.

I desperately wanted to be with Amber and hold her close to me. Lana quickly finished with my injuries and carried me inside.

You are safe! Amber rushed to me and took me from Lana's arms. *I am so very happy you are safe!*

I nearly fainted, but from what I was not sure. It could have been the multiple waves of intense emotions crossing our link, or her hug crushing the air out of me. If I was to die, in her arms was the place to be.

Most High One, he needs to breathe, Lana said.

Are you damaged? She held me at arm's length to examine me.

Your mother healed me. She held me close to her again. *Amber, I want to return to the landing area.*

No! You will stay with me. No one will take you from me again.

Will you go with me to the landing area?

Why do you want to go there?

We must confirm the former queen and her followers are on the long walk. Would you leave them in the suns like she did her challengers?

It is too dangerous for you to go outside.

The males were protecting me when they rescued me. You need to be out there, showing no fear when you send the former queen and her followers home. We must go to the landing area.

Most High One, he is correct. The males will not harm you or him. We should go and have Core record what is there. Then it can be sent to everyone, including the females in the detention domes. If the former queen is on the long walk, her followers will not do anything else because there is no one to reward them, Lana said.

Are you certain you want to do this? Amber said.

I have to. We have to, I replied.

When we entered a transport, Kaa, Lana, and Elder went with us. Another transport of guards joined us as we flew to the landing area. The fading light made it difficult to see.

Core, I need some light.

When the large shuttle in front of us began to glow, I wished I had not returned. The carnage was ghastly to look at. The bodies of males not lying down were propped up by their dead neighbors as they squatted, shoulder to shoulder, in loose circles. When I looked at the rivulets of blood flowing away from the gruesome scene, I felt as if my heart had been ripped from my chest. They had died for me.

Feeling my anguish, Amber said, *You must leave this place.*

No. No. Core, how many are on the long walk?

Twenty-one females and forty-four males are on the long walk. There are many damaged males afraid of being repaired by healers.

Why? I said.

Any male involved in sending a female on the long walk will be summarily sent on the long walk.

It is our protocol, Amber said.

They are not responsible, I am. Everyone, listen to me! I am the only one responsible for this! Please, come out and be healed! I am the only one responsible. No one will be punished except me!

You are not responsible! Amber shouted.

Most High One, they were defending me, and I am responsible for them.

I left the transport and Amber's guards quickly formed a ring around me when males began appearing from the shadows. I left the guards' protection and went to one who had deep claw wounds on his neck and shoulders.

Call in every healer in the area! I shouted.

It is done, Lana said, and began treating the male I was standing in front of. Several females ran toward us carrying their medical bags. I was surprised they had responded so quickly, and in so many numbers. While the wounded were being treated, I went to the carnage.

Core, is anyone still alive in there? I said.

They are all on the long walk.

Bring transports here immediately so I can take them home.

Command accepted.

Who will help me carry them home?

I will! Several hundred male voices thundered inside my head.

I want the females taken home, I said.

We will take them home, several females said.

When the dead males had been carefully loaded, we made our way across the city to an immense field of grass. In the light of our glowing transports, we laid them on the grass, and it quickly consumed them.

When we returned, the remains of the females had been removed, except for one. I barely recognized the dismembered corpse as the former queen.

Most High One, why is this female still here?

She will not be taken home! That is my command!

I walked to Amber and offered the gesture of respect.

Most High One, it is time to bring peace and dignity back to the people.

She grabbed my arm and roughly pulled me to the transport. When she stepped inside, I turned to the males who remained, offered the gesture of respect, palms up to them, and said, *Thank you!*

A deafening roar burst from them and they melted into the darkness. When I entered the transport, I felt confusion as everyone looked at me in surprise. I was being myself, just as I was told, but I had done something wrong again.

Amber dropped me in her lap, and we flew to the Place of the Most High One. I followed her to our sleeping dome, but she did not invite me to lay with her. I curled up alone with the memories of the carnage indelibly burned into my mind. I desperately needed the blissful forgetfulness of sleep, but it was an elusive commodity until I found myself in the workspace with the puppet in front of me again. A string dropped toward the puppet, and I fell into a deep sleep.

Chapter 18

CORRUPTED

The next suns, Amber was still giving me the silent treatment, and I felt she was afraid of something.

"Why are you not talking to me?" I was suddenly flooded with so much information, it left me disoriented.

Is that what you want, Raymond the Most High One?

"What do you mean?"

Why are you trying to take the rule of Draasen from me?

"I cannot challenge you."

You commanded Core, and it obeyed you. Many females obeyed your commands, including my mother. Males follow your instructions without question, and you defend them, as if they are yours. They consider you their Most High One.

"Let me bring this into perspective for you. If the males had done nothing, your eggs and I would be somewhere out in the void with the former queen, never to be heard from again. Those males went on the long walk for you, by saving me. I honored them for their sacrifice."

You have violated many protocols. There may be a call for the Council of Five.

"If the Council disagrees with what I did, then maybe I should be punished. Perhaps the Council will order I be sent on the long walk, but if they do, I will be sent by your claws and no one else's. Shall we bathe?" I concluded calmly.

That is what I fear most. To give you final claws would send me on the long walk as well.

Core appeared through a wall and said, *Most High One, a Council of Five has formed. They demand you bring your surrogate to them immediately.*

They demand? Send an Oracle to inform the Council we are going to bathe and have first feeding before we consider coming to them.

Yes, Most High One.

***

When we arrived at the bathing pool, Amber was speaking with someone I could not hear.

"Am I allowed to know what is going on?"

A group of females agreed to form a Council without my approval. They are testing me.

We should go to them.

They will wait for me, or they can dismiss themselves.

After bathing and feeding we casually walked to the plaza, where the Council of Five formed a semi-circle near the entrance. Beyond them, the plaza was crowded with bystanders. When we approached the waiting Council, I saw the leader was much younger than the others.

Ambrisseethsss, kneel before this Council!

Does this Council wish to challenge me for the position of Most High One?

No!

Show respect to me or I will dismiss this Council for disrespect, as is my right under protocols!

The older females looked worried, but the young leader's face was like stone.

Most High One, your consort is accused —

Since I am not accused, you have my permission to proceed with your accusations. When you make your judgment, remember he is still my surrogate protecting my eggs.

Amber did not stand behind the Council like she had at the colony. She placed her hand on my shoulder and started a private conversation.

This is wrong. Be careful what you say.

She walked to a nearby wall and turned, her guards forming a semi-circle in front of her.

Before I had the chance to kneel before the Council, the young leader said, *Male; you are removed from all positions to the Most High One. You have violated many protocols. You have violated more protocols than this Council will list. The violations are not in dispute. You are guilty. This Council has summarily ruled you will be sent on the long walk.* Two of the elderly females snapped a look at Council leader.

Hey! I have the right to respond!

Silence! Guards, detain this alien thing. Most High One, you will now kneel before this Council and face judgment as the one responsible for your male.

One of the former queen's guards had called me an "alien thing" at the landing area. It was possible the Council was loyal to her. I had to take the chance I was right, because Amber's life depended on it, as did mine.

Core! Come to me!

Core, you will maintain your place! The Council leader shouted as Core flew to me and landed on my head, starting a private conversation.

How many know the former queen has gone on the long walk?

Only those who were at the landing area.

Core, obey me! Male, I will not allow you to disobey protocols any further. I will carry out the judgment of this Council. She sprang at me, claws extended.

When two of Amber's guards tackled the Council leader, the air was suddenly filled with males as they jumped in from every direction. Kaa landed beside me, picked me up, and bounded to the top of the nearest dome while the plaza became a scene of chaotic activity. It looked like a riot as females started jumping in, knocking males over.

Stop fighting! Stop it! Stop! Amber and I shouted.

The mass of Draasen slowly stopped struggling, carefully watching each other.

See what you have done? You have turned the males against us! You must be sent on the long walk! Release me! the council leader shouted while she was pinned down by the guards.

I have to get down there and face the Council.

You do not need to face them. They have violated protocols, and their duty, Amber said.

I was not allowed to respond to their accusations. This must end in accordance with protocols. Kaa, help me get down.

Kaa jumped to an open area near the restrained Council.

Will your queen obey protocols and allow this Council's judgment to stand?

I have faced a Council of Five before, and I know I have the right to respond to the Council's accusations. This is my response. All of you will face a Council of Five because of your violations of protocols. I am a birthing animal. I carry the Most High One's eggs, and you tried to send me on the long walk. We know you are loyal to the former Most High One. Do not look so surprised. We know of your communication with her last suns.

It does not matter. The true Most High One will reward me when she takes the rule of Draasen back for herself. Release Me! she said, struggling against the guards.

I do not think so. Core, show the landing area, and the disposition of the former queen.

Core projected the scene of carnage directly into every mind in the plaza, ending with the dismembered corpse of the former queen.

Most High One, these five females are loyal to the former queen, I said.

Amber's voice rang out, *Guards, restrain the former Council members in the detention area.*

Most High One, I request you send healers to repair the damage some have, I said.

When healers came to treat all who needed it, I had to ask the hard question, *Core, how many are on the long walk?*

One male.

The report hit me like a sledgehammer. Too many were dying for me, far too many.

Most High One, I have one thing to do before I submit myself for punishment.

Most High One, I will go with him, Elder said.

No, you will stay with me, for now. He has endured much more than any consort should. I felt a brief conversation between them I was not allowed to hear.

I will go with you, Kaa said.

Do what you must and return quickly to me, Amber said.

I walked to the dead male and knelt beside his head.

I am so sorry, I said, tears streaming down my face. *Who will help me carry him home?*

Every male voice in the plaza thundered inside my head saying, *I will!*

A transport arrived and settled in the plaza. Several males and I gently placed the dead male on the transport, and we took him to the field of grasses; we took him home. On our return, I had the pilot stop the transport and open the door. I stood in the open door and offered the gesture of respect.

Thank you! I telepathically shouted, and a deafening roar came from tens of thousands of male voices all over the Drassen capitol.

I felt very old and worn-out as I thought about those who were on the long walk. Too many had died for me, and the worst thing was, I could not stop any of it. It made me question why I was here.

When we landed, I rushed into Amber's arms and said, *When will it end?*

The unfolding for you is not yet complete. There is one more thing for you to endure. During the former queen's rule, billions of our people were sent on the long walk when she abandoned our colonies to the Baleorans. There is much blood on her claws for that. The blood of those who have gone on the long walk for you is on her claws, not yours. No consort has ever done what you have. You have gone far beyond the limits of protocols, and you have been raised to a much higher acceptance by everyone. I was afraid you would take my position by using the males to help you. It is why I was worried when we returned from the landing area.

Most High One, you asked me to be myself, and I did what I needed to do.

I have seen many of your decisions are guided from a dark and disorganized place in your mind. I feared that place, because I thought it might influence you to take my position from me.

I would never take anything from you. You are my queen. I do not need anything else.

I know that now. I never should have doubted you. She picked me up and carried me inside.

Core, prepare links for everyone to see and hear me. Set links to all colony planets.

Most High One, the links are set, Core said as Amber stepped up to the dais.

People of Draasen, the former Most High One has gone on the long walk. This visual is provided. Through all the Oracles, Core showed the carnage at the landing area. It entered my mind as it did across the home world, and the six remaining colony planets.

The former queen's cruelty has had its way with her. Those who remain loyal to her must make a choice. You can come to the Place of the Most High One, where I will hear your acceptance of my reign, or you can go on the long walk. Make your choice quickly.

Most High One, will you hear a request from me? I said, offering the gesture of respect.

What is your request?

A Council of Five claims I have violated many protocols, and they have ruled I am to be sent on the long walk. I submit myself for punishment.

She started a private conversation when she held my hands. *Why are you doing this?*

I am a male, and you must obey protocols. We must set the example.

I did not have a death wish, but the deaths of so many weighed heavily on me. Amber released my hands and stood to her full stature as Core hovered near her shoulder.

Male, a Council of Five has removed you from all positions to the Most High One. You have violated many protocols and a Council of Five has judged you guilty of violating those protocols. It is my duty to send you on the long walk as the Council ordered. I will send you on the long walk at a time of my choosing. Until then, you are reinstated as my escort, consort, and my surrogate. That is my command.

Command accepted, Core stated, and returned to its position at the top of the dome.

It was as if everyone had been holding their breath, and let it go in relief when she gave her decision. While everyone was relieved I did not die on the spot, I felt like the Sword of Damocles was ready to fall on me at any moment.

Surrogate, take your place. When I walked to her side, she placed her hand on my shoulder and said, *Do not do that to me again.*

If you did not follow the judgment of the Council, you would not be trusted. We must do it the right way. We must do it by protocols.

Who made you an authority on protocols?

You did. I looked up at her and smiled. Her smile was slow to come, but when it did, it was meant just for me.

I will hear requests after first feeding of the next suns, she said, and Oracle terminated the links. *Now, we will go to Core's center and I will release the seventy-three telepathic commands.*

You should take your time doing that, I said.

The commands you separated are a concern. You will wait outside when I release them.

258

I was so surprised by her statement I stopped short, and Lana had to hop around me.

You will wait outside. Her tone, and regal gaze, did not allow room for argument.

***

Amber was in Core's center for several hours, and we had no idea of what was happening. Being unlinked from Amber always unnerved me, and knowing what she was doing did not help.

"Core, what is happening in there?" I said for the hundredth time.

The Most High One has completed releasing the telepathic commands.

"Finally. When is she coming out?"

I do not know.

"Open the door."

The Most High One has not authorized entry.

"Core, open up! Amber!" I shouted, pounding on the door.

Surrogate to the Most High One, that may not be the correct way to enter. Core, please inform the Most High One we are concerned for her, and we would like her to authorize entry.

I was relieved when the door opened and our link reconnected.

"You can lose the smug look," I said to Lana.

When we walked in, Amber was squatting in the center of the dome; her chin was on her knees, arms wrapped around her legs, eyes staring forward.

"What is wrong?" I said.

Her eyes swiveled to me, and I was so overwhelmed by sadness and fear I burst into tears.

We have been betrayed by the former queen, Amber said.

"She was bad for everyone," I said, wiping the tears from my eyes.

You do not understand. She betrayed all of us to the Baleorans.

259

"How?"

When the Baleorans took the first of our colony planets, she ordered Core to contact them. They agreed not to come to our home world if she gave them the locations of the colony planets.

"Is there anything you can do?"

My training did not prepare me for this.

Most High One, you should let your surrogate become the warrior I know he is, a familiar voice stated from the open door.

"Tikan!"

She walked past me and offered the gesture of respect to Amber. Then, she turned to me and offered the gesture to me, palms up.

"I am glad you are here. Did you hear what is happening?"

Yes, what is your command?

"My command? I do not have any authority here."

Most High One, he needs access to Core if we are to protect ourselves from the Baleorans.

Core. I want to give my surrogate access to you. Can this be done?

Most High One, I do not agree with this, Lana said. *He has been given weapons. Now, you want to give him access to Core. A male has never been given access to Core.*

As Most High One you can give any access. I recommend restrictions be applied before granting access to any male, Core said.

Amber briefly looked at me, and then said, *Grant my surrogate access to all information. Reserve commands to me. That is my command.*

Command accepted.

With that access, you can defend the Draasen people, Tikan said.

"Whoa, whoa, wait a minute! Defense is something to be handled by your generals and such. I do not have any experience with this!"

Neither do I, so we will do this together, Amber said.

"Let me see if I understand what you want me to do. You want me to take charge of the defense of the Draasen people with no experience and no training. You want me, the...alien thing, to defend the Draasen people. Is this what you want?" A burning fear settled in the pit of my stomach.

You would not do it alone. We have many warriors waiting for your commands, Tikan said.

"We? Are you volunteering to help me?"

Yes! It sounds exciting.

"Exciting is not a word I would choose."

I wondered why Amber was letting Tikan make the arguments she should be making, until I felt a very subtle influence just on the edge of my awareness. It stopped when I felt it.

"You are doing the influence thing on me again."

The Draasen people need you. I need you, Amber said.

"Most High One, can I have a free hand to do what I need to do?"

Do what you must, but any decision you make will be approved by me.

"When you found the agreement with the Baleorans, was there any mention of when the next colony planet would be taken?"

Yes, the next will be taken within two suns. Core has the location.

"Core, did the former queen remove the defense platforms from that planet?"

They were withdrawn thirty-eight suns ago.

"Do we have enough time to evacuate the planet?"

Full evacuation will take approximately forty-nine suns.

"Can we move defense platforms back to that colony world?"

If they were sent to tunnel immediately, they would arrive within one suns.

"Do you know how many Baleoran ships will arrive at the colony planet?"

Probes report twenty large storage vessels, five vessels containing several thousand-drop ships, and two very large armed vessels.

"So, they have container ships, aircraft carriers, and battleships. Core, how many defense platforms are available?"

The former queen stationed forty-six defense platforms in orbit around this planet.

"Send eight platforms to our colony planet immediately. Position them in low orbit on the opposite side of the planet, where the Baleorans cannot see them when they approach. When the Baleorans come within weapon's range, spread the platforms apart an equal distance from each other, and orbit the planet to appear at the same time to concentrate their firepower on the two armed vessels. If the other vessels attempt to escape, have two of the platforms split their firepower between the armed vessels and the others."

Command confirmation from the Most High One is required.

What are you doing? Lana said.

"I am preparing an ambush. I want to hit them with surprise and overwhelming force to destroy them quickly, with minimal damage to our own."

When they discover we have violated their agreement, they will come after us.

"Do you think they will honor the agreement with the former queen and not come here after the last colony planet is taken? We have to make a stand now, while we can."

We must inform the Baleorans there is a new Most High One, and we will defend our colonies, Lana said.

"Do you think sending a message like that will make them go away and leave us alone? A swift kick in the teeth will send a better message."

Core, send eight defense platforms as my surrogate has suggested. That is my command.

Command accepted.

It is time to rest, Amber said to me.

"I have too much on my mind. I will probably stay awake until this is all done. Can we go outside?"

Where do you want to go?

"Nowhere. Just out for some fresh air."

When we went through the archway, I was glad to see the decayed Draasen heads had been removed. When we walked in the plaza, people stopped and squatted when we walked by. A feeling of peace had replaced the fear and oppression I had felt when we arrived. It was a comfortable feeling being outside and not worried about danger.

We walked until it was completely dark and I could see the stars, thick and bright overhead. I was safe and comfortable in Amber's arms, free from the cares of the day.

My last recollection was Amber carrying me.

Chapter 19

BALEORANS

When we woke the next suns, I worried about the disastrous outcome if my plan failed, but Amber was still not concerned as she listened to requests from our people in the throne room.

Near the end of the suns, Core said the defense platforms had arrived and were being positioned at the colony planet. The announcement sent my anxiety soaring to new heights.

You need to relax, Amber said.

Dee, Kaa, and Tikan came with us when Amber carried me to her transport. We flew far outside the capitol and landed in an area of open fields and trees. Tikan, Dee, and Kaa bolted out the door and hit the ground running.

"What are they doing?"

We come to places like this where we can exercise and run. We do this to relax. We could not run very far at the colony because there was not enough room.

"You should run if it relaxes you."

I do not like leaving you alone.

"Oh, go ahead and have some fun. Even a Most High One should relax."

When she hesitated, I swatted her on the back of her thigh, and she sprang into the air in surprise.

"Run!" I shouted.

She smiled, and ran like the wind across the field toward distant trees. Kaa and Dee came running toward me, foot claws digging in as they controlled their turns. Dee tackled Kaa from behind, and they tumbled to the ground together. When they sprang to their feet and ran again, Dee complained as Kaa bit the tip of her extended tail.

When the suns slowly disappeared, I leaned back against the transport, looking for the constellations I was familiar with from Earth, but the shapes of the constellations were not recognizable from here.

After all our time together, you still look for those pictures in the stars, Amber said.

"I like knowing which way is north, but I really do not need to because you are my direction. I follow you, not because you are my queen, but because I love you."

Amber placed me in her lap and wrapped her warm arms around me while we waited for Kaa, Dee, and Tikan. I was not sure how long we waited, because at some point, I fell asleep.

***

After first feeding, Core called us to the throne room and announced the defense platforms were moving into attack positions. Fear caused my stomach to tighten into a painful, sour knot.

Most High One, how would you like the visual displayed?

My surrogate will decide.

"Can you show the region as a spherical display, with the colony planet at the center?"

The dome darkened and the colony planet took a prominent position behind Amber's head. The defense platforms were moving from behind the planet. In front of Amber's nose were the two Baleoran battleships leading the other ships. When Amber moved to get a better view, the defense platforms appeared to be smaller than any of the Baleoran ships.

"Core, show me the comparative sizes of the Baleoran vessels and the defense platforms."

The Baleoran battleship was at least three times larger than a defense platform. The container ships were larger still.

Surrogate to the Most High One, the Baleoran vessels have a limited supply of energy to power themselves and their weapons. The defense platforms are near a planet with a strong magnetic field. They have unlimited energy to draw from, Oracle said.

This was no computer game. There was no restarting this nightmare to get a second chance. If my plans failed, hundreds of millions would die.

Suddenly, the Baleoran battleships opened fire with bright blue beams, hitting two platforms squarely in the middle. A second volley struck the same targets again.

"Are the defense platforms going to fire anytime soon?" I said.

They will begin their attack when they reach optimal distance, Core said, as the Baleoran ships fired a third and fourth volley.

One defense platform was on a straight course, away from the others' curving trajectory around the planet.

"Core, what is wrong with this one?" I said, pointing at the wayward platform.

It has ceased to operate. Another beam struck the inoperable platform.

Suddenly, the room lit up with multiple beams of light as the defense platforms finally opened fire. The rate of fire from the defense platforms was faster than the Baleorans. Multiple simultaneous hits tore a gash down the side of one battleship. Despite the firepower coming from the other defense platforms, the Baleorans concentrated their firepower on only the two platforms rising over the poles, until one of them broke apart. A Baleoran battleship suddenly exploded with a blinding flash.

Surrogate to the Most High One. Baleorans have landed on the colony planet.

"What? How did that happen?" I could see they were in low orbit, streams of drop ships heading toward the planet.

Priority instructions were given to destroy the Baleoran vessels if they attempted escape. There were no instructions given if they continued toward the planet.

"I knew I would forget something. Tikan, will the warriors fight?"

The Most High One has given permission to defend their colonies.

"This is not going well. Core, the defense platforms must destroy the carriers and container ships immediately," I said, going into full panic mode.

Central has received priority instructions from the Most High One to destroy the Baleoran armored vessels. When this instruction has been completed, they will revert to their original programming, and destroy any Baleoran vessels within range of their weapons.

A second defense platform was inoperable and continued out into the void just as the second Baleoran battleship exploded in a bright flash. Core reported two other defense platforms were damaged, but continued to fire on the remaining vessels.

"Core, are there any Draasen on the container ships?"

Central has released armed pods from all colonies, and they are keeping Baleoran capture vessels on the planet surface. Warriors have been armed and are defending individual colonies.

"How many Draasen are on the long walk on the planet?"

None reported.

"I thought Baleorans took populations for food."

Baleorans do not immediately send populations on the long walk. They are captured and placed in stasis to be consumed alive at a later time.

I shuddered to think about the billions of humans who had been taken by the Baleorans. When they woke up, they were fresh meat on the table.

While I watched, the defenseless carriers and container ships were destroyed. They did not explode, but broke up into many large pieces.

"Core, what is happening on the planet?"

Baleorans are being neutralized.

"It looks like it is time to clean up. We do not need to repeat what happened on our colony planet. Core, order the platforms to destroy the pieces of the Baleoran ships before they fall into the atmosphere."

Command confirmation from the Most High One is required.

Destroy the wreckage of the Baleoran vessels. That is my command.

Command accepted.

The Baleorans must be informed there is a new Most High One, and they must be warned if they approach another colony planet, they will be destroyed, Lana said.

We have kicked them in the teeth. Now we have to tell them about it, Tikan added with a vicious smile.

"Most High One, how can we do this?"

Core will handle the communications. What message should we send?

"Core, can the Baleorans receive images like we have seen here?"

They can receive them, but it is uncertain they will understand what they see.

"Tell the Baleorans the former Most High One has gone on the long walk. Tell them the new Most High One will protect her people from anyone who approaches any of our colony planets. Any who do will be destroyed. Send the images of what happened to their vessels with the message. Since they already know which planets are ours, it should make them think twice before they approach any of them."

I felt a link wavering in my mind. I heard a shuddering breath come from Elder, and I realized it was his link that was wavering. I ran to where he squatted, his head between his knees, his nose nearly touching the floor. Dropping to my knees, I placed my forehead on his.

What is happening? I said when he appeared in front of me.

It is my time to go on the long walk, he said with complete inner peace.

You cannot leave me. Lana!

Please, do not deny me this last privilege. It is my time and I am grateful. My mated pairing waits for me at the end of my walk. Please, let me go.

I need you, old man.

You have our queen, and she loves you. You have our people, and they need you. You have my love, and that will never leave you. You have our memories, so I will not be forgotten.

Can I come with you?

I would welcome your company, but I must walk alone. Will you take me home?

I would be honored to take my best friend home.

He smiled and walked into the darkness, his retreating figure becoming smaller and smaller, until it became a tiny spot of distant light. The spot grew brighter and silently exploded into millions of stars, slowly fading until I was left in darkness. All that Elder was had gone.

To be with him as he went on the long walk was the greatest thing you could have done for him. The unfolding for you is over. It is time to return from the dark of the long walk, Amber said gently.

The darkness was replaced by light. I was still on my knees with my forehead on Elder's. I stood and turned to the gathering of people in the dome.

"Elder was my friend and I will honor him. Who will help me carry him home?"

I will! Thousands of voices resounded in my head.

Use my transport to take him home, Amber said.

Kaa and three other males picked up Elder's body. I held his hand when he was carried to the transport and sat beside him as we traveled to the field of grasses. It seemed the aggressive nature of the grasses held back as I gently positioned his hands on his chest.

"You are home. Goodbye, my old friend." I did not watch when his body was consumed by the grasses.

When we landed inside the Place of the Most High One, Amber was waiting for me. When I left the transport, she squatted, placed me in her lap, and comforted me as I wept for the loss of my friend.

***

The next suns, Amber brought the journal to the feeding table where she, Lana, and Core helped me write the events of the past seven suns. The task stretched past the end of the suns while I was helped with the details. When it was finally completed, I could enjoy the peace and love Amber brought to everyone as the Most High One.

Chapter 20
END OF ALL THINGS

In a recent conversation with Core, it reminded me that it has been over sixteen years since I last wrote in this journal. I guess I have been distracted and forgot to update it. Amber said I should end this journal, this final link to my past.

Amber is a very popular queen, much loved by our people. I fondly remember everyone's excitement during the birthings of our last two daughters, because Core set links for everyone to experience the birthings. Everyone was invited to experience the birthings, including the males, at my request. Since then, there has been a baby boom. It was the first time in many years that the Draasen wanted to have children, because the cruelty of the former queen had tainted everything, even the desire to have children. The former queen did not know, or even care, that she was slowly destroying her own people without any help from the Baleorans.

No one challenged Amber for the position of Most High One, which I was very happy for. I feared any challenge, because the events of Amber's rise were still fresh in my mind, as if they had happened only last suns. Amber assured me a violent challenge was extremely rare, and would not happen again, at least in our lifetimes. She would rather step down quietly than allow anything to happen to me, because she knew I would vigorously defend her position as Most High One, even though I would be acting out of my place.

I considered the Baleorans to be an ongoing threat. To make sure we would never be caught off guard, I presented a request to build one hundred thousand deep void probes and scatter them around our colony planets and our home world. Core already had thousands of probes out there, but more of them would offer better coverage.

As we spread the new probes deeper into the void, one of them located a Baleoran transport with seven drop vessels still attached to it. A scan proved the occupants were humans. I made sure a probe followed the vessel and reported when a building was dropped off so we could quickly recover them and add them to our existing colony. With my queen's permission, I initiated an ongoing effort to locate other human buildings. Selected probes had been programmed to seek out planets with conditions compatible for Draasen colonization, and were given additional instructions to look for any human populations when they discovered a new planet. I had Core send other probes back to planets already discovered to search for any humans who may have been dropped there. With the advanced support and assistance of my people, the human species would not disappear and be forgotten.

***

As near as I could figure, I was seventy-four earth years old. I had severe arthritis, and Lana frequently beat me with her blue glowing rod to heal it, although I think she did it with a little too much zeal. The temporary cure was almost as bad as the arthritis. I had been walking with the help of a cane, and Amber had a ramp built behind her dais so I could more easily get up on it to stand beside her as her consort.

The thought that I had condemned Amber to a long life alone began to haunt me, for I knew she would not pair again. Although she did not seem to be concerned about it, it frequently crossed my mind and she was quick to send comforting thoughts and feelings across our link. She would not discuss it, and I had learned long ago when my queen did not want to talk about something, we did not talk about it.

After a recent medical examination, Lana and Amber had a private conversation. When Amber and I went to bed, Core sent one of its Oracles to settle on my head.

***

The suns began normally enough. Amber carried me to her bathing pool, where we had our usual long and leisurely bathing. The hot water always felt good on my old bones. After first feeding, Amber carried me to the throne room and gently put me on my feet behind the dais. As the Most High One, she stepped up first and I followed her, struggling up the ramp with my cane.

When I reached the top of the ramp, a crushing pain in my chest took me completely by surprise. I did not have time to call for anyone before I crashed to the floor and blacked out. In brief moments of consciousness, I felt the crushing pain. Then, the pain was gone. I opened my eyes to see Amber and Lana looking down at me in the hospital. Lana was tapping one of her devices on my forehead.

How do you feel? Lana said.

Tired.

Any pain?

No.

Most High One, there is nothing more I can do for your consort.

I caught a glimpse of Core as it settled on my head.

My queen, my human frailty has condemned you to a life of loneliness. I am very sorry.

Always thinking of others before yourself. It is one of the many things I love about you, and it is why you are so very popular with our people. When it is time, I will take you home, she said, and gently nuzzled my cheek.

If there is any justice in the universe, I will see you again, my beautiful queen, my love.

My arm was too weak to scratch her chin. She always enjoyed it, and I would have liked to do it for her, one last time.

I could not keep my eyelids open because they felt as if they weighed a ton. I stopped breathing, but felt no pain. A light became brighter as it surrounded me. The light washed over me and filled me with a wonderful feeling of peace. I felt something pushing in my neck as my link with Amber dissolved, and I was left alone as the light faded into darkness.

Chapter 21

RESURRECTION

I am hungry. Is this what it is like to be dead? How can I be dead, and hungry? What is that buzzing? Do I have to suffer with an annoying buzzing all the time? I do not like it here. I am hungry!

Transfer is complete. Pathways are set. I detect resonance from intellectual activity.

I did not like that voice. I was being punished. That was it. I was being punished and the voice was my eternal tormentor. There was always the possibility I might end up down here. Well, maybe not, because it was not hot. I am hungry! The buzzing stopped.

Can you hear me?

Now, that voice could punish me all it wanted. It was soft and gentle. I knew who it was.

Amber?

Yes, he has returned! I felt waves of relief and happiness.

Why is it dark? I want to see you.

Your eyes are covered. We are still testing your functions, a different voice said.

Lana, I was on the long walk. Why did you bring me back? I cannot last much longer.

Most High One, this will be a surprise for him, and you know he does not like surprises.

I want you to keep your eyes closed until I tell you to open them, Amber said, and I felt her take something from over my eyes. *Now, slowly open your eyes.*

As I did, my vision was blurred, but quickly focused.

What is wrong with my eyes? I see double!

Close your eyes. Now, open this eye. Only this one. I felt her gently touch my left eyelid.

When I opened my eye, I could see clearly. I smiled when I saw Amber looking at me, but my smile felt wrong; I felt wrong. When I looked forward, I was looking at a long, dark gray nose. I briefly closed my eye, hoping it would be gone, but it was still there. I opened my other eye, and I saw double images again.

Close your eyes. Now, open the other one.

I looked along the same, long nose again. Hoping it was some kind of optical illusion, I opened my other eye and tried to cross them to find my own nose. I saw two separate images again as they crossed over the long nose. It would not go away. When I tried to move it, I saw a dark gray hand with three fingers and a thumb. I thought I had lost my mind when the hand responded to my movements.

Close your eyes. Please listen to me before you try anything else. Do you remember, just after you rescued the human colony, I said I had a gift for you? This is the gift I have to give to the one I love.

My mind was filled with the image of a very young, very thin male lying on a table, and I watched Amber gently rub his chest. Even though I felt her touching me, fear gripped my heart because I thought I had been replaced; I was jealous of the male who had my queen's attention.

It is you. You are the only one who has my attention.

What happened to me?

Core saved your memories and restored them into this Draasen body.

A Draasen went on the long walk to save me again? Too many have walked for me already.

No, you saved a male from the long walk.

How?

Do you remember our sixth birthing?

The reminder of our lost hatchling made me feel like crying again.

Your intellect, personality, everything you were, is now in the body of this male, who was like our sixth birthing. You saved this hatchling from the long walk.

I am hungry.

Feeding is here, Kaa announced when he walked into the dome.

Help him sit up, Lana said.

My balance was completely off, and I had to be steadied while Amber tried to feed me.

You can feed him easier if he is squatting. Help me put him on his feet, Lana said.

It was a bad idea. I was disoriented by the dual images I saw, and I could not coordinate my two pair of knee joints going in opposite directions. Despite the support, I collapsed in an uncoordinated heap.

It might be easier to feed him in the bathing pool, Kaa suggested.

Amber picked me up and carried me to the bathing pool, where she placed me in the water. Kaa brought me to the surface and Amber fed me. I could not eat fast enough, even though I swallowed every mouthful whole.

More. I want more! I insisted when the tray was empty.

Another tray was brought and Amber continued to drop food into my open mouth. Just before I finished my second tray, I was still hungry, but so full I could not eat any more. I looked around, being careful to keep both eyes looking straight ahead. While I held on to the edge of the bathing pool, I remembered what Kaa had done while he was in his pot of water just after his birth. I turned to look for a tail and sure enough, there it was, extending from my lower back. I watched it in fascination as I tried to move it around.

Can you move to the scrubbing ledge? Amber said.

I will try, I said, but I was getting sleepy.

I shuffled my hands alongside the bathing pool until I stopped to look at my hand again. I slipped off and sank to the bottom, landing on my toes in a semi-squatting position. I had to crawl along the bottom to the scrubbing ledge and work my way up the side.

You are learning, Amber said.

What did I do?

Look down.

I was standing upright with all four knees cooperating with each other. When I thought I should not have another pair of knees, they folded.

Stop thinking and accept what you have.

I felt Amber guiding my thinking away from my human mindsets. It felt strange, and somehow comforting at the same time.

It will take time for you to adapt, and you will learn from experience, just like all hatchlings.

It was the last thing I remembered, because I fell asleep in the bathing pool.

***

When I woke again, we were back in our dome. I was so hungry it hurt, but Amber and Kaa were ready with a tray of food. I rolled on the bed and tried to squat, but I was only partially successful. Kaa steadied me while Amber dropped handfuls of food into my open mouth.

How did this happen? How did I become this?

I love you, Amber said, as if that was enough.

Actually it was, but I wanted a detailed explanation.

Core said, *When birthing colony High One Ambrisseethsss requested a way be found to keep her surrogate alive longer than what was normal for your species, I researched my databases and* found a very old procedure to transfer intellect from one species to another. I downloaded all of your memories over several suns while you slept. When you were close to going on the long walk, the Most High One commanded I search for a healthy, empty male. When you were assisted on the long walk, an empty male was located and hatched. The male was brought here, and I restored your intellect.

Amber, what does it mean I was assisted on the long walk?

When you were judged by the Council of Five for violations of protocols the second time, I assured our people I would carry out the Council's judgment and send you on the long walk at a time of my choosing. Just as you started on your walk, I gave you final claws. It was the hardest thing I ever had to do.

I have never heard of this happening to a Draasen.

Core said, *Draasen cannot endure the process because the telepathic organ is unique from the moment of sentience. Your human body did not have the organ. The one you have now is unique to you.*

Amber, I was on the long walk. You cannot bond again.

If you had a Drassen telepathic organ, I would not be able to bond with another. No telepathic organ could accept that, but your human body did not have one. Your intellect and memories have been restored into this body, and we are bound together in ways you could not experience before.

I can feel the difference, I said, looking at my tail that had stiffened and quivered behind me, almost tipping me over. *What happens now?*

You will to learn to walk, and talk, and go through the education process again. You once thought you would never know what it would be like to be truly Draasen. Now, you will, and I am looking forward to us, Amber said with an excited smile for me.

Chapter 22

FINAL ENTRY

Amber's gift of a new life, a second life, was difficult for me to accept because of my linear human thinking. Dead was dead, and there was no returning from it. Yet, here I was, alive in another body. I was the third person to have accepted being a Draasen birthing animal. I was the second to have been given another life by the Draasen. Others may have considered it to be a gift beyond measure, but I was the first in the heart of my queen, and that was the greatest gift of all.

Shortly after I relearned to walk, I received a message from High One Ann. When she appeared, I was surprised by the creature speaking to me until I realized it was someone I knew from my human past. Ann said everyone saw what happened, and she congratulated me on successfully cheating death. She also said Cherie was happy for me, but was disappointed with her decision not to stay with Kaa. Amber told me Cherie would not have been given the gift of a second life. I decided not to tell Cherie what Amber said because it might come back and bite me in the tail, now that I had one.

My education had finally been completed, and it took a lot less time than usual because everything I had learned came with my intellect when it was transferred into this body. My second education filled in many gaps I had suspected were missing, and among the lessons, I learned of a probe appearing to the Draasen very early in their history. I asked Core about it, and it said there had been several recorded attempts to time jump in the magnetic tunnel, and only one was thought to have appeared in Draasen history. It was known that the Draasen of the distant past had embraced the advanced technology of an alien probe, and Core suggested it may have been the root of its own beginning.

Amber said we should send my journal on a time jump to warn Earth about the Baleorans. Initially I disagreed, because sending my journal back to earth might alter my past, and my future. I might cease to exist in this life as I knew it, and I did not want that to happen. Amber and I discussed several possibilities at great length, and she convinced me nothing could change what had already happened to me. I decided that if my journal was found, it would be regarded with skepticism at best, and at worst, it would be seen as the wild imagination of some demented writer off his rocker until the events of the Baleorans began; only then would it possibly be taken seriously.

In a sudden flash of revelation, I realized someone would find this journal. I remembered the newspaper headline stating the Baleorans had taken the ninety-third building. How could anyone on earth know who was taking them? The Baleorans would not have told them, so it stood to reason I had told them through this journal.

Core and I had many discussions while we prepared the probe, and we decided to have the probe confirm the location of Earth using the image of the gold plaque from the Pioneer Ten spacecraft, because we knew it was accurate. Core and I toyed with the idea the probe could fly back to Drassen after the delivery of the journal with the details of what I was going to do, and Core could hold on to it for the seven-hundred some odd years until I arrived. Amber quashed my very creative idea because the former Most High One might access it and know we were coming before we did. There was no need to sabotage the future, so we had Core program the probe to fly into the sun after the delivery was successful.

Before we seal this journal in the probe, I will make my writing permanent with the magnetic process that is used, so these will be my last entries.

The Draasen are my people. I am one of them in heart, mind, and now, body. I think I had a good run in my human form, and I did many things of interest to me. I enjoyed most of them, but I never did anything worthy of remembrance by human history; not that it matters anymore. I should offer hope, or write something meaningful, or inspirational, but I have nothing to offer because I have seen the future; your future. Instead, I will write a goodbye to my human wife. Even though she will never see this message, it will be on Earth when she goes on the long walk, which is as close as I will ever be to her again.

***

My dearest Kim,

My life has changed so much since I was taken from you, and I wish I could show you what I have done and tell you how much I still love you. You are never far from my thoughts, and when I think about you, my feelings are still the same.

I love you. I do not think I said it enough.

I love you. That never changed, and it never will.

Ray.

Epilogue

When Tanner finished reading, he was certain of only one thing. The book was handed to him by the silver pod. Still believing he was the victim of an elaborate joke, he took the stylus from the binding and wrote his name on a blank page. Then, he pressed the stylus on his name, drew it across, and it disappeared. In a like manner, he tried to erase a word from the book, but it didn't work.

"Excuse me, Mister Watson, the president has arrived," an aide said from his open door.

Tanner tucked the book under his arm and left the office.

***

"Good morning, gentlemen."

"Good morning, Mister President."

"General Thomas, I hear we had some excitement this morning."

"Yes sir. An object of unknown origin appeared —"

"Wait. Do you mean a UFO?"

"Yes, sir. The object suddenly appeared on radar at twenty thousand feet. It didn't fly in from any direction, it just appeared and hovered. Two F-16's were scrambled to intercept it. The pilots reported it was silver in color, oval shaped, about twenty feet long and fifteen feet wide. It didn't have wings, rotors, or markings of any kind. The pilots reported they were under attack, because something shot past them at close range. They were authorized to fire their sidewinders, and made four direct hits, but it did not appear to be damaged. Then it flew straight up and disappeared. Radar indicated it was flying toward the sun before it went out of range."

"How many people know about this?"

"It was very early, sir. I doubt anyone saw it, other than our pilots."

"There's no need to create a panic so investigate quietly, please."

"Yes, sir."

"Mister Watson, I have one for you. A building has vanished in England, and the British Prime Minister has asked for our help."

"You don't mean a whole building, do you, sir?" Tanner said, clutching the journal under his arm.

"Yes, an entire two story building. The press had the story before we did. Turn on the television, closed circuit two."

A news report showed an aerial view of a dark circle in the ground. The caption crawling along the bottom of the screen read: "…where a popular English pub once stood. The building disappeared late yesterday, filled with revelers celebrating a soccer match victory. There is no evidence of an explosion—"

"Excuse me, Mister President. I think you should read this," Tanner said, handing him the oversized journal.

Before You Go...

Share your voice and help guide other readers to these wonderful books. Even if it's only a line or two your reviews help readers discover the author's books so they can continue creating stories that you'll love. Login to your favorite retailer and leave a review. Thank you.

About the Author

Having been born on December 24 created an important life lesson; choose wisely, the best is not always the largest. I followed a family tradition of military service, and despite my tours in Vietnam and Desert Storm, I continued to pursue my favorite activity of reading science fiction. I am a late starter to writing and have found writing as enjoyable as reading. I write the type of science fiction I like to read: believable, without incredibly ridiculous situations that suddenly appear to solve all the character's problems.